Air:
The Elementals
Book One

Printed in the United States of America

First Printing, 2020

ISBN: 9781952422072[1]

Imprint: Imagine Nation

Imagine Nation

Chenoa, IL 61726

AuthorJenniferLush@gmail.com

---

1.   https://www.myidentifiers.com/
title_registration?isbn=978-1-952422-07-2&icon_type=Assigned

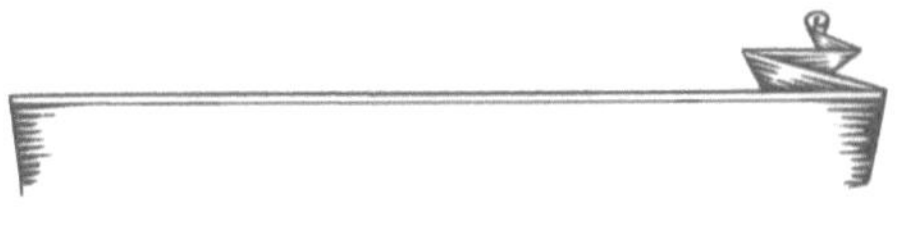

Dedication

To my mom and dad for their unwavering belief in me. I only wish you were here to hold the first autographed copies in your hands.

To Mr. Tom Wells who is without a doubt the most amazing and engaging English teacher a teenager could hope to have.

And last but not least, to all of you reading this because I wouldn't be able to continue in my chosen craft if no one was interested in the worlds my mind creates.

Chapter One
The Arrival

He stepped off his corner of the flat rock and saw the light pouring into the entrance of a cave. The sun was high here and blinding. His eyes closed almost instinctively at the glare. He stepped back into the shadows to allow his eyes to adjust. The dampness from the cave spread over his skin, yet he could also feel the heat from the rays of light that danced across the cave floor inches from where he stood. His senses were alive and responding to each new sensation flowing through his human form.

Slowly he made his way to the front of the cave and emerged. He placed both of his hands over his brow to shield the sun from his eyes. The warmth of the sun penetrated his light bronze skin. There was a vast forest in front and below him filled with trees that would tower over any man. The sky was a hazy blue with a few scattered clouds that looked more like thin wispy horse tails than the fluffy balls he had imagined. He turned round and round taking it all in: the sky with its bright warmth, the forest with its autumn colored paintings, the shadowy darkness of the valley floor below, and the earth tones of the hill and dirt beneath his feet. Each held a different stunning view. Each had a different feel.

A blue jay flew overhead, and he was captivated by the blue on blue contrast against the sky. He followed the bird with his eyes, turning his head to keep sight of it until he almost lost his balance. Steadying himself, he took a deep breath letting the clean air fill his newly made lungs. *'Has air always carried a smell such as this?'* he wondered. It was like inhaling the sycamore trees and fertile soil with each breath. Their aroma was so strong.

He was alone on the side of the hill by this cave at least for now. He needed to remember the location to be able to travel back when the time came. He walked several feet down and turned back to fortify the image in his mind. He trusted that instinct would bring him back even without burning it in his memory, but he wasn't going to risk the chance. He had no way to know yet that the route home would always find him when the time came no matter how far he may venture.

The forest spread out below him. He was fascinated by the multitude of textures that intertwined. Shades and hues that he had never seen. Not like this. It was beauty in a way that he had never known existed. He never really had an opinion on this expedition and wasn't at all affected by whether or not the Elements would get this chance, but he was glad now that he was here in the mortal realm. It far exceeded his expectations and in only the first few minutes.

He surveyed the landscape and could pick up on two villages within miles of his cave. The larger village held more promise for learning, but he chose the smaller one because it would lead him through the thick grove of sycamore trees. He found their scent enticing and breathing them in to be almost intoxicating.

Every experience was exhilarating. Each step found soft warm blades of grass tickling his feet. Bird songs were echoing through the canopy like a symphony in his ears. He made his way down the side of the hill to the valley floor below and placed his palm on the trunk of the closest tree. He could feel the shade from the tree providing immediate relief from the rays of the sun, and he became aware of the tiny droplets of sweat that formed on his forehead and were now dripping down into his eyes.

Using a piece of cloth that draped over his arm, he wiped his face. With the tree supporting him, he leaned back and looked up the trunk until he could see light peeking through the branches nearer to the top. Every moment was filled with enticing new sensations that lingered around him, and he would have chosen to stay out his year there in the valley if he could. It wasn't an option. He had to follow orders and find a group to observe to gain knowledge and understanding.

His walk through the valley was steady and deliberate. He spent several hours keen on making it a slow exploration. He was eager to experience everything. How did grass cooled by the shade compare to the feel of bark from a fallen tree? What if he placed a foot on each at the same time?

Then which sensation would be the primary? He continued heading east at a leisurely pace until a new sound approached him from the distance.

It was like melodic laughter meandering through the forest. He quickened his pace and the smell of the air became heavier and damp. As he neared the burbling stream, he could already begin to feel its coolness softening the temperature around him. It finally came into view when he stepped over a log and walked between two tall giant oaks to reach the bank. The water flowed past him cutting through the sides of the bed and lapping around rocks.

Birds were singing to each other and branches snapped from unseen animals that lurked nearby. He scanned the growth along both sides of the stream, but he could only hear movement. Whoever these new creatures were, they were careful to remain out of his view. This water source was a necessary gathering place for all life in the valley, and he must be seen as a threat for them to hasten their retreat.

He walked down the bank to a shallow point with a bridge of rocks cutting across. Some were fully emerged, jutting out from the water. He eased his foot down onto the stone nearest to him and felt the cold chill of the fresh water cover it. He lifted his foot and watched the water drip down and flow away with the current. A breeze picked up and the air instantly chilled his already wet skin. He silently chuckled over the near tickling sensation it caused as he quickly set his foot back down on the ground.

He knelt down along the edge and held his hand against the flow of the water, watching it separate to both sides to surge around his fingers. Using both hands, he formed a cup to collect enough to drink. He brought his hands to his lips and sipped the crystal clear liquid. He could feel the chill from the water as it moved down his gullet. He sipped from his hands again and collected more water from the stream savoring another new sensation.

A few feet downstream was a large rock that jutted out of the side of the bank. He walked over and sat down allowing his feet to dangle in the water. He continued to rest while taking in all he could of his surroundings. He noted how the trees' branches would sometimes interlace with each other as they grew. He watched and listened to the forest creatures flittering from one branch to another. He spied through the grass and other foliage of the valley floor hoping to catch a glimpse of one of the animals he'd yet to only be able to hear.

A warning shot through him suddenly as he picked up on another presence nearby. This was definitely a human, and he couldn't be spotted. He couldn't see anyone, but his intuition told him they were close. Quickly he scrambled up and back into the cover of trees where he had exited not long ago. He stood in the shadows and waited. Moments passed before he saw a young woman approach on the opposite side of the stream. She carried with her several makeshift wooden buckets. He sat down on the log hidden in the darkness of the shade and peered around the trunk of the larger of the two trees to spy on her undetected.

She emerged from a path through the trees about twenty feet upstream, but she was close enough that he could tell her body was barely covered. She wore a type of animal skin skirt, but that was the only covering on her body besides her feet. Her chest was exposed to all that was around her including him, and he could feel a stirring come from below his waist under his robes. He darted his eyes away ashamed.

She knelt down to the stream and took a drink in the same way he had just minutes earlier. She continued to kneel by the stream looking down at her hands resting on her knees. He watched her filled with intrigue and wondered what she must be thinking sitting there alone. He could, of course, read her thoughts if he chose, but there was something about the mystery that tantalized him. Slowly, she stood up and removed the small piece of cloth from her waist. He turned his head and wouldn't allow himself to look back until he heard the small splash as she lowered herself into the stream.

Her back was to him when he peeked out again. She was bent over rinsing off her arms in the cool, clear water. She stood up and cupped both hands together lifting them to splash a gentle spray over her face. The water didn't fully come up to her waist, so his eyes followed her long hair down her back to the top of her round and taut bottom. His face flushed, and he carefully moved over and sat on the forest floor. His back to the tree that stood between them. He remained this way for a very long time fearing the thoughts that would entertain him if he dared to take another look. He could hear the splashing of the water as she climbed out.

Quietly he sat faced away from the stream unable to bring himself to move. There was no sound at all, but he continued to wait. He fought the temptation to see her through his mind's eye as he was afraid of what she may be doing and what he may accidentally witness. After several long minutes with his heart beating faster and faster, he turned. She was fastening one of her foot coverings, but the rest of her garments were in place. He let out a long exhale, relieved that he would see no more than he already had.

She finished tying the coverings. Then, one by one, she lowered the buckets until they were filled with the crisp, fresh water. Before he could begin to wonder how she would be able to carry all of these back by herself, she tied the handles to the ends of a vine rope. The other ends of the rope were attached to a long pole. She crouched down and placed the pole across the top of her shoulders at the back of her neck. She wrapped each arm around one end of the pole from the back then slowly stood up. The buckets of water were perfectly balanced on either side of her small frame.

He was impressed by how simple yet ingenious this device had been. It made light of heavy work allowing anyone to accomplish tasks that their physical prowess may have otherwise limited them from performing. His curiosity had been piqued, and he decided to follow her back to her village to learn more, knowing full well that was not the real reason he chose to follow her. She was the only reason his interest had been stirred.

It was necessary to be cautious. He waited until she slowly disappeared out of sight before departing from his cover in the trees. He walked back to the rock bridge and hesitantly crossed the stream. The rocks were slick under his feet, and he feared falling in would grab her attention enough to investigate the noise which would give his presence away. Once on the other side, he walked quickly until he caught sight of her again then he slowed to match her pace to be able to keep a safe distance.

He was thankful that she was facing away from him as he was already imagining how the weight of the carrying stick pulling her shoulders back would lift and push out her round breasts. A similar stirring began to grow inside of him under his robes. He closed his eyes and shook his head. It was only day one, and he was already being exposed to temptations that were trying to overpower him. He must learn to control these thoughts, or else he may fail at his task.

She continued to walk along the worn path about a hundred yards before she turned to exit the tree cover. He was keenly aware of the village that wasn't much farther off. He hung back knowing he could find it on his own, and he wanted to give her time to disappear amongst the huts before he approached. His aim was to observe these societies functioning as a whole, not to devote his attention to any one person. There would be no harm in learning about the daily life of these people by concentrating on one he thought. He was already trying to reason with himself why it would be acceptable for him to devote all of his time to her.

Trying once more to push thoughts of this beautiful woman from his mind, he slowly made his way back into the forest marveling again in the feel of the cool grass under his feet. He leisurely circled the village at a distance that kept everything out of his sight, but nonetheless an occasional sound or excited yell from a child would reach his ears. He didn't have to be within view to be able to see them. His gift was sight.

He could see the mud huts that housed each family. The village was larger than he originally expected it to be. Some of the children were playing, but the older ones were helping with the work. He could see the women cooking and sewing. Only a few men were in the village, and they were resting and talking. He knew the rest of the men were hunting. They wouldn't return for hours, and when they did, he would be safe on the southern edge for the hunt was to the north. All of this he could see before he walked close enough to bring the village within view.

Circling the village a second time, he noted how the children wore no clothes at all. The men wore loin cloths, but the women wore a type of skirt fashioned around the waist that was short enough to reveal everything as they moved. He found the girl from the stream. She was helping her mother prepare a midday meal. He found himself relieved that she was not married even though he knew he shouldn't care.

He continued around until he was back on the southern edge. He understood he would need to find a place close to the village to use for cover from anyone who wandered near him. The cave would be too far of a trek to make daily. He searched through the woods until he found a massive tree with a hollow trunk that was wide enough he wouldn't be able to wrap his outstretched arms halfway around. There was a very large opening in the base of the trunk allowing him to hunch over and enter. Once inside, he could stand up with ease. There was enough floor room that he could sleep comfortably and be protected from any weather.

The tree would not be considered safe, but he knew it would be several years before it toppled even with the added stress of him using it as a home for a year. "A year?" he asked himself out loud. "Is it wise to spend the entire year with only one village?"

He knew it was because of her that he would even consider it, and he knew it was because of her that it was exactly what he would do. He would rationalize the logic behind this thinking later. He would convince himself that it would be better to study the same group then multiple ones, as it would allow more understanding than the small fragments of insight acquired off of several groups would provide. This would be the internal conversation that would keep him awake many nights over the next year, but not today. For now, the top priority would be making this space livable.

Leaves from the forest floor would have to make do for a bed. The robes he wore would work both as a pillow and a blanket while he slept until he could make new ones. The rumbling in his abdomen told him he needed to find food fast. He stepped out of his new home and focused on the village. No one would be entering the woods again tonight. He could forage without care.

The valley was filled with nuts, berries and other fruit. He held each one in his hand to feel whether it was safe to eat. There was an occasional corn stalk or other plant growing wild. Seeds must have been scattered from the nearby village either on the wind or through animals. These plants were safe for him to pick from because their bounty wouldn't be missed by anyone. It didn't take long before his robe was gathered to use as a pouch and had been filled. He ate as he searched to cure the hunger pains attacking him. On his way back to the tree, he grabbed a few large sticks to begin making tools for hunting. The weather would turn cold soon, and the foliage would stop producing. He needed to be prepared.

Once he had safely stored his findings in the trunk on a flat piece of wood from a nearby broken log, he set his mind on water. He would need a way to store it. He saw in his mind that if he went back to the stream further down than where he had started, he would find what he needed. He set off immediately because the day was growing old, and it would be dark soon. He made his way back to the rock bridge he had crossed merely a couple hours ago and kept going. It only took a few more minutes until he saw it. A wooden bucket was bouncing on the surface caught between two large rocks.

When he picked it up, he could see the bucket's previous owner. She had tripped many miles upstream, and the bucket went tumbling from her hands. She tried to find it, but gave up thinking it had washed too far down. She was much older than the woman he had followed earlier, and it would have been too far for her to explore safely. He gathered water in the bucket and held it up checking it for leaks. It appeared to be in good condition, so he headed back to his tree as shadows began creeping in everywhere.

It was dark before he returned, but he could sense every rock and protruding root around him to avoid tripping. He made his way into his tree and sat down. He looked around at the bed he had made, his bucket of water, and the food he had collected. He beamed proudly at the great progress he had achieved on his first day, and he hoped the others had been successful in their attempts as well.

He took off his robe and bunched part of it to place under his head. He then draped himself with the rest. When he closed his eyes, his thoughts ventured back to the village and the woman he couldn't forget. He could see her in her hut laying down with a blanket of woven vines over her. Even with the blanket and the darkness that encompassed her, he could see she was completely naked underneath. Every curve of her body was visible to him, and he took it all in from her head to her feet. Her bronze skin was smooth and soft, and her hair draped over her shoulders barely covering her bosom.

His eyes shot open, and he blinked several times as though the images were imprinted on the backs of his eyelids, not his mind, and blinking would rid himself of them somehow. He could not understand his fascination with this woman. He had seen nudity all the time from the spiritual realm, and he had never been affected by it. In fact, he had oft wondered why people bothered covering their body for any reason except to protect themselves from harsh weather conditions. It had always seemed like a large waste of time and resources to bother with clothing. Yet he had been here less than a day, and it consumed his mind. He was making progress on his quest. He was beginning to learn and understand at least where the need for garments was concerned.

Perhaps the naked form would be something he could adjust to seeing regularly as the members of the village were not at all preoccupied by the nudity around them. This was quite truly his first time seeing nudity in the flesh, and he hoped it was the reasoning behind how it distracted him. In time, it should be no different than admiring the beauty of the trees.

Thinking about the days to come and all he would need to do to prepare helped get his mind off of her. Tools needed to be made to allow him to hunt and trap. He would have to devise a way to gain meat for survival. He invaded the thoughts of the hunters who had come back, spying on their weapons and the means they used to secure food. He searched their memories of the hunt for a quick tutorial on how to accomplish their feats. He would need to work fast to gather enough stores for the approaching winter.

No matter what he tried, his thoughts always found their way back to her, and he would do his best to stay focused. It was growing more difficult, and he hoped that as time passed, his fascination with her would become stale. As he tried to clear his mind of thoughts of the woman from the village, he heard a deep voice whisper only one word to him inside his head, *'Marcus.'*

Marcus wondered why a name had been given to him at all since his orders were to only observe. He would never need to use it. No one on this plane of existence would ever know who he was or why he was here. The decision was not his to make, and he knew he should not question it. He was Marcus, Air Element, sent by the Divine Spirit to study one of the newest species evolution had created.

Chapter Two
The Others

Lilah looked out the passenger window of her mother's car like she had been doing for countless miles through the Midwest backroads. She longed for something to change. Anything that would break up the monotonous fields she'd been staring at for hours.

"We've switched from wheat to corn, Lilah," her mom teased, reading her mind.

"I hate when you do that," Lilah glared at her mom.

"I hate when you give me the silent treatment, but yet here we are. Stuck in a car together with hundreds of miles left to go."

Lilah turned back to the scenery passing by. *"It's not silent treatment,"* she thought. *"I have nothing to talk about."*

Her mother sighed and switched through radio stations until she found one that was playing a new pop hit. She even turned the volume up.

Lilah felt a twinge of guilt. She knew her mom was trying. She had to be to put on a station that was playing music she hated. Lilah turned her head and looked out the windshield for a moment before closing her eyes. She repeated the mantra to herself she had been saying since they left Florida two days earlier. *'This is bigger than me. The family needs us. It is only temporary.'*

Her mom looked at her. "You can talk to me, you know. Just because I can know your thoughts doesn't mean you can't voice them yourself."

Lilah kept her eyes closed and tried to keep her mind empty. It was a blessing and a curse. Being able to communicate with each other without speaking was great most of the time. Lilah could tell her mom anything she wanted no matter who was around, and no one else would be able to hear.

Other times, like this, when she just wanted to be left alone to mope, it enraged her that she hadn't learned how to shut her mom out yet.

Someday soon her powers would heighten. She would be able to read anyone's mind not just her own family when they allowed her to, and her ability to see the future would strengthen. That would always be limited however. Whenever someone tried to foresee anything, they couldn't delve too far. The possible outcomes were almost limitless when you factor in the freewill that every person is afforded. Their visions would branch off, and if they tried to see too far, it could result in unconsciousness and convulsions at best. Her family had learned centuries ago to practice extreme caution when traveling inward through their mind's eye.

It was probably still years away before she could even attempt to see more than simply what an evening had in store for her. She could only communicate telepathically with her closest family still, and she couldn't read their minds unless they were intentionally sending messages to her. It frustrated her not because she couldn't read their minds, but because she couldn't stop them from reading hers.

"I understand that we have to move. I know we can't stay in the same place more than a few years because people will become suspicious of us. I understand that we have to move to the middle of nowhere because of something going on with the family. I don't understand exactly what it is that is going on because you won't tell me. I get it, mom. I do. But I'm allowed to be unhappy and miserable about it." Lilah's voice grew steadily louder and more pointed as she spoke.

Her mother drew a heavy breath. "It's not that I won't tell you, Lilah. I can't tell you what I don't know myself."

"Then why are we going? Why can't we move to New York or California instead? Anywhere other than this." Lilah's voice filled with disgust, and she motioned to the fields out the window. "Why come here when you don't even know why?"

Her mom sighed. "We have to come here because Marcus summoned everyone. I don't know why he wants us all together, but Marcus–"

"Marcus is God," Lilah rolled her eyes cutting her mom off in the middle of her sentence.

"No. Marcus is not God," her mom's voice was stern. "He's the eldest of us. You know that. That's why he's the one who created our code to keep us safe."

"He's met God."

"So to speak," her mom corrected.

"And we have to drop everything to come running the moment he snaps his fingers," Lilah didn't try to hide her irritation.

"You do realize this isn't something that's limited to us, don't you?"

"What do you mean?" Lilah turned to face her mom for a moment, holding the belief that more than just their family would be involved.

"I mean people do this all the time for their own families."

Lilah let out a long exhale and sunk back in her seat. This wasn't what she thought her mom had meant.

"When someone's elderly family member is ill or needs help, they come to their aide. It doesn't have to be someone older either. It could be anyone in need."

"Yeah," Lilah nodded, looking out the windshield. "And do they sell all of their belongings and move halfway across the country too?" Her disdain dripped from her mouth.

"Sometimes!" her mom practically yelled then calmed herself down. "Sometimes they do, Lilah. Marcus rarely calls us all together. This is the third instance in my lifetime that it's happened. It's only if there is something that concerns all of us, or that could have a devastating effect on one or more of us."

Without moving her eyes away from the white line running down the side of the two lane highway where she was focusing all of her anger, Lilah's attitude was in full force, "Maybe he should get with the times. He could just as easily send a group message."

Her mom gasped and gripped the steering wheel tighter until her knuckles turned white. "We were due to move soon anyway. You know that. This is just a detour on our way to a new location. Why are you acting like this?" her mom hissed.

Lilah didn't respond. There were a million reasons why she was against this move, any move, but none of them mattered. Moving in general had grown old long ago. It made it impossible to form friendships when you know you're going to have to leave in a few years without a word. You can't tell anyone anything that is honest about yourself. Every little detail is a cover story.

"Do you want to stop for the night or push through until we get there?" her mom asked with a sigh, not wanting to continue the argument.

"Neither," Lilah thought.

Her mom gave her a pleading look.

Lilah rubbed her temples with her fingers before answering. "How about we stop to eat then get back on the road till this trip is over? I'd rather see what I'm being moody about instead of only imagining how bad it will be."

Her mom laughed softly. "Okay. We can do that."

Almost two hours later, they pulled out of the small café's parking lot. The large sign on the side of the highway read Fairview - 184 miles. It seemed like every state had a Fairview, but Lilah knew this wasn't entirely true. Her mom played with the radio until she managed to find yet another talk station. Lilah lay her head against the seat's head rest and closed her eyes. If she fell asleep now, she could skip some of the dread she'd been feeling for the entirety of the trip.

¹

LILAH'S EYES SHOT OPEN from a sound sleep, and she leaned forward in her seat.

"You felt it too?" her mom asked with apprehension in her voice.

"What was it?"

---

1. http://www.clker.com/cliparts/7/6/9/b/13309573511112670181decorative-lines-2_large-md.png

"An energy surge near as I can tell. As soon as we came over that ridge back there, it hit."

"What caused it?" Lilah asked, looking around trying to see if she could tell where they were.

"We're about ten miles out," her mother read her mind again. "And I don't know what caused it."

"Do you think-?" Lilah saw her mom's head shake slightly. It was a little cue telling her that her mom was trying to focus. Lilah waited. It would be no use to try to concentrate on the source herself because her powers weren't matured enough. She was only twenty-one years old in both appearance and years. Her mom easily passed for Lilah's slightly older sister even though she had lived for almost three centuries before Lilah was born.

Finally her mom relaxed to some extent. "I wasn't sure at first, but now it would appear we're not the only ones gathering here."

"You mean we're not the first to arrive?"

Her mom shook her head. "No, we're the first of our kind. Your father and a few others went to help some of the family because we could leave more easily than the rest were able to. They will come later."

"Then what do you mean?"

Lilah thought her mom wasn't going to answer her, but finally, as the car's speed slowed at the entrance of the town, her mom replied, "I mean there are others here as well."

"What others?" Lilah asked silently, remembering their earlier conversation when she thought this is what her mom had been trying to tell her. There were other Elementals involved.

"Try to feel them."

"You know I can't!" Lilah was irritated over how limited she still was in her capabilities.

"You might not be able to pick up everything yet, but you should be able to tell who they are."

Lilah rolled her shoulders and arched her neck back and forth as though psychic thought required stretching. She closed her eyes and tried her best to focus on any energy she could pick up as they drove down the quiet, empty street. She could see one large two story house ahead vibrating with bright light. It was off the main road about a block, but the top eaves peaked over the nearby houses and could be seen through the tree tops. Her eyes flew open.

"Witches?" Lilah whipped her head to the side and faced her mom.

"Yes. Lots of them. There are many in that house alone."

"Is it a coven gathering?" It would make sense with Halloween approaching. She didn't know all the ins and outs of Earth, but she did know Halloween was the equivalent of their New Year which meant traditions and celebrating.

"No. They're familial."

Lilah was puzzled. She could sense these witches were young. The oldest was in her early twenties. No, there could possibly be an older one, but it was hard for her to tell. How could there be so many from the same family in one house? Unless they were using aging spells. Or it could be possible their grandmother had a lot of children. That would explain it. Witches skip a generation, and only one is given the calling in each family.

"In times of trouble, more witches will be spawned," her mom explained. "Something big is coming for there to be five so young in that home. It's no wonder Marcus summoned us."

Lilah thought she could hear just a faint tremble of fear in her mom's voice. "Unless none of them are siblings," Lilah pointed out.

Her mom continued to watch the road with a distant look in her eye. "If I've learned one thing in all my years, it's that coincidences are rarely ever just that."

They made the rest of the drive in silence into the country just on the other side of town. The inconvenience over moving to the middle of nowhere that Lilah had been feeling gave way to anxiety and alarm. She had thought this only affected her people. She thought it only affected Air. Her mom was right. The large amount of new witches in the same area her family had been summoned to couldn't be a coincidence. She realized whatever was happening must affect all the Elementals. This was a lot bigger than she had anticipated.

Her mom turned down a long gravel road a few miles west of Fairview that went uphill to a very large old farmhouse. *"It belongs to an uncle,"* Lilah could hear her mom answer before she could ask.

They pulled up and sat still in the car a moment before either one of them attempted to get out. Lilah stared at the house through the windshield for several minutes thinking about how isolated she would be here. It was a far cry from the bright and loud cities where she was used to living. Safety in numbers. A large population meant they could go unnoticed easier and longer.

A small smile broke on Lilah's face, and she squealed, "It's my turn to pick!"

Lilah closed her eyes, concentrating on her image. Her blonde locks slowly changed to black. Her deep Florida tan lightened to a much paler tone, and when she opened her eyes, they were emerald green instead of hazel.

Her mom laughed. "Snow White? Is that the look you're going for? I believe her eyes were blue."

Lilah looked in the mirror on the visor. "I love it! Mock all you want. We're *sisters,*" she emphasized. "You have to match me close enough to at least look like we're related."

"Or...I could claim I found you lost and alone. Maybe I'll just tell everyone I took you in out of pity."

Lilah scowled. Their agreement had always been they would rotate who got to choose their new appearance until she was on her own. It was bad enough that day wouldn't be until after she learned to control all of the capabilities that she didn't even have yet, but now her mom was fighting her on this look when it was up to her to decide.

"Change back," her mom ordered. "We already have our new identification," she said, patting her purse which contained a large manila envelope sticking out that held everything they would need to start over including new names.

"But it's my turn!" Lilah pouted.

"I know it is, and you can choose when we move on from here. We left in such a hurry that I just told your Uncle Todd to surprise me."

"Well," Lilah said defiantly, "just call him up and have him redo everything."

"Lilah! He has to create new identities for the whole family."

Lilah wasn't moved by that statement. It wasn't her fault she wasn't consulted in this, and she should have been if it's the image she is expected to portray as her own.

"Plus he has his own affairs to get in order before he can join us," her mom added. "You get to keep the name though."

"I do?"

"Yeah, it simplified things. Our first names didn't change."

It wasn't much of a consolation prize. "There will come a day, mom."

"When what? You won't have to listen to me anymore? I'm well aware. You remind me of it almost constantly."

"No, I was going to say when I will be able to turn into a bird and poop on your head." Lilah smarted off the first thing that popped into her head.

To Lilah's surprise, her mom broke out into a large grin and began laughing. She joined her. It would be comical, and now that she had the thought, she wondered if it was a threat she could ever be able to carry through.

"It's not," Abby said, wiping a tear from the corner of her eye. "I believe I had the exact thought about my mom once myself, but once I had the ability to do it, I no longer wanted to."

Lilah sighed. She took a deep breath and allowed her skin tone to change back to the deep Florida tan she had sported the last few years.

"Your hair too," her mom sounded annoyed.

"We can always say I dyed it, mom."

Her mom sighed in defeat. "It's late. Let's unload the car and go to bed. We can grab breakfast in the morning on the way to the store."

They had packed light. Moving was nothing new to them. This was Lilah's ninth move although she barely remembered half of them. Lilah carried the boxes to the porch while her mom grabbed their suitcases. That was it. Their whole lives were tucked away in two boxes and three suitcases. Halfway up the steps, Lilah froze.

Her mom bumped into her back. "What-?" she started to ask.

"Shh. Look."

She followed Lilah's gaze to a squirrel that was on the rail on the side of the porch. It appeared to be watching them unafraid.

"It's a squirrel."

Lilah shot her mom a glance. "I know it's a squirrel," she said quietly, but the irritation in her voice came through loud and clear.

"So why are you so fascinated by it?" her mother whispered.

"It's white."

"Yeah?" Her mom walked past Lilah up the rest of the steps to make her way to the door.

"I've never seen a white squirrel before, and it doesn't seem frightened by us."

"It's a squirrel," her mom said, motioning for her to keep moving.

Lilah walked up beside her mom. She balanced the boxes on top of each other, and she used the front of the house to support them while her mom unlocked the door. Her mom held the door wide for Lilah to walk inside. Lilah walked through the front room a few feet down the hall then turned to set the boxes on the dining room table. She looked around the room and then across the hall into the kitchen. It was nothing like she expected.

"I know. It's old."

Her mom's voice made Lilah jump.

"Why couldn't we move somewhere more modern?" her mom whined, mocking her.

"It's not that."

"Then what's wrong?" her mom asked.

"It's clean."

Her mom stared at her blankly before erupting in laughter. "And that's a problem?"

Lilah shook her head and smiled. "No, but I thought we had to prepare. I thought we were the cleaning crew that had to get the musty dank old house back in livable order."

"Marcus and Leena had been here for close to two months before he had other matters to tend to, and they left. They took care of all that."

"Then what sort of preparations are we supposed to be making?" Lilah asked out loud more to herself than to her mom.

"I'm tired. Let's rest and discuss it more in the morning."

Lilah sighed. She knew better than to pester her mom with any more questions right now. It would do no good anyway. She had been asking questions since the news of their move was announced, but there were never any direct answers. Lilah understood how people her age felt. Treated like a child even though you are an adult except in Lilah's family, she was still very much a child. She was the youngest by hundreds of years. That wouldn't change until long after one of her cousins had a child to take Lilah's spot as the baby.

They headed up the split level stairs that turned back at the landing, bringing them to the rooms at the front of the house when they got to the top. They looked down the hall at the number of bedrooms. There were five in this large house plus room in the attic. "You can pick any one you want for now, but as more of the family arrive, we're all going to have to share rooms," her mom informed her, walking into the first room at the top of the stairs.

Lilah checked out the rest of the rooms. She chose the one at the far end of the hall near the back stairs. It was the smallest one which meant fewer people to crowd her. The bed was a double with a small nightstand beside it. A door in the corner opened to the tiniest closet she had ever seen.

She set her suitcase on the bed and picked up a pillow. She held the pillow to her face and breathed in the scent of lavender. Marcus and Leena really had readied everything. Lilah opened her suitcase and hung the few items of clothing she owned in the low ceilinged closet. There was no dresser, so she left what couldn't be hung up in the suitcase on the closet floor. Besides, now there really wasn't any room to share the tiny space with anyone else. Her one little suitcase and its belongings was enough to fill it completely.

The last couple of moves Lilah had stopped unpacking and decorating. It seemed pointless to make a room her own when she was only going to have to leave everything behind almost as soon as she finished. She would live out of a laundry basket instead. It infuriated her parents, especially her mom, but it was her way of communicating how much she hated not having a steady home and consistency.

This move was different. Even if no one ever clued her in as to what was going on, she knew something big was happening in the family. Family came first at all costs. Their code that had been set by Marcus for everyone to follow made it clear that everything they did had to be what was best for the protection of all. This was why they moved regularly. This was why she had to always be aware of what she said or did to not draw questions or raise suspicion from others. This was why she was not allowed social media accounts and had to try to avoid being the subject in anyone's pictures at all costs. This was why her life was miserable.

Being social and being young go together like air and breathing. Her heritage was extraordinarily rare and different from any of the people she had been around in her life, but some of the aspects of other cultures were the same no matter where they lived. Teenagers and young adults want to be a part of things. She wanted to be a part of things too, but that could never be.

Lilah looked around the bedroom again. There was one tiny window, and she struggled to open it. Once she got it unstuck, she opened it halfway. The window stayed open on its own, and she hoped she would be able to get it to close. It was rather chilly out, but she wanted some fresh air. Her parents had mostly kept to the warmer climates, so a crisp Midwest autumn evening was a new experience. This was about the coldest it got in the dead of winter where they used to live. She tried to shimmy the window shut again before it cooled her room off too much. It stuck at first then came down with a loud bang. She waited to see if her mom was coming to investigate, but she didn't.

'She's probably reading my thoughts again and knows I'm in my room safe without having to check,' Lilah thought while rolling her eyes. Her parents had preached to her since the day she learned about who she was that having abilities doesn't mean you have to use them. They constantly reminded her that private thoughts are meant to be private. Granted, it was usually when she asked one of them to tell her what someone was thinking or if a boy liked her or not. Still it seemed their whole view of private thoughts went out the window when it came to their own daughter. They never stayed out of her head.

There was a heavy presence in the bedroom. Lilah knew it had once been a room meant to house servants, and the energy of the spirits from days past still lingered in the tiny space. Most of their souls had long since moved on, but their imprint remained. If her powers had already blossomed, she would be able to see them as clearly as when they had lived if she chose.

Her powers. The notion distracted her again. She wished she could turn them on by merely willing it to happen, but that's not how it worked. They would slowly increase over a long span of time. Each gift would develop in its own time and take years to reach full potential. If she could just go ahead and begin the process, it would be enough to satisfy her for now.

Chapter Three
Preparing

"Why can't we just hit a drive thru?" Lilah pleaded.

"That garbage? It'll clog your arteries."

"Really, mom? Really?" Lilah was irritated. The one perk she enjoyed the most after learning of her own immortality was not having to worry about living healthy. Her body would heal itself. It would cleanse itself. It would rejuvenate all damaged cells. To Lilah, this meant she could live off of chocolate shakes and french fries alone if she chose.

Her mom pulled in to a parking space of the small town family restaurant off the highway a few miles from the farmhouse. "Get us a table. I'm going to try your dad," she instructed Lilah.

"Sure thing, *Abby*," Lilah said with a smirk. There could be no mentioning of the word mom while they were in public together. They could almost pass as twins.

Lilah entered the restaurant and saw the 'Please Seat Yourself' sign. She scanned the room and found a private booth near a television mounted on the wall. She sat down, and the waitress approached the table right away and handed her a menu.

"Anyone joining you?" the waitress asked.

"My sister is still outside."

The waitress plopped another menu across the table and laid out two rolls of silverware that had been tucked in her apron. "Can I get you something to drink?"

"My sister will want a glass of ice water and coffee," Lilah scanned the restaurant. It didn't look too busy. "Would it be too much to ask for a chocolate shake?" Lilah leaned toward her and whispered, "I'll tip well," with a smile.

"Nah sweetie. It's no trouble," the waitress said before heading to the kitchen.

Lilah knew the waitress probably wasn't happy about the shake, but she couldn't read her thoughts. Even if she could, she would always be reminded not to do so. *'Private thoughts are private for a reason,'* Lilah repeated her mother's words again in her head.

"You ordered a shake, didn't you?"

Lilah's head quickly turned to face her mom who was standing by the booth scowling at her. "I wanted to hit a drive thru. This was your choice."

Her mom slid into the seat across from her. "One of these days, you are going to work a waitress to death."

"That's not possible," Lilah clenched her jaw.

Her mom stared at her a moment then shook her head. "Did you order me a coffee?"

"Yes, Abby, I did." Lilah's eyes twinkled with delight at using her mom's first name as the waitress approached with coffee pot in hand. She was still young enough to find enjoyment in being able to act as though her mom were an equal when others were around.

The waitress left again promising to return after they'd had a few minutes to look over the menu. Lilah glanced at it then put it down. "Did you talk to dad?"

"Yeah, but only for a moment. He was busy."

"Where is he?"

Her mom slowly looked up and set the menu on the table. "He's been with your uncle working on a cover story for our cousins in Texas. They'll join us in a few days or so."

The cousins were actually aunts and uncles, but their family didn't use relation titles accurately. Everyone appeared about the same age, so it was easier to call each other cousins without raising suspicion. Marcus and Leena had twelve children, eight boys and four girls. Only the girls were able to have children of their own, and there were only five of the boys who were still alive. The first generation of Air were the only family given the title of Aunt or Uncle.

Lilah hadn't seen her Uncle Todd since she learned about the family history. There were only phone calls and texts. He came to help her mom and dad guide her through what it meant to be an Air descendent. Lilah never met more than a handful of family members in her life, but Uncle Todd had always been her favorite.

The waitress strode up to the table with her order book out. "You all set?"

Abby ordered a Julienne salad with Italian dressing on the side.

"Why?" Lilah pleaded silently. *"Why not order something that has real flavor?"*

"And you?" The waitress jarred Lilah from her thoughts. "Are you ready?"

"I'd like a patty melt and fries."

"Would you like soup or salad with that?"

"What's the soup?"

"We have vegetable and chicken dumpling."

"Chicken dumpling," Lilah grinned. *"Maybe it wasn't such a bad idea to skip the drive thru."*

Abby took a deep breath and looked at Lilah before shaking her head.

Lilah laughed. "What?"

"Do you ever think about anything besides food? Besides junk food to be more specific?"

"Of course I do!"

Her mom shot her a challenging look, "Like what?"

A slow mischievous grin began to spread across Lilah's face. "Boys, of course."

Abby threw up her hands and smiled. She added some ice to her coffee then stirred it to cool it off.

Lilah turned her attention to the television and the breaking news story that had come on. She read the words scrolling across the bottom of the screen.

"Did you see this?" Lilah asked her mom.

Abby craned her head around to see the screen. "I heard about it on the radio this morning before we left the house."

"Are we causing it?" Lilah asked, still reading the captioning that wasn't quite keeping up with the newscasters.

"What do you mean?"

"They're talking about a tornado that hit thirty miles from here during the night."

"And you think we did that?" Abby looked puzzled.

"No. Not *us*. They're saying it's the twelfth tornado to hit this state in the last week."

"It is tornado season, Lilah. That's what happens in the Midwest."

"That's in the spring I thought."

Abby cocked her head to the side. "Primarily I suppose, but they occur all year long."

"So, it's not because of us?"

"You just said you didn't think it was us causing them."

Lilah looked around to make sure no one had started listening in on their conversation, and then she lowered her voice even more. "The family are coming here, right? Everyone is focused on this area. Couldn't that cause a rash of storms like this?"

"No. I mean there are enough of us to cause a tornado if we tried, but just thinking about a place or even being in the same place isn't enough to cause one," Abby explained, understanding now what was on her daughter's mind.

"But twelve in a week? That doesn't sound excessive to you?"

Abby shrugged. "Maybe a little. It's not unheard of for so many to come through close together like this. And-"

Abby's mom stopped before she could finish her thought as the waitress approached with Lilah's soup. "Here you are. Chicken dumpling," she said as she sat the bowl in front of Lilah. "Enjoy."

"And what?"

Abby looked up at her daughter confused.

"You started to say something."

"Oh, it was nothing. Don't worry about it."

Lilah added salt to her soup. She stirred it in then cut a dumpling with her spoon. She lifted the spoon toward her mouth, but stopped and looked at her mom. "Balance. That's what we need to remember. Is that what you were going to say?"

Lilah put the spoon in her mouth and savored the taste. Chicken dumpling was definitely one of her favorites. She eyed her mom carefully wondering if she would even answer.

Finally Abby spoke. "Yes. Balance. That's what I was going to say."

Lilah nodded then continued to eat her soup in silence while watching the television for more news of the storm. "One confirmed death and several are still missing," the reporter was saying. She looked at her mom worried.

The waitress returned. "Okay, a salad for you," she said setting the plate in front of Abby. "And a patty melt with fries for you," she turned toward Lilah and set it down. "Can I get you ladies anything else? More coffee?"

"Yes, please," Abby looked up and smiled.

Lilah turned her attention back to the television and sat quietly trying to hear what was being said this time. "At least one tornado touched down in the Greenville area west of Fairview overnight, tearing through structures, overturning vehicles and leaving thousands without power."

She moved her fries around on her plate not feeling as hungry as she had before. It was unlike her to ever lose her appetite.

The news reporter continued, "Power companies have crews working to restore power. The National Weather Service said the tornado touched down around 3 am southwest of Greenville and continued on a path through the town leaving dozens of businesses and homes damaged."

Abby turned back to her salad and picked up a strip of bell pepper with her fingers. She took a bite of it, but she wasn't feeling too hungry herself. *"Four will be confirmed dead by noon,"* she notified her daughter silently.

Lilah studied her patty melt for a moment wondering if she would ever learn what was actually going on, or if she'd just be forced to piece bit by bit together herself. Finally she picked up half the sandwich and took a bite. As she did, she noticed a group of friends walk into the restaurant. They were all close to her age. One of them stood out from the rest. She was beautiful with creamy mocha skin. Her hair was pulled back tight. Lilah secretly watched her and the rest of the group take a table across the restaurant while drowning her fries in ketchup. She picked up one and right before she popped it into her mouth, she turned back to her mom, *"Can they sense us as well?"*

"Not as easily. They could do spells to find us if they ever had a need to. The spells would only give them a general area. No exact identification. But no, she doesn't know who we are."

Lilah ate her meal in silence after that thinking about the witch house they had past the night before on their way into town. Surely this girl was part of that group. *'How many more witches could there be in one town after all?'* She thought to herself before shooting a look to her mom that screamed don't answer that.

Witches weren't new to Lilah. She had seen them many times in passing before without them ever knowing who or what she was. She'd only ever met one witch who was a friend of her Uncle Todd's. It unsettled her running into one today given the circumstances.

Lilah looked back at the group who were now giving their order to the waitress. She couldn't help but wonder if this witch knew more about the events that were to come than she did.

AFTER BREAKFAST, LILAH and Abby sat in the car in the parking lot working on a game plan. They had to stock the house for about twenty adults which would not be an easy task. It would take several trips in their car no matter what, but they needed to go about it in a way where no one would question their purchases. This meant they would have to go to different stores in nearby towns. It was going to take all day.

---

1. http://www.clker.com/cliparts/7/6/9/b/13309573511112670181decorative-lines-2_large-md.png

Abby had already made a list of what was needed, hoping it would be enough for a week even though she didn't know how long they were going to be there. The list covered everything from food and toiletries to air mattresses since there weren't enough beds for everyone.

Lilah would have much rather stayed home. By the end of the day, she knew she would only be bored and exhausted with nothing good to show for it. Her mom didn't like to buy anything fun. Ever. Since she knew there was no way out of helping, her plan was to sneak as many snacks as she could get away with tricking her mom into buying.

They went to the first store in the next town to begin shopping for supplies. Abby was on a mission as though she were going to feed an army. Every cashier kept asking if they were having a party. Her mom would play it off so innocently and easily saying that she had family coming in from out of town to visit for a few days, or some other explanation that came easily for her. Her mom was an expert at thinking of a cover off the top of her head. She should be with her centuries of practice.

The two of them went to over a dozen stores total in several nearby towns. Every couple of stores, they would have to return to Fairview to unload the car to make room for the next haul. It took them all day to finish shopping and stocking the house. Loads of paper goods filled every closet. The deep freezer was packed. The kitchen cabinets overflowed, and staples had to be packed away in boxes on every surface available.

By the time they were through, family had already begun to arrive. Uncle Brian and his wife Marie were first. Lilah hadn't spent much time with them up until now. Before long, some of her favorite cousins Claire and Michael, and Sara and Gene were there. They helped put away items and inflate the air mattresses her mom had purchased for when they ran out of beds for the new arrivals.

They started to hand out room assignments. Two couples would each share a bedroom while Uncle Todd, Sara and Gene stayed in the attic. Lilah would share her room with Maddie when she arrived. This was all she needed to hear. Maddie had been the youngest in the family line until Lilah was born. She had been ordering Lilah around her whole life because Lilah is the only one young enough for her to treat that way. She'd rather give up her tiny bedroom altogether and join the others in the attic, but not before Maddie arrived. She was going to enjoy the private room until then.

After the last load, they came home to a delicious aroma stemming from the kitchen. Claire had made her famous clam chowder. Lilah wasn't hungry. It was the second time inside of a day she felt that way. It would usually be very alarming except she had been snacking since leaving the restaurant, begging her mom for something at every store. Still, there was no way she could resist something that smelled this good.

Lilah sat in the front room letting others do the work for a change. She had unloaded the car enough times for this visit. While she sat, a small silver car came up the driveway, so she moved to the window for a closer look. There was no mistaking the man who got out.

"Uncle Todd!" Lilah bounded out the door and down the steps. This had been the one and only thing she was looking forward to about coming here. It had been too long since she had last spoke to him in person.

"Hey, runt!" he teased, picking her up in a tight hug.

"Where's dad?" Lilah looked at the empty car.

"Sorry. It's just me."

"I thought he was with you."

"He was. There was still a little bit left to do. Myles stayed to finish up and told me to go ahead and leave."

Lilah was disappointed her dad wasn't with him, but it was made up somewhat by being able to visit with her uncle again. They walked inside to join the family in the kitchen.

All of them sat for hours after eating, talking and catching up. There really was no need to ever keep anyone posted in their family. Everyone could always easily know what another was doing or going through. It was merely a polite formality on the rare occasion they visited with each other that they did it. Tonight they were just trying to keep their minds off of anything especially the questions that no one had any answers to yet.

It was getting late, and everyone was starting to think about turning in for the night when Uncle Joseph and his wife Leona arrived. Some of the elders and older family members adjusted to the changing times over the centuries better than others. Joseph and Leona were not amongst them.

Uncle Joseph found room at the table to squeeze in a couple of chairs. His wife set about fixing them a meal because there was nothing left of the clam chowder. They never had a quick bite to eat. She always made him a full meal as had been the traditional way of the time when they were born.

He greeted everyone and checked that they all had safe journeys. Again, questions that were asked only out of polite courtesy, not necessity. Once the formalities were out of the way, he began the deep conversation.

"Has anyone been able to garner anything from Marcus or Leena?"

The group replied no or shook their heads in a round robin. The last anyone had heard from Marcus was weeks ago, shortly after he called for them to come together.

"Has anyone else tried?"

The response was the same. They wouldn't be able to pick up on Marcus. He was an Element which meant he was invisible to anyone's abilities. Leena was as well for she were Marcus' human match which was the equivalent of a soulmate except that matches also gained immortality as well as the rest of the powers of Air. They could easily read the minds of anyone else in the family who wasn't actively blocking their thoughts except for those two.

"He will contact us in time," Abby said measuredly.

"Marcus has never been silent this long. I'm afraid something has happened to him."

No one looked at Joseph. Everyone had thought this at some point themselves. But what could have happened? The four Elements could not die. They were spiritual creatures. Marcus' descendants did have the luxury to enjoy immortality provided they were careful because there were ways their lives could end. A handful of them have passed on. It was an unanswered question as to whether Leena was also completely safe from death as she was not an Element herself, but as his match, she may also be able to be spared. It was a question no one ever hoped to learn the answer to.

"I've been trying everything to find a way to locate him," Todd told Joseph.

"It's not enough!" Joseph yelled and slammed his fist on the table.

The outburst took the family by surprise. Joseph was normally quiet and gentlemanly. This was out of character for him.

"Marcus is my father..." Joseph whispered, and you could hear his voice cracking.

"Our father," Todd interrupted.

Joseph nodded and rubbed his hand across his forehead. "Yes, our father. What if something has happened to him? And so close to the Return?"

"Like what?" Lilah asked innocently.

Her family glared at her, but she wasn't entirely sure why what she had asked was so wrong. Nothing could happen to Marcus.

Lilah looked at them like they were overreacting and said, "Even if something happened, he would heal. Leena would be able to communicate with us. I agree with mom. He'll contact us in time."

Joseph's head was still resting on his hand. He lifted it slowly and looked at his brothers Todd and Brian. "Aye, but what if he's been detained?"

"Detained?" It was Sara who voiced how baffled she was by Joseph. "What do you mean detained?

"Captured," Joseph told her dead faced.

"By who? Why? And how would anyone be able to block his ability to communicate with us?" Sara was getting very worked up.

"Maybe if he were-"

"Even if he were unconscious, we still wouldn't be able to sense him. It's not like it is for you or me, but Leena would be able to reach us." Sara didn't let him finish. "Someone would have to know who Marcus was and would have had to devise a way to block his thoughts externally, or medically, or in some I don't know what kind of way!"

The family sat in silence. Some agreed with Sara, but a few wondered if it were possible to accomplish.

"Maybe they did!" Joseph's face reddened as he fired back.

Sara took several deep breaths trying to calm herself, but it did no good. "Most of the world doesn't believe there are people with the natural ability to see into the future. Who would believe there's an entire race of ancient immortal shapeshifters with virtually unlimited psychic power?" she rambled sarcastically. "Think, Joseph! Think."

"Other Elementals know about us," he said without missing a beat.

"Witches," Lilah muttered under her breath.

"Exactly," Joseph said pointing at her. "Witches-"

Abby cut him off this time, "Enough!" She shot him a look that warned him he better watch what came out of his mouth next. "We have no reason to think something is wrong. Witches or no witches, why would anyone want Marcus? Or Leena?"

"You know damn well what the reason is, Abby. It's the one thing we've feared almost our entire lives of people discovering about us."

Everyone quieted again. They were all thinking it, but it looked like no one was going to say it out loud. People had been searching for the fountain of youth almost since humans first appeared on earth. If anyone learned that their essence was it, they would be guinea pigs who would never leave the science lab again.

"Okay, Joseph, you're right. I won't rule out the possibility that something has happened to them. I just don't think it's the most logical solution." Abby was trying to keep the peace.

Joseph seemed satisfied that she acknowledged it was at least an option. "We need to try to be proactive," he told them. "I have no doubt something big is headed our way. It's the only reason we would be summoned like this. We need to be prepared."

"How do we prepare when we don't know what we're preparing for?" Gene asked him.

"Prepare for everything." Joseph was serious.

"It's late," Todd spoke before anyone could object to Joseph's apocalyptical strategy. "Some of us have traveled quite a bit more than others in the last couple of days. We're all exhausted. Before we start making plans to go to war against unknown forces, why don't we get some rest. Maybe sleep will help us all think a bit better in the morning."

The family murmured their agreements and headed off to their rooms one by one, including Lilah until only Todd and Abby were left. "Have you heard anything?"

"No," he answered.

"Well, no news is good news, right?" She put on a fake smile that quickly faded when she saw the look on his face.

"Not necessarily, Abby." Todd's face was racked with worry.

"What's going on? What aren't you telling me?

"I've heard nothing of Water for months. It wouldn't be a concern because that alone isn't highly unusual. I haven't been able to get ahold of any of my Fire contacts for weeks. It's like they've gone radio silent as the old saying goes."

Abby tried to understand what it could mean. "Do you think they are plotting something? Either of them?"

Todd glanced at her, and she knew that he was as lost as she was by the look in his eyes. "I really can't say. I want to say no. What would be the reason for there to be trouble? But the reality is our groups have barely had an acquaintance for four centuries now or more."

"When all the Elementals were hunted," she looked off, remembering the stories she had been told.

"Not all," Todd corrected her. "We weren't. We were the only ones saved from the wrath of the time."

"You think this is some form of revenge?"

"Now? After all this time? I don't think it makes sense, but I can't be sure. Earth insisted we distance ourselves when the witch hunts were in full force for our own safety. Plus, almost all of the witches who were murdered weren't real witches anyway. It was just an over-precaution or in most cases, an excuse to get rid of an enemy, whether they be personal or business. Regardless, Earth escaped pretty much unscathed only suffering some fear and future precautions from the ordeal."

"Then why?"

"That's what I'm saying. I don't know. None of us do because the Elementals have kept their distance from each other for so long. I can tell you that I haven't been able to track down Luke for over a week. And Meredith..."

Abby gasped, "Is she okay?"

Todd and Meredith had long been close. "She's MIA as well. The only people I've been able to communicate with as of late are our family. Not a single one of the other Elementals has answered my calls or returned my messages. But Meredith? Well her family is just down the road. She should be here."

"Maybe she's with Luke."

"Yes, of course, but why are they ignoring me?"

Abby's eyes danced with mischief, but Todd didn't seem to understand her reaction to what he had asked. "Well, when a man and a woman love each other very much..." she elaborated.

Todd closed his eyes and begged her to stop. When he opened them again, she was forcing her smile down. "Are you finished?"

Abby bit her lip and shook her head yes.

"I wouldn't worry about their silence because, yes," he emphasized, "sometimes couples need to be alone. This has been going on since Marcus first called for us. Then add their silence to everyone else's, and it's alarming."

Abby knew he was right. Most of the groups did stay fairly separate. There were exceptions of course all over where different Elemental groups got along and coexisted. Air was the exception. Their family had the fewest numbers, and they kept primarily to themselves.

Todd had contacts everywhere. Since the middle ages, Todd had wanted to say on top of any developments with any of the other groups.

"You think whatever is coming affects us all then?" It was something that had been gnawing at Abby since before she left Florida.

"Either that, or it's caused by one of us. Maybe more than one."

"Why would there suddenly be a fight between the Elementals?"

"The Return," Todd answered as though it were obvious. "It's less than a week away."

Abby looked up out of the corner of her eyes. "But we're not the problem in the Return. Why would this affect us?"

Todd leaned back and stared at the table. "Abby, I know no more than you do now. It's a hunch. The timing is too coincidental for it not to be connected to the Return."

She didn't want to admit it, but it had been on her mind as well. The Return always weighed heavily on her thoughts, on everyone's thoughts because there were so many unknowns concerning what would happen if the Return was ever completed. It did seem to be connected somehow.

"We should get some sleep," she told him when she couldn't think of anything more productive to say.

Todd agreed. Abby headed to her room. He went toward the attic stairs, but never went up. Instead he quietly headed down the back stairs into the kitchen where he continued to try to find answers well into the early hours of the morning. He thought no one was aware of what he was working on because he blocked his thoughts, but he also paid no attention to the others in the house in his distraction.

Lilah had still been awake when he quietly passed her room. She snuck down and sat a few steps from the bottom of the narrow staircase trying to gather any information she could. Her mother was keeping something from her. She could feel it. There were too many shared looks amongst her family, and there had been too many times the conversation seemed to be quieted on account of her. She intended to find out the truth one way or another.

She kept her mind as quiet as possible hoping that nothing would give her away. Her uncle sat at the table and began making phone calls. He was leaving one voice message after another. Lilah didn't recognize any of the names he was saying. Whoever her uncle was calling wasn't family, and she couldn't yet read him to find out who these people were.

"Hey. Meredith, when you get this, call me. I'm worried. Neither you nor Luke have answered my calls for days."

Lilah did know Meredith. She was the witch who was friends with her uncle. They had even met a couple times. She had never heard anyone talk about someone named Luke before now. *'He's probably a witch, too,'* she thought before quickly clearing her mind again thankful her uncle didn't notice her.

The calls continued. Todd must have left a couple dozen messages before the kitchen grew quiet. Lilah was about ready to try to sneak back upstairs before her uncle came through the slightly cracked doorway and found her. She assumed he would probably head to bed soon. Then he started talking again, and Lilah wasn't sure if it was to himself or if he finally managed to get an answer.

"I've tried everyone. I can't get ahold of any of the vamps."

Lilah gasped, and that was enough to give her away.

Footsteps approached, and her mother tore open the door to the stairs. "What are you doing here?" her mother was livid.

Lilah hadn't heard her mom come back down. She jumped to her feet filled with surprise and stood eye to eye with her mom. "What does Uncle Todd mean by vamps?" Lilah fired back.

"Nothing," her mom told her. "Go to bed."

"I heard him..."

Her mom stopped her. "Camps. He said camps. You'd have heard it clearly if you weren't trying to eavesdrop through a practically closed door."

"Camps?" Lilah asked more to herself than to her mom. *'Maybe that is what he said,'* she thought.

"Yes. Exactly. Bed. Now."

Lilah walked up the stairs. Her mom was too angry for her to try to press for information tonight. It would have to wait. She wanted to know what her uncle meant by camps. He had to know more about what was coming then he had let on at the table earlier.

She walked into her room and laid on her bed. The only thing she could think about was what did her mom and uncle mean by camps. It didn't make sense unless there were known enemies somewhere lying in wait. If that were the case, the family should be working on some sort of defense strategy.

The only other possibility would be a quasi-refugee camp. If there were any family members in that kind of trouble, they would surely be helped by now. It only left the witches. It didn't make sense they wouldn't come together to help them if they were in need.

Lilah closed her eyes and tried to concentrate hard to focus on her mom, but there was nothing. She was blocked. Trying a different tactic, she tried to pick up on something psychically, anything that would help her figure out what Uncle Todd had been talking about downstairs. It was no use.

Taking a deep breath, she tried once more. This time she simply saw the letter V behind her closed lids. That was enough to convince her even though she knew it was just as likely a coincidence caused by her worried mind than it was any kind of vision. Besides, it was her mom who had recently told her coincidences are usually anything but just a day ago. Lilah stared at the window knowing there could only be one explanation. V is for vamps. Vamps as in vampires.

Lilah ran down the stairs again to the kitchen to confront her mom and uncle, but they weren't there. She looked around downstairs then went to her mom's room. No sign of her. She hesitated before checking the attic because she didn't want to disturb Sara and Gene, but she couldn't resist.

The attic stairs creaked and groaned beneath her feet, and she tried to walk them as quietly as possible. The only people she saw were her cousins who were sound asleep. She had no idea where her mom and Uncle Todd would have gone, but she had no doubt they left to continue their conversation about vampires in private. *'Vampires,'* she thought, shaking her head as she quietly retreated to her room. *'Could it possibly be true?'*

Chapter Four
My Leena

Marcus awoke in the makeshift hut inside the trunk of his tree unaware of the blistering cold outside. He kept the air around him warm protecting him from the harsh winter. A small haze of light penetrated through the bark. The dawn was still young.

It was clear what woke him so early. Leena was up again. Her father had taken ill, and her mother was adamant about marrying her off to a warrior in their tribe who could provide their family with meat from his hunts. The warrior was twenty years her senior and already had two wives. Leena had nightmares about the pairing, but found no way to escape its eventuality.

Marcus often became blinded by the rage and jealousy he felt over the thought of his Leena forced to marry a man she did not desire, but he knew intervening was forbidden. '*Observation only,*' his mind repeated.

"My Leena," he said to himself. Marcus dropped his shoulders and looked to the ground. "She's no more mine than this tree I call my home," he thought. "Less so as this tree can know my presence, something that Leena can never know."

More light was cutting through the trunk now. Marcus cupped his hands into his water pail to lift a drink to his lips. When the ripples stopped, he gazed at his reflection on the surface. His light bronze skin was just as smooth as the day he arrived. His brown eyes stared back at him. A beard covered his square jaw. He had made futile attempts to keep it cut with the sharp rocks he'd found to form spears, but had long ago given up. The man staring back at him was still quite striking even with the scruffy hair hanging from his chin, and Marcus sometimes had difficulty separating himself, his true self, from the image he saw clearly before him.

He rooted through the floor of the tree to find his provisions of nuts and some assorted vegetation that faired the cold weather. His last hunt supplied him with enough meat to last for weeks stored in the snowbanks outside. With the snow easily collected to melt for water, cooking and cleaning, Leena had not made daily trips to the stream with her buckets since a few weeks after Marcus first spied her. In fact, she rarely left her village at all. Marcus felt no need to leave his home if not to see her again.

Spring would break soon, and Marcus knew he should leave to learn from other villages. He also knew that was something he could never do. His connection to Leena was too strong. He worried about failing the Divine Spirit, but he had followed all of the rules laid before him. He only used his powers for safety and survival. He had not made anyone aware of his presence. Still, Marcus had fallen in love as much as he hated to admit it.

"Isn't that part of the human experience?" he wondered out loud. "Love."

Marcus convinced himself that having these feelings did not break the rules set for him. It actually could be considered part of what he was sent here to do. He was to study human interaction and experiences to understand them better. Marcus had definitely accomplished the latter. His feelings for Leena kept him confined to this tree most of the winter where he followed her with his mind's eye instead of experiencing anything for himself.

He rested his head back and began a breakfast of pecans and his own version of pemmican. He learned how to make it from watching the women of the village combine fruit and meat to make bars for the men to take on their hunts. Marcus didn't have everything they used, but what he managed to make tasted good and kept him satisfied. Fire couldn't be chanced this close to the village, so he had to travel a great distance to cook. He could prepare a week or more's worth of pemmican at a time, so it was his main staple.

While he ate, he watched her again. Marcus couldn't keep his thoughts away from her for long. She was layered in animal furs stoking the fire for warmth as well as to melt snow to drink. Leena was drained, and it showed on her face. Marcus wanted nothing more than to go to her. He wanted to hold her and comfort her. He wanted to take her away from the cruel fate that awaited her, but take her where? All he could do was watch over her and dream of a life that couldn't possibly exist between them. His time was limited. Not only would giving in to temptation and meeting her surely be suffered by severe punishment upon his return, but it would not help her in the long run. He would be interrupting her life only to abandon her in the fall when he had to return to the spirit realm.

He watched as Leena laid cool cloths on her father's wide forehead. Even with the cold that snuck in their hut overnight, he was still burning up. She propped his head with a bundle of fur and slowly fed him some broth to sip. Marcus knew her dad's end was near, but he would first improve. He would recover from this illness initially, but the toll it was taking on his body would bring about his demise in the autumn of the year. Marcus worried about how he would be around to witness Leena's grief because he was uncertain he would be strong enough to not go to her then. He could barely stay away now.

Marcus decided to spend the day exploring. He needed to try to get his mind off what his heart was feeling. He could keep the air around him warmed, so the temperature outside was of no concern to him. Marcus placed the shoes he had crafted on his feet. It was another trick he had learned from watching the villagers. His shoes were not as impressive. They were simply two sheets of animal hide from his first successful hunt tied around his feet with smaller pieces of hide tucked inside. They were inferior to what the villagers wore, but he had little time to construct anything before winter had settled in the area.

He removed the door of branches and vines from the opening of the tree. Marcus allowed the bitter air to burst forth and startle his warm body before controlling the air around him again. The cold was almost cleansing. It cleared the thoughts of Leena from his mind completely.

Marcus stepped outside and looked at the snow cover. It glistened in the morning rays that cut through the tree branches. The snow sparkled like it had memorized the starry night sky and was mimicking it on its surface. There was a light snowfall, and he liked the feel of each cold flake that landed on his skin before melting from his body heat.

The trees were silent and had been for months mostly. Most days the only sound was the night owl that rocked him to sleep each evening. Occasionally, a deer would make its way close enough for Marcus to spy, but they seemed to be aware not to travel too close to the village. Even without their constant chittering and running through the valley, Marcus was keenly aware of the animals that slumbered nearby. Many snakes, squirrels and other animals had made their winter homes in the vicinity. Marcus was careful not to hike near enough to disturb their homes or their rest.

The glistening white terrain was forgiving, but he slowly hiked for miles giving no real thought to where he was going until he reached the small clearing he used for preparing food. He no doubt walked there out of habit as opposed to intent. This location suited a fire perfectly as it was too far from the village for the smoke to be detected. He looked around and found the sycamore he had used to hide a small stash of coconuts before winter began. His supply was dwindling, and he would soon have to use the bucket to gather snow for melting to conquer his thirst.

Clearing a spot in the snow, Marcus drew warm air to the earth before sitting. He reached into his robes and pulled out a piece of pemmican. Marcus had been so mesmerized by the beauty of winter in the forest around him that he had not realized how much time had passed or how hungry he had become. He ate and drank from the coconut as he thought about how great this walk had been to help him organize his mind. He hadn't even thought about Leena for hours.

"Leena," he whispered. "Here I go again."

Marcus distracted himself by clearing his fire pit of snow. He had no trouble seeing wood beneath the snow or preparing it to burn with the forced dry air he summoned to it. Soon he had a small fire going, and he allowed the bitter air to chill his body so the heat from the flames could warm him. Leena escaped his thoughts again as quickly as she had entered them.

He stared into the flames for a long time thinking about nothing and everything. Marcus had always known that he and his companions controlled the elements, but he was amazed by how much humans could control them as well. It was evident how much they depended on them and their ability to manipulate them. Life would not be able to survive without the most basic uses of the four elements here. Fire meant survival. It provided heat and prepared food. Water was needed for everything to grow and thrive from the smallest blade of grass to the largest bear. Earth provided fruit and vegetation, poultices, and shelter. Air scattered seeds for life to continue and breezes to cool you. It also contained the very breath you needed for survival.

People found a way to harness these elements themselves. These villages didn't wait for air to disperse seeds. They harvested the seeds in the fall and planted them every spring. They had learn how to add nutrients to the ground to help the plants grow even if the earth was not that rich. They interfered with the natural course of water, so it would flow through fields. They created fire with tools of their own design.

It impressed him considerably. He knew the humans' ability to manage the elements were limited by comparison, but their accomplishments were nonetheless magnificent. No other creature had ever made such progress.

His thoughts on the inhabitants' progress were cut short, *'The fever has broken.'* Marcus continued to stare in the fire, but he could see the hut where Leena's family were excited and relieved to see her father doing better for the first time in days. He knew the relief would be short lived, but they still had a little time before they would see just how much he had weakened.

Marcus blocked the air from the fire, and it quickly died out. He covered his fire pit with snow and began the walk back. He decided to take the long way by walking across to the stream before heading north to his home. Winter was almost over, and he wanted to see the ice covering the stream again while he still could. It was one of many sights that he hoped would never fade from memory after his Return.

As he walked toward the stream, a branch snapped near him. It startled him, but he knew before he looked that it was a buck. Marcus had sensed the deer while he was still sitting by the fire. He stopped and turned to face it. It was close, but it was still at least fifty yards away. The buck saw him as well of that Marcus was sure. Marcus could sense the apprehension the deer felt, and knew it was unsure as to whether he was a threat. The deer bowed his head for a moment obviously deciding that he meant him no harm.

Marcus stood very still not wanting to cause an alarm. He knew that as soon as he moved, the deer would run. Marcus was awed by the buck's size. It's different seeing one like this than when you are watching from afar. He already knew how people and animals compared in size, but it didn't prepare him for experiencing it himself. The buck lifted his head again and turned away. Another noise had caused it to take heed. It turned back to Marcus before bolting off into the trees almost as though he was trying to give warning of possible danger nearby.

No more creatures made themselves known as he continued his walk toward the stream. Light was fading. There were still a couple hours before dusk, but the tree cover blocked most of it. Even after they shed all of their leaves, they still prevented a lot of the light from peering through. He knew he was getting closer even without being able to hear the bubbling of the flowing water. Marcus used his intuition to see the rocks and limbs that scattered the ground under the snow. He knew exactly where to step to avoid tripping on them. However, he hadn't yet learned to watch for ice.

The ground was slick where he stepped down with his right foot on the bank of the stream, and it slipped up in the air bringing his other foot with it. Before Marcus could react, he was falling and twisting until he landed on the ice covered stream with enough force to break through the surface into the near freezing water below. The forest was awakened by the sound, and every living thing scrambled for safety. Marcus could hear every one retreat even as the cold penetrated his entire body stinging like a thousand little mosquitos biting him at once.

Marcus clambered for the bank trying to pull himself out of the water, but he slipped back into the icy drink. He tried again and was able to grab hold of a large sturdy rock to pull himself up on. His right ankle shot pains up his leg, and his right foot jutted out at an awkward angle. The pain from the break was almost enough to distract him from the ache that ran down the length of his back.

He wound the air around him into a warm dry personal tornado to dry himself and his robes. It was the one problem he could easily fix. Sitting on the rock stunned with paralyzing fear, he wondered how the villagers faired in this weather. A fall like that would surely be fatal for them. They would freeze before reaching the warming fires of their home especially with injuries like his. Even if they did reach their home, a broken bone such as this one could lead to a permanent disability or death from infection.

The muscles in his back loosened first, and the ache quickly faded as it healed. His ankle would take more time. Marcus was unsure as to how long it needed or if he could do anything to help it along. Carefully and slowly, he moved his foot back to the correct position as best he could. The torrents of pain that rippled through him rocked him hard, and he almost slipped back into the stream.

Shoving his fist into his mouth, he bit down hard to prevent any screams from being released. The fear of his voice echoing far enough for anyone to chance hearing him was still a possibility that he couldn't risk. The aftershocks of the jolt started to fade, and he regained control of his breathing until he was once again calm. Time passed, and he had no way to tell how long he sat waiting for the ankle to heal. The only indication was the darkness that started to cover the valley like a blanket.

He ventured to move from the rock to the other side of the water before darkness fully took hold. There was a risk of falling in again, and it would amplify once all light was gone. It was easier than he expected. His ankle still cried out at him in the form of painful throbs that could be felt up to his knee, but it was not as intense as it had been when he moved his foot.

On the bank, he sat down again to rest and gave his ankle as much time as it needed. There was no way to tell how long it would take. All of his previous accidents had been minor by comparison. A pulled muscle or perhaps a scratch was the extent he had suffered. They had healed within minutes. This would likely take quite a while. Even when the veil of nightfall covered him, he continued to wait. He wouldn't attempt to make it home until the hunger in his abdomen became worse than his pain.

Slow and steady, he walked back to his tree as carefully as he could. Night was upon him. His faith in seeing the hidden obstacles in the covered ground had been shaken. Marcus wanted to reach the safety of his tree, and he vowed to stay there until spring came to light the wilderness with beauty and expose all of the hidden dangers once again.

Chapter Five
Vampires and Werewolves

Lilah didn't see her mom or her uncle until late the next evening. She was waiting on the front porch when the car pulled in the drive. "Where'd you guys disappear to?"

"We went to Trinity to meet with the rest of the family this morning," her mom answered.

"You had to drive all the way there? You couldn't have talked to them any other way?" Lilah was suspicious.

"It's nice to visit in person too, Lilah," her uncle told her.

"In the middle of the night?"

"It was morning when we arrived," her uncle explained.

"What are you getting at, Lilah?" her mom sounded irritated.

"I just thought you might have been checking on the camps."

Todd looked at Abby. "I told you it was a bad idea. Are you going to tell her or should I?"

Lilah shot her mom a look with her arms firmly crossed over her chest. *'They better not try to lie again this time.'*

"I won't lie to you," her mom said.

Lilah threw her hands up and groaned. "Would you stop already?" She stormed over to the swing and sat down so hard she worried for a second it might break from where it was attached on the ceiling of the porch. "Stop listening in on my thoughts all the damn time! You're always telling me private thoughts should stay private, but you never practice what you preach!"

"You're right." Her mom had that condescending appeasing tone to her voice that grated Lilah's nerves. "I'll stop."

"So get on with it," Lilah demanded. "What is it you claim you're not going to lie to me about?"

"You heard your uncle correctly last night. It was vamps that he said like you thought."

"Vamps?" Lilah looked at her uncle.

"Yes. Vampires." He swiftly looked back at Abby regretting getting into the conversation as soon as he spoke.

"You are saying vampires are real," Lilah asked incredulously.

Her mom started nodding slowly before finally saying it out loud in a hushed voice. "Yes."

"They were real at any rate," Todd saw how difficult it was for Abby being forced to have a conversation she wasn't prepared to have. "How many are actually left is still unknown."

Lilah was amused. Surely they were playing a trick on her. They were getting her back for eavesdropping last night. "Where did they go, Uncle Todd? Have you tried checking Transylvania? I hear they like to winter there."

"Enough," her mom's voice returned loudly. "You wanted to know, so we are telling you. Now, shut it and listen."

"The vampires are all dying off at an alarming rate," Todd went on.

"We don't know that," Abby insisted.

Todd walked over and sat next to Lilah. "She's right. We don't know for sure what has happened to all of them, but they have disappeared. That is a definite."

"Oh okay," Lilah rolled her eyes. "Sure. The vampires are disappearing. Whatever you say, Uncle Todd. Next, you're going to try and convince me the werewolves ate them, right?" Lilah said in a spooky voice while waving her fingers like she was telling a ghost story.

Her Uncle Todd looked baffled. "Why would the werewolves eat them? Water and Fire get along for the most part."

Lilah looked at her uncle confused. It dawned on her gradually that maybe what he was saying was true, but she wasn't sure. She crossed her arms over her chest, "I'm not falling for it, Uncle Todd. I know I'm still a baby compared to the rest of the family, but I'm not a kid anymore."

Todd looked at Abby who opened her mouth to say something before looking down. "I think I'm going to leave the two of you alone out here for a minute," he said, opening the screen door of the farmhouse and disappearing inside.

Lilah looked at her mom leaning against the porch rail across from the swing. Her thoughts were racing. Her mom just stared ahead rubbing her hands together in slow circles. Lilah tried to focus first on her mom then on her Uncle Todd who was now in the kitchen. It was no use. She couldn't pick up on their thoughts, and the only thought she had was the vampires are disappearing. Maybe even dying.

"That's right," her mom said, cutting into Lilah's thoughts. "Some of them are dying and in record number too. We can't be sure of the amount because the rest seem to have gone into hiding."

"Vampires," Lilah said weakly, ignoring yet another mind invasion committed by her mom.

"Yes."

"You told me–"

"I know what your father and I told you," her mom broke her train of thought. "You were young. You had just discovered witches were real. The pop culture at the time..." her voice trailed off.

Abby closed her eyes and swallowed hard. "The pop culture painted all of us out to be so different than what we are. It still does. You were caught up in all the myths, legends, the school for magic, and the vampires that sparkled. We thought it would be best to break everything to you slowly. Knowing you, you'd have wanted a werewolf as a pet."

Lilah gasped as the words slipped out of her mother's mouth. Her mom looked directly at her, and Lilah said more to herself, "They're both real." Everything was sinking in.

"Yes. I didn't plan for you to find out this way, but," her mother didn't finish her thought.

"But something's happening?"

"Exactly."

"What is happening?"

"I don't know."

"You know more than you're telling me! Will you ever stop treating me like a child?" Lilah jumped from the swing and walked away from her mom. "I know at twenty-one years old, I'm still a kid compared to the rest of the family, but I'm an adult as far as anyone else's standards are concerned. How old do I have to be before this family, before you, treat me like one?"

Lilah walked to the end of the porch and looked around. "All I've had to go through my whole life. No real friends because I can't let anyone discover our truth. Not to mention we never stay anywhere very long! I couldn't do anything like the other kids because if I got injured, I would heal too fast. People would ask questions." Once she started to vent her frustration over not knowing the truth sooner, everything started pouring out. She stared down the field that ran along the driveway toward the road. Part of her wanted to run. She wanted to leave and never come back.

"What would that help anything?" her mother asked.

"And that!" Lilah yelled, turning back to her mom. "You are aware that almost every other person on this earth are allowed private thoughts, aren't you? Just because you can eavesdrop in my head doesn't mean you should! Much less, it wasn't five minutes ago you told me you would stop!"

With that, Lilah ran inside the house and upstairs to her room. She paced the floor of her small bedroom for several minutes growing angrier by the second. *Vampires? Real. Werewolves? Real. They told me Water and Fire were different versions of us!*

The thought stopped her in her tracks. *Different versions of us!* Her anger continued to boil. *All this time, I thought Water and Fire were different versions of Air and Earth, psychics and witches. They're different versions of the Elements. Of course! Mom's favorite game to play was semantics, so she can say technically she wasn't lying.*

Lilah had never before felt this emotional. She was angry at her parents for not trusting her with the whole truth. She was embarrassed that she believed them blindly to the point where she would even doubt her Uncle Todd when he tried to tell her. She was humiliated that the whole family was probably downstairs right now laughing over how everyone treats her like a baby. She didn't try to block her thoughts. She wanted her mom to hear everything that was on her mind if she chose to eavesdrop in on what she was thinking.

'How could she lie to me like that? This isn't just withholding information. Her favorite excuse is, "I didn't LIE to you Lilah; I omitted something." I asked you point blank if vampires and werewolves were real, and you said NO! You LIED!'

Lilah could hear the voices of her mother and uncle trickle up the stairs. They were in the kitchen now and obviously had no intention of trying to talk to her again just yet. Lilah sat on the edge of her bed not sure what to do. She only knew she didn't want to be here in this house with them anymore. A cool air drifted in through the small drafty window and gave her a plan.

It wasn't hard at all for Lilah to climb out of the window onto the roof of the back porch. She hung over the edge and lowered herself down until her toes finally made contact with the rail on the side of the porch. Lilah jumped to the ground and looked around listening closely to hear if anyone was coming after her for a minute.

They must be giving her some much needed privacy and not paying attention to her thoughts. No one seemed to notice her except the white squirrel who was eyeing her intently from the other side of the house. Lilah started slowly away from the house staying on the grass next to the gravel drive to not make any noise. Halfway down the drive, she took off at a sprint.

Lilah ran out onto the state road at the end of the drive and began the two or so miles toward town. She kept running until she could see the lights of Fairview growing brighter in the distance. She slowed her pace and only then became aware of her pained side and her chest that was working hard to keep up in the brisk fall air.

Slowing to a walk, she knew it wouldn't be much longer until the restaurant came into view. It was the only place in town she knew. She only hoped she would have enough time to get there and calm down a bit before her mom realized she had left.

'I hope she worries,' Lilah thought. *'I hope she goes to check on me and is scared when I'm not there.'*

Lilah knew even if that happened, it would only be fleeting. Her mother would find her easily since Lilah couldn't block her thoughts yet.

She was aware of the sound of an approaching vehicle behind her and knew it might already be her Uncle Todd with or without her mom. It was coming toward her fast. Lilah turned to look back just as the pickup truck took notice of her and swerved to avoid hitting her. She jumped out of the way and wound up falling into the ditch. The pickup swerved back and forth. Its tires screeching before the driver finally regained control. About half a dozen boys were in the bed yelling and laughing. High schoolers? College? Lilah couldn't be sure.

Lilah tried to stand up, and a pain shot through her arm as she tried to push off the ground. She sighed in frustration. She managed to climb out of the ditch to the side of the highway. She sat down on the shoulder of the road and looked her arm over. It was already starting to bruise and swell, possibly broken. It wouldn't matter. It would be healed soon.

The rest of the trip toward town continued at a very slow pace. Her wrist throbbed relentlessly with the vibration of each step, but she reminded herself with every second, it was already healing and would soon be back to normal. The pain was taking her mind off the argument with her mom and how angry she had been when she left. It also gave her a chance to realize how cold it had become that evening and made her regret not grabbing something heavier than a jacket to wear. It seemed to take forever, but she finally saw the restaurant come into view.

As she neared the parking lot, she saw the same full size red pickup that nearly ran her down not even thirty minutes ago. Her anger started creeping back. *'Idiots,'* Lilah thought. *'Why do people always have to go out acting dumb, trying to impress their friends? They easily could have killed me tonight.'*

Lilah stopped near the door of the restaurant and smiled devilishly. *'Well, not me, but they could've killed someone.'*

Her wrist still looked bad, so she pulled her sleeves down until she held the ends in her palms to prevent them from rising back up. The last thing she needed was for someone to notice the injury especially if she stayed here long enough for them to see that it healed itself.

She walked through the door of the restaurant and looked around. She saw the occupants of the pickup gathered in a corner booth. She would have known it was them even if she hadn't seen their truck outside. The one with the blue hair and white hoodie was just as loud here as he had been in the bed of the truck as it was flying down the highway. She decided to sit at the counter on the other side of the dining room.

"You okay, sweetie?" the waitress asked as Lilah was pulling out her stool.

"Yes," Lilah replied, assuming the waitress was only concerned about a young woman out alone and obviously upset.

The waitress looked her over before shrugging and walking away. Lilah looked after her puzzled. She turned to sit on the stool and saw her reflection in the front window. She was covered in dirt and grass from her tumble in the ditch.

Lilah headed to the restroom and could feel every eye on her from each table she passed. Once in front of the mirror, she took off her jacket and shook it out. Lilah brushed her jeans off and picked grass and leaves out of her hair. She wished she had brought a brush with her, but her decision to run out wasn't exactly planned.

Heading back to the counter, Lilah could feel her anger boiling over again. Her cheeks flushed with embarrassment from being the center of attention, and she was certain she would be the topic of small town gossip for days. Everyone continued to stare. She wished she could read their minds, but she really didn't need that ability to know what they were thinking. Who was this stranger, and why did she look like she just fought a scarecrow in the middle of a cornfield and lost?

The waitress walked up to her from behind the counter and handed her a menu. Lilah wasn't hungry. *'This is becoming a trend,'* she thought. She continued to look through the menu while waiting for the waitress to return. The guys in the corner were being obnoxious, and she wondered if the rest of the diners were as annoyed by them as she was.

Lilah turned her head slowly toward the group. She glanced at them one at a time until she saw him. He was on the end facing her. Their eyes met briefly before he looked away, and Lilah felt the entire room move around her as though the stool she was on suddenly shot across the restaurant toward him. She didn't realize her breathing had stopped until she gasped for air, and everything returned to normal, leaving her a little dizzy. She wondered who he was. She could sense witches, but no one had ever had that effect on her before.

"Maybe she's homeless," Lilah her a voice behind her say. She whipped her head around to look, but couldn't tell who was speaking.

Her waitress appeared again and asked if she needed a few more minutes. "No, I'm ready. Could I just get a chocolate shake?" Lilah smiled, "I'll leave a good tip."

The waitress nodded and took the menu. As she walked away, Lilah heard her make a remark about how she should have told her the milkshake machine was broken.

"If it's too much trouble," Lilah called out to the waitress's back, "I'll just have iced tea."

The waitress turned to her and smiled. "It's no trouble, sweetie. I'll be back in a few."

Soon the waitress was busy writing in her order pad. "All these kids ever want are milkshakes. They don't care how long it takes for us to make them, or what a bother it can be especially when we're busy. Leave a good tip my hind end. None of them know how to tip."

Lilah stared toward the direction where the waitress had disappeared behind a divider. Her mouth hung open. *I can't believe she said that! I guess I'll be one of the kids who don't know how to tip tonight.*

A throbbing pain in her wrist brought her thoughts back to the matters at hand. Lilah figured she probably got what she deserved for running off like she did. She was still angry and embarrassed, in pain and could feel a headache coming on from all the commotion around her.

The restaurant was loud. Everyone was talking, and Lilah wondered how anybody could follow their own conversation with all the noise around them. She could hear bits and pieces of everyone's conversation. There was a woman who was worried about a sick friend. Another woman was actually talking about her husband cheating on her. Loudly. In public! She could even hear the group of guys in the corner talking about girls, homework, and football.

Then she heard it. Or rather, then she paid attention to it. One guy far off was talking about her.

"I'm going to do it. I'm just going to walk over there and introduce myself to her. That's what I'm going to do. Just as soon as I can will my legs to move me in that direction."

It was the same young guy she had noticed minutes ago. She didn't remember seeing him in the bed of the pickup truck. '*Maybe he was in the cab.*'

He glanced back her way again and when he saw she was looking at him, he glanced down and nervously played with the straw in his glass. Lilah heard him, "She's looking at me. You idiot! Go talk to her!"

He never moved. Instead he took a pen that was laying on the table and glanced at her again before writing something on the corner of the paper placemat. He ripped the corner off and looked directly at her. "*Just go give it to her. You can do this.*"

'*Wait,*' Lilah sat up straight. '*He's not talking. How can I...?*'

She turned away so as not to stare and tried to concentrate. He was mad at his friend. Kent? Trent. Trent was the driver. Trent hadn't seen her walking, but he did. He saw her, and grabbed the wheel to prevent an accident. He felt horrible that his friends didn't seem to care about their near miss.

Lilah slowly turned around and looked at the people in the tables along the front windows of the restaurant. She could hear bits of actual conversation and other pieces that she couldn't be sure if the words were spoken or merely thought. She saw a man sitting alone and tried to focus on him without noticeably staring.

'*Nothing. It's been a bad night. You're upset and-*' Lilah's thoughts were interrupted when she heard him.

"*Might as well go home. Alone here. Alone there. What difference does it make?*"

Lilah was watching the old man the whole time. His lips never moved. She watched him pull out his wallet and put some bills on the table. He got up and headed toward the door. Lilah couldn't help but stare now. As he passed her, she watched as his mouth stayed closed, but she could hear him, "*She'd be quite a pretty little thing if she owned a hair brush.*"

Lilah looked down at the floor. Everything came at her at once. It felt like an entire stadium yelling not just a couple dozen people in a small restaurant. She pulled out her phone and sent a text to her mom, "Come get me. NOW!"

The room started spinning, and Lilah began to feel sick. Her stomach churned out a warning that she needed to get somewhere private immediately. She stood up and took a step toward the door thinking she should go outside to get some fresh air. One step was all she managed. The last thing she heard before passing out was the voice of the young man across the room, "Is she okay? Something's wrong." Lilah couldn't even be sure if he said it or only thought it.

When Lilah opened her eyes, she was on her back on the floor in front of the counter. She lifted her head, but her mom stopped her. "Keep still, sis," her mom said. "Don't try to get up just yet."

From somewhere behind her, Lilah heard a voice say, "Show's over folks. Move on."

Lilah looked around. She recognized a few of the faces from the restaurant, her mom and uncle, and then she saw him. On the other side of her mom was the guy from the pickup. As soon as she recognized him, her face flushed. Lilah glanced back to her mom then to him again.

"This is Jackson," her mom told her. "Lucky for you he was here. He got you on your back and your legs raised above your heart before Todd and I arrived."

Lilah started to move again, and this time no one tried to stop her. Instead, she felt her uncle's hands move beneath her arms to help her sit up. She was only a few inches from Jackson now. "Thank you," she said to him in barely a whisper.

He looked down, "It was nothing really. Glad you're okay." Slowly he lifted his head and flashed her a smile.

Lilah couldn't pull her eyes away from him.

"Let's get you home," Todd said.

Lilah knew her uncle was nervous about the attention this could draw to them.

Todd and Abby helped Lilah to her feet. They paused to make sure she was alright then they all headed to the door. When Lilah stopped for her mom to open the door for her, she felt someone grab her hand. She turned back quickly. It was Jackson. He was pressing something into her palm, and she wrapped her fingers around it. "Thanks again," she told him before following her family out to the parking lot while tucking the paper she held into her pocket.

Once in the car, the silence was deafening. Lilah knew they were mad and an argument would begin soon. She deserved it. What she had done was stupid. Anything could have happened. She had unloaded on her mom about treating her like a child then she went and acted like one.

"I think it'll be fine," Abby said.

"With your story that she went for a ride on her bike and wrecked it? I doubt anyone will wonder why someone new to the area would be riding their bike this late in the dark. And in this weather! Top notch cover up, Abby."

Lilah couldn't help but giggle. Her uncle's sarcasm always amused her.

"What?" her mom asked.

"Nothing," Lilah replied.

"Didn't you say something?"

"I just laughed. That's all. Sorry."

"This is funny to you?" her uncle was irate. "We had no idea where you were. Your mom thought you went to bed until she got that text."

"I know. I'm sorry," Lilah began.

"Not sorry enough. We thought you were dead. We couldn't find you."

Lilah was mystified. It must've been after she passed out, so they couldn't get clear details from her mind. "You found me though."

"Only because Abby knows you well enough to think you went for a milkshake!" Uncle Todd was almost yelling now, and he hit the steering wheel.

"I passed out right after I sent the text," Lilah said more to herself to try to understand why they would have any difficulty finding her.

"We figured as much, honey," her mom soothed.

"No, Abby! She wants to be treated like an adult. Stop babying her!"

"You're right, Uncle Todd."

"I know I'm right! And now you're in the backseat giggling because you think this little stunt you pulled tonight is funny."

"That's not why I laughed. I laughed at what you said."

"What did I say?" Uncle Todd looked at her through the rear-view mirror.

Lilah deepened her voice and mocked her uncle, "Top notch cover up, Abby."

Abby's mouth dropped and looked at Todd who was still eyeing Lilah in the mirror. "I never said that."

"Yes, you did."

He shook his head and gripped the steering wheel tighter.

"I heard you, Uncle Todd."

"I never said anything, Lilah. I thought it."

"Oh," Lilah wasn't sure how to respond.

"You're not surprised?" her mom asked.

"At the restaurant..." Lilah began then stopped.

Uncle Todd eyed her in the mirror again, "You could hear people's thoughts at the restaurant?"

"Yes," Lilah rubbed her temples which were beginning to pound again. "At first, I thought I was just overhearing conversations, but then I started to realize that some of them weren't speaking."

There was an uncomfortable silence that returned in the car. "What is it?"

Neither her mom nor her uncle answered.

"What?" Lilah repeated more demanding. "What's wrong?"

"Nothing's wrong, honey. It's good that your abilities are developing. You should be happy. You've wanted this for a long time."

"Then why are you two acting like this?"

"Like what?" her mom asked.

"I don't know. I can feel something between the two of you. Like it's worrisome."

Her uncle cleared his throat. "Everyone is different, Lilah."

"I know," she groaned. She had been hearing this her entire life. "Some have stronger psychic abilities. Some heal faster. Some develop younger or older."

"Close," he said, glancing at her in the mirror again. "Usually, it begins with your immediate family like your parents."

"It did," Lilah chimed in.

"Yeah, but then it's other family, friends, neighbors or other people you see often. It usually takes years before you're able to hear the thoughts of complete strangers."

Lilah thought about it for the rest of the drive. Her abilities turned on a like a light switch. One minute, she could hear nothing then she could hear everyone.

"What are you thinking about?" her mom asked as her uncle put the car in park at the farmhouse.

Lilah snapped to attention, shocked. "You can't hear me?"

"No, and I've been trying ever since you went silent."

"I blocked my thoughts from you?" Her voice didn't hide her shock.

"And me as well," added Uncle Todd.

"But how?"

"Well, for me, what I do is-"

Lilah interrupted him. "I didn't do anything Uncle Todd," her voice strained.

"It's okay," her mom told her. "It's been an eventful night, and you had a lot to say about privacy earlier. I'm sure you're blocking us without realizing you are doing it."

Lilah mulled it over for a while. They got out of the car, and she was quickly reminded about her injured wrist when she pushed open the car door without thinking. The pain had lessoned, but she still winced. Crossing it over her stomach and keeping it still with her other arm, she headed up to the porch.

Todd raised an eyebrow then nodded as though he answered his question before he could speak it, "You fell tonight. It'll be fine by morning."

Abby extended a hand to help Lilah up the stairs, and Lilah looked at her and deliberately thought, *I was thinking that my abilities came on at once like someone flipped a switch.'*

Her mom smiled, and said, "Exactly. Like a switch."

Lilah breathed a sigh of relief at the familiarity of her mom invading her mind. She was happy knowing that her thoughts could be blocked now. Once she figured out how she did it.

Chapter Six
History Lesson

Lilah was still struggling to wrap her mind around the news that had been dropped on her like a bomb well into the night. Vampires and werewolves were real. She waited for her mom, Uncle Todd or Aunt Akalah to say something. Akalah was actually her great-great-great grandma, but they never went by typical familial labels.

It was Akalah who finally spoke. "Each of the Elements were punished in their own way."

"Not Air," Lilah said.

"Oh yes, Air too. That's why Marcus has been trapped here for a millennium." "But I was always told he followed orders?"

"He did. That is why our line has the least of the punishments doled out by the Divine Spirit."

"Why was he punished at all?"

"It was a risk for the four of them to be here on this planet as mortals. They were each made aware of the chance they were taking. If one did not make the Return, none would be allowed home."

"So that's the punishment? Being stuck here instead of returning to their spiritual form."

Akalah nodded. "Mostly, yes. Air's punishment is the annual denial of being able to go back. It's also the unknown of what will happen to us when the Return does occur."

This was something Lilah was highly aware of and tried not to dwell on. No one knew what would happen. Would they die instantly? Would life continue for them as it always had? Would they become mortal?

Her uncle added, "None of us really know what the Divine Spirit's reasoning was when he punished the Elements. We're not supposed to know any more than humans can figure out their own divine plan. Some of us have had a few more years to think on it then others to try to decipher the meaning of it all."

"Why don't you enlighten us, Uncle Todd?" Abby said in a tone that hinted this was not the first time she had heard his explanation.

"Don't mind if I do," his eyes twinkled.

"Wait," Akalah interrupted him. "She needs to learn the basics first."

Todd sat back and crossed his feet at the ankles. "Okay. Carry on."

Akalah "Air and Fire are immortal. Earth and Water are not save for the two Elements who rule their lineage. Fire stays young as do we. Earth can change their appearance with spells. Water Elementals are unable to change except for their transformation during the full moon which cannot be stopped no matter how hard they try. I'm told natural born Water's can change at will though I've never met one."

"And they've tried everything," Abby added. "There's always rumors that some have figured it out," she shrugged. "Who knows?"

Lilah's aunt and uncle agreed. "Most importantly, to me at least," Akalah continued, "we have natural human counterparts. Some are more real than others. There are people who are born more sensitive to the spiritual energy that connects us all. That is how a mom knows that the ringing of the phone will bring terrible news involving her child before the phone actually begins to ring. Or why there are mediums who assist police in solving murders because they communicate with the spirit of the deceased."

Spiritual energy had been explained to her before, and Lilah tried to remember what she had been taught. It was like a web in a way. Everyone, even the Elements, were all created from one collective spirit energy source. We were all connected by it. The human body created a blockage that cut them off from the source. Some people were more in tune with the web that connected them than others. Throughout history even before the Elements arrival, people had felt that connection, and they were usually hunted down and killed if their secret was discovered.

Akalah went on, "There are those who choose to practice witchcraft and declare themselves witches. There is an innate power in all of nature. These self-made witches are able to harness a fraction of that power, but they do not possess the magic that lies inside a true Earth descendant."

"There are even people who claim to be vampires and drink their partner's blood. Choosing to drink a human's blood does not a vampire make, but if they're happy in the world they created, let them enjoy it."

"Vampires and werewolves can actually be created although the practice has been frowned upon for centuries. Still, there is the occasional werewolf attack survivor, and vampires still take mates who they turn in order to have an immortal companion. Love is the only acceptable reason for Fire to turn a human today."

Akalah stopped there. She knew there was more that Lilah had not yet learned, but it was a lot to take in at once. She felt that after a time when Lilah had digested this new information, she would fill her in on the rest.

"So how do the punishments fit the crime, Uncle Todd?" Lilah asked when she was sure her aunt had finished.

"Well, in order, it was Air, Earth, Fire and Water from who followed orders the most to least. Air and Earth got off fairly easy. True, Earth isn't immortal, but their spells allow for a lot of aide and ease in life. Fire is immortal, but cursed to be persecuted and alone. Water has the worst of it. The agonizing bone breaking transformation every lunar cycle."

"What did Water do?"

"No one knows," he answered. "Marcus hasn't seen Water since the first night they left the rock as far as I'm aware. Any of the Water clan I've ever met have been tight lipped about their Element as well."

"I've always believed it was for protection. Water probably feels like everyone is pointing fingers," Abby added.

"Fire wasn't there that night either," Todd pointed out.

"No, but Fire has made the Return attempt hundreds of times since. Water disappeared without a trace."

"What will happen if they never make the Return?" Lilah asked.

Akalah shook her head as though she wouldn't entertain the thought of it never happening. "It's not good whatever it is I know that. Balance in everything is brought about by the four Elements. Without it, things have moved off course. It started slowly then picked up speed and is ever increasing in magnitude. Look at the number of natural disasters. There was a volcanic eruption just last night in Iceland! I fear that if they don't manage to make the Return soon, this planet may not survive much longer."

"Why aren't we friends with the others?"

"What are you talking about?" joked Uncle Todd. "One of my best friend's is a witch."

Lilah smiled. She had met Meredith several times and was utterly fascinated by her.

"You've always been the strange one," Abby teased.

"Exactly!" Lilah looked at her uncle. "You're the only one of us to befriend a witch. Why is it so rare for the groups to intermingle?"

"Protection and habit," Akalah was the one who answered her. "Earth, Fire and Water have all suffered persecution at more than one time. Assumed witches were burned at the stakes. People were drowned out of fear of them being a witch or a werewolf. People's graves were dug up and stakes driven through their heart to make sure they stayed dead. The groups separated to keep themselves safe then it became habit for us to stay apart."

Lilah thought it over, but something was still plaguing her. "There's one thing I don't understand."

"What's that?" her mom asked.

"None of this started with us."

"How do you mean?" Uncle Todd furrowed his brow.

"Well, there are legends of vampires that date back long before the Elements came for one."

"Ahh," he smiled. "I see now." Uncle Todd leaned back and appeared to be deep in thought.

"Are you going to explain this or not?" Abby asked him confused by his initial response.

He nodded while continuing to stare off at nothing.

Lilah sat and waited for someone to explain to her how vampires could begin with Fire when they were already here. She was starting to wonder if anyone would.

"Alright," her uncle looked at her. "Have you ever heard of the term 'dead ringer'?"

"Isn't that when someone looks like someone else? Like exactly like that person? A doppelganger."

"Yes. Its origin dates back to the origin of the phrase 'saved by the bell' as well. Familiar with where the phrases got their start?"

Lilah shook her head.

"Way back, medical care was rustic and harsh at best. Sometimes people would be declared dead and buried when they were actually still alive, just unconscious with a faint heartbeat."

It clicked with something she had learned in school. "People became aware of this and started tying a string to the fingers of the deceased that ran above ground to a bell."

"And if the bell rang, they would dig up the body thinking the person was still alive," Todd finished. "Mostly, they would in fact not be alive because the body's muscles do twitch and contort after death. However, in the rare event the person would be alive, they would have been saved by the bell. Also, anyone who saw them on the street afterward, not knowing they had been saved from a horrible fate, would think they were a dead ringer for the person they believed to still be buried." Todd sucked in a long breath after getting all of it out.

"What's that have to do with vampires?" Lilah had no idea what it had to do with Fire in the least.

"Before humans had the knowledge that sometimes people were accidently buried alive, graves would be exhumed for various reasons. It was mainly grave robbers back then doing the digging. They would see the unusual twisting of the bodies. Sometimes there would be claw marks on the coffin if the person had indeed been buried alive. Plus, your hair and fingernails continue to grow. All of this added up to something that the minds of the people of the time couldn't comprehend."

Lilah opened her mouth then stopped. She thought she had it, but couldn't be sure. Her uncle looked at her encouragingly wanting her to grasp what he was trying to explain. "So, what you're saying is people created vampires to explain all of that?"

"In part, yes. There were other unexplained mysteries and oddities that they had to make sense of as well."

"Like large quantities of cattle disappearing or being killed near the time of a full moon," her mom added.

"Must be werewolves," Lilah threw the thought out.

"Now, you're getting it," her mom smiled.

"Okay, I kind of already knew the false myths. People would stake the corpses in the coffins to make sure they didn't resurrect or hang garlic nearby to stave off vampires."

"Garlic came later. That was Fire's doing," Uncle Todd told her.

"It was around before him," Abby corrected.

"No, I distinctly remember that Fire started that rumor," Uncle Todd argued.

"He may have encouraged it, but he didn't start it," Abby insisted.

"Were you there? I was there, Abby. I know he spread that rumor like wildfire."

"Yes," Abby agreed. "He spread it; he didn't start it."

A sharp whistle cut through the morning, and they turned to look at Lilah.

Her eyes were round as she looked at both of them before pointing to Akalah. "It wasn't me."

"You two," she spoke as if they were children. "You keep talking in circles, but have said nothing to answer this poor girl's questions."

Lilah was enjoying watching Akalah treat them the way everyone had treated her throughout her life. She didn't even try to hide the amusement from her face.

"Fire and his descendants are not vampires. No more than Water is a werewolf. The myths existed long before they did, but it's where they fit."

Lilah put her elbows on her knees and her face in her hands. She rubbed her hands across her skin tightly to grotesquely move and distort her face in frustration. "That's even more confusing."

"Vampires and werewolves existed before the Elements came. They just had various myths and legends associated with them, but weren't actually real," her mom tried to explain it better.

"So, you're saying the Divine Spirit punished them based on the existing myths?" Lilah suggested.

"Perhaps," Uncle Todd said. "Or the myths evolved based on their true attributes after they arrived."

The corners of Lilah's mouth pulled down, and she rocked gently as she said, "That actually makes perfect sense."

"It does?" her mom asked.

"Yeah. The two merged into one."

"Something like that," her uncle agreed. "Only there are still so many exaggerated tales throughout all parts of the globe that don't come close to being accurate."

"Right. I get that," Lilah was still processing everything. "But Water does change into wolf form?"

"It's a very askew human and beast cross form. Not exactly wolf, but definitely not human," Akalah described.

Lilah struggled to picture it, but it was no use. "Is there any imagery of a werewolf that comes close?"

"Yes," Akalah was quick to respond. "In fact, some have to be based on real life experience. It's too uncanny. I don't have any of my books here to show you one, so you can see for yourself."

"Do they use two legs or four?"

"Either," Uncle Todd quipped. "Whichever they choose. They're faster on four, of course."

"Covered in fur?"

"Not entirely, and I wouldn't call it fur necessarily," Akalah took the lead. "They have terrific muscle build and a mouth of razor sharp teeth. No tails."

It was like she knew the questions Lilah was going to ask next.

"I'll try to find a picture that comes close for you," her mom offered.

"And vampires?"

"What about them?" Uncle Todd asked.

"What's true about their myths?"

"Almost nothing," he laughed.

"Forget everything you thought you knew about them," her mom told her. "Their blood heals. Their blood will turn you. They do change form slightly, but only in their face and teeth. They have superior strength at all times, and their speed tops even the fastest of us."

"Cool," Lilah mumbled to herself. She hoped to meet them someday. Fire and Water both. She wasn't sure if that was something her family would approve of or not, so she kept the thought to herself.

"Are the wolves disappearing too?" the thought came to her suddenly.

"Not as far as I can tell, but I haven't been in contact with them either," Uncle Todd looked forlorn again.

"Then how do you know Fire is in trouble but not Water?"

"I don't," Uncle Todd said bluntly. "I have more Fire associates, generally speaking. The last I heard from any of them they were growing increasingly concerned that something was happening to their people. When I stopped being able to contact them, I tried in vain to get ahold of any of my Water contacts."

"So why wouldn't you assume the same is happening to them as is happening to Fire? Whatever that may turn out to be."

Uncle Todd stretched out his legs and sighed. "That is a possibility, but there's also the chance they've chosen to go into hiding for protection as all of the Elementals have done throughout centuries when one group is being persecuted."

"But you just said you don't know what's happening, so why are you now saying they're being persecuted?"

"I'm not, Lilah," he looked to Akalah for help, but she shook her head. "I'm saying they may be hiding just in case."

Lilah thought it over pulling her knees up under her chin. The white squirrel was back, and she watched him scurry over the side lawn to the tree cover. It made sense what her uncle had explained even if it still left a lot of unanswered questions. She knew no one would be able to answer them for her.

"What is it?" her mom saw the worried look on her face.

"I was just thinking."

Abby let out a light laugh. "I know that. What about?"

It wasn't that easy to put it into words. Lilah could find the words to describe her thoughts fine, but saying them out loud was the hard part. It was like admitting something she didn't want to face, and it would make it real. Once she said it, she would never be able to go back to how it was before the words were spoken.

She looked up at her mom and realized her uncle and aunt were focused intently on her as well, waiting for her to say something. They weren't going to drop it until she told them or let them into her thoughts. "It's just... Well, you know how much I didn't want to come here?"

Her mom laughed until her side started to pain her. "Talk about an understatement!" She clutched her sides and looked at Todd and Akalah. "I seriously thought I might wind up having to hog tie her and toss her in the trunk at one time."

Lilah glared at her. "I felt that way even though I thought this would be temporary."

"It is temporary," Uncle Todd didn't understand.

"Yeah, but I mean... I thought we'd all get here. Marcus would tell us what was going on. There might be a few days to do something he needed us to do or whatever," Lilah shrugged.

"You thought it would be in and out?" her uncle clarified.

"Exactly. A quick pit stop on our way to the next place we would live."

"What do you think about it now?" her mom wanted to know.

She put her face down into her knees trying to hide from what was becoming more and more clear. Turning her head to the side she said, "Now, I think we're going to be here awhile."

"What does that mean?" Akalah was never one to abide people not getting to the point.

"There's no Marcus or Leena. No vampire or wolf contact. It's something much bigger than I expected. I can feel it."

"I'm afraid of that too, child." Akalah reached out and patted the top of her head. "We shouldn't fret about what we don't know. There will be plenty of time for that later when we learn more."

Lilah looked up at her and asked, "How do you do that? How do I not worry about it now?"

Akalah looked at her seriously. "I was hoping you'd teach me."

Chapter Seven
Dangerous Exploration

Spring dawned, and Marcus had enjoyed spending most of his days since the first signs that winter was over watching the forest come to life. The buds and blossoms began appearing slowly, but now most of the forest was covered in brightly painted flowers and green leaves. The animals had emerged, bringing their children in tow to explore what nature had created while they slept.

Each morning the thick grass was wet with dew, and Marcus enjoyed walking through the trees barefoot until the sun dried the ground again. Today was no different, and yet he knew it was far from the same. He walked down to the stream to what had become his usual spot. Marcus sat on the log on the far side of the stream that was well hidden in the shadowy overcast of the forest. This had become his morning routine since the snow melted, to sit and wait for her to appear.

He had spent over half of his year outside Leena's small village, and he knew he should move on to explore other areas and learn from other groups of people. He couldn't. It's as though an invisible tether was attached the moment he first saw her on the day he arrived. Marcus had been unable to stray too far from her ever since.

Marcus knew she was heading to the stream long before he could hear her approach. She rested the buckets and the carrying rod on the ground before kneeling at the water's edge like she had so many times in the past. Leena didn't manage this with the same ease she normally possessed. Her body was exhausted from lack of sleep.

As she knelt, the tears began to flow. Marcus felt the tug on the unseen rope that bound him to her, but he had to resist the urge. As much as he would like to, he could not go to her. Not now. Not ever. He could feel her pain, and it danced with his own until his face became wet with the streaks of his own silent tears.

Leena was betrothed to a man she did not wish to marry. After her father's recovery a few months ago, she had believed she was safe from the union. Her parents realized that the time for her to wed and raise a family of her own was at hand, and they decided to go through with the marriage of their only daughter to the best warrior in their village.

Marcus longed to go to her, to comfort her. He wanted to cradle her head against his chest and stroke her hair while promising her that she would never suffer pain like this again, but he knew he couldn't. And he knew it would be a lie.

The wedding was to occur after the harvest. Leena had pleaded for it. She would already be married now if the man her parents chose for her hadn't allowed it. It was not unheard of to marry throughout the year, but most marriages occurred in early spring. It was considered a blessing upon the couple's happiness and ability to bear a large family to wed when the ground was ripe with fertility.

She had begged to push the wedding back under the pretense that her favorite time of the cycle of life was when the colors of nature reflected the burnt gold and rust of the sun. Yaxkin had been named for the sun and took Leena's pleadings as a desire to honor him and his legacy. Even though he was eager to have his young wife lay in his bed, he allowed the delayed marriage with pride wrongly thinking Leena was not only agreeable to the union, but longed for him as well.

Marcus smiled at the thought and wiped his tears with his hand. Leena was no more agreeable to this marriage then the animals were agreeable to give their life to provide nourishment to the people of the village. He knew Leena's plan was to run near the end of harvest season. She was going to load as many supplies as she could easily carry and take off through the hillside finding shelter in the caves. The approaching winter would cut short the search for her giving her a chance to succeed.

The smile quickly erased as his thoughts drifted to what her escape held for her. He couldn't think about that now. He couldn't let his mind linger on it at all for fear of what he may do to prevent it. There was still time for something to happen to change the course her life was on. He could hope for such an interference.

Forcing these dangerous images from his mind, he watched Leena as she composed herself on the bank. She ladled water in her cupped hands to splash her tear stained cheeks. Marcus watched as the water dripped down to her exposed chest. His eyes followed two tiny droplets as they rolled down one supple breast before curving to glide down her side.

Leena wasn't fazed by the water that fell and ventured down her skin. She slowly grabbed each water pail and filled them one by one. She took her time making each movement deliberate and as slow as possible. Marcus knew she was in no hurry to return to her people. He knew the feeling all too well because each passing day brought him closer to his own Return.

Slowly she adjusted the carrying rod and placed it over and across her shoulders. When she first began to stand, she lost her balance and toppled over. The buckets drained small rivers into the ground all around her.

Marcus leapt to his feet wanting to rush to her aide, but quickly stopped and sat down again. He knew she was drained from the lack of sleep. The nightmares that tortured her when she was finally able to drift off didn't allow her any rest either. He couldn't offer her assistance despite how it pained him to stay in the shadows. He had to stay hidden.

Leena stood up and looked down at her legs that were covered in dirt and mud from the spilled water. She placed her hands behind her on the small of her back and drew her shoulders tight to stretch. Leena righted the buckets again and placed the carrying rod over top. Slowly, she slipped her animal skin skirt over her long bronze legs and laid it over the top of the buckets.

She carefully walked into the stream staying in the shallows. Marcus watched as the cool water chilled her causing her nipples to harden. He was undeniably aware of how his own human form was reacting. He could feel the throbbing beneath his robes, but Marcus could not turn away. Not this time. He continued to watch, etching every inch of her naked body to his memory.

Leena rinsed off her legs then ventured a little deeper in the water. She finally sank below the surface which surprised and frightened Marcus until she reappeared. She smoothed her long wet hair back with both hands before dipping below the surface again.

She didn't enjoy the clear, cool water long before returning to shore. Someone would look for her if she didn't return soon. Marcus watched the water as it glided down her back and over her round tan bottom as she walked. Marcus clenched his fists to the side, quelling the urge to run to her and lick every drop of moisture off her body.

Leena slipped back into her skirt then filled the buckets a second time. She attempted to affix the carrying rod again. This time she managed it successfully, and she slowly walked from Marcus' view. He would normally follow her at a distance with the excuse that he wanted to make sure no harm befell her. He knew it was just that. An excuse. Marcus already knew she'd be back in the village safe and sound in no time.

Marcus hung back today because of the massive problem left to him. Walking would be awkward. He contemplated handling the matter himself as he had considered many other times since his arrival, but he was afraid to give in to the lust he felt for Leena. He worried that it would only grow his desire for her until he eventually approached her.

Instead he chose to swim across the river on his way to his makeshift hut instead of taking the rock path in the narrows he normally used. The cold water did the trick. Marcus knew he shouldn't have these thoughts about Leena. He could never intervene, not even though her life was in danger.

Once Leena had safely returned to her people and his robes were again dry, Marcus set off to explore more of the valley around him. It might keep his mind occupied and off of the woman he desired for a change. There was another village to the west, but it was a day's hike with leaving at sunup and not resting. To the south was only more wilderness, and that was the area he had explored the most up till now. He decided to head west in the hopes of experiencing something new and exciting like possibly spying a new forest creature, or finding a new source of food.

The hike through the territory seemed to be just what he needed. Soon all thoughts of Leena and her village were far from his mind. Marcus was watching the brush along a line of trees move and shake as an animal made its way through the overgrowth. He watched in anticipation even though he knew a young jackrabbit was about to appear. A low noise far off was missed by him in his captivation of the little creature. If he hadn't been paying such close attention to it waiting for it to finally emerge, he may have had more warning of the danger that approached in enough time to avoid almost being found.

When the rabbit broke through the branches and sniffed the air around him, it took immediate notice of Marcus who reclined against a nearby tree. The rabbit didn't recognize him as a threat and cautiously continued to move away from the safety of the thicket where he had been covered. It didn't come much closer to Marcus directly, but he did continue to explore the area near him. Sights such as this were invaluable. He could not remember a single time when he had paid attention to an animal so small from the spirit realm except for possibly when they were first created. It would now be locked in his memory forever how the eyelashes on this creature could compete with those of any human in length.

Something spooked it. Marcus watched its ears shoot straight up as it tried to hone in on what it had heard before it suddenly vanished in a flash. That would just about do it for the day. He needed to head back before much longer, or he would never make it home in time to get any sleep before morning. He had already ventured farther than he had intended when he left.

As soon as he stood up, he became aware he was not the only person in this section of the valley at the moment. They couldn't yet be seen, but they were drawing closer. Their movements were so light they couldn't be easily detected. Marcus realized if he had been distracted by the jackrabbit for much longer, he may have been seen. He needed to hide and quick, but there was no real option available. They'd be close enough to spot him in minutes, so the only way to avoid detection would be to run. Marcus was sure he wouldn't be able to mimic their quietness which would draw unwanted attention to himself through the noises he would make running away. Surely, someone would be sent out to investigate.

In a panic, he believed there was only one option available to him. Marcus put his hands on the trunk of the tree and gripped tightly. Bounding with all his strength, he shot up the tree with amazing speed, moving his hands and feet in unison up the trunk until he came to the lowest branch of the cypress and began pulling himself up, swinging through the canopy until he neared the part of the crown where it became too narrow to hide him well. The branches this high wouldn't support his weight, so he crossed his legs around the tree and watched the movement below with his mind.

It took only seconds once he was in place for the band of warriors to move into view. There would be around a dozen or so in the party walking through, but a few young men led the way keeping an eye out for the rest. Marcus slowed his breathing even with being safely out of sight. The warriors would be hard pressed to see him if they scoured the tree canopy at any time, but the overcast sky of the late day would make it impossible to spy him. His light bronze skin and aged robes blended well in the treetop.

The hope that the group would pass through swiftly leaving Marcus free to climb down and head to his home before it grew to be too late was crushed. The warriors in the front of the pack found a small area nearby surrounded on two sides by hills and a wall of trees. It was a good location to set up camp for the night. Marcus was trapped.

Night wore on, and Marcus still clung to the tree. Every muscle in his body ached for relief, but he was too afraid to even reposition himself. Several times he had considered scampering down slowly and as quietly as he could manage then running as swiftly as he could through the darkened wilderness. He didn't fear the outcome of a confrontation if one occurred. His speed was greater which meant the likelihood of being caught was marginal, and his healing rate would be invaluable if it came to be needed.

There were only two things keeping him in the tree. The first was the one order he had to follow to not be detected. Even if the group never caught up to him, they would still be aware of his presence which was enough for Marcus to not want to risk moving. That wasn't even his main concern. There was only one direction he could head. The southern and northern routes were blocked by hillside which would make his attempt to flee even more difficult. To head west would be to head toward the village this group came from which would mean he could be seen by others of their tribe. That would leave his only option of running east toward Leena's village.

Even if he turned south at the stream where the hillside was not as steep, there was no guarantee all of the warriors in pursuit would follow him. Marcus was unaware if they knew about her village, but none of them had thought about it since they arrived near him. It was a risk he couldn't chance. The last thing he would ever want to do was bring more hardship to Leena's life.

They were on an expedition to a salty spring, and this was the first phase of their journey. There would be several more nights spent camped along the way before they made it to their destination. The group would spend several weeks there gathering supplies and hunting before making their way back to their village. All Marcus had to do was survive the night in the tree, and they would depart in the early morning.

It felt impossible many times throughout the night. Two men were on guard at all times taking turns on watch with the rest. Only the women were allowed to sleep undisturbed. Several times he felt like he would not be able to hold out long enough. At those moments, he let his mind wander to his beloved Leena, and the visions of her in his mind would give him the strength to keep going.

In the hour before dawn, he stretched each limb carefully one at a time. His bones and muscles were stiff and achy from being cramped together and tightly wound around the tree. It did little to increase his comfort more than a few minutes.

Light started to break through the trees illuminating the ground far off below him. The group awakened and packed up their camp while a meal was prepared. Minutes seemed to stretch out forever, but soon the group was on their way through the valley.

Marcus waited until he was certain it was safe then waited some more. After what he had already endured, staying in the tree a little longer to be assured would be child's play. When he did begin to stretch and move before his descent, the pain was enough for him to consider jumping to the ground. He would survive the fall, and his body would heal fast enough. It wouldn't do. There would be a risk the he would be heard by someone or something who may come to investigate. In that case, it would be hard for him to flee with the injuries he'd suffer.

The climb down was much slower than his ascent had been because of how difficult it proved to get his limbs in working order again. It took him around twenty minutes, but his feet were once more on solid ground. He stretched for quite some time before beginning the long walk back. The thought of finding a spot to rest nearby was a constant in his mind, but he wouldn't be able to fully relax until he made it to the familiarity of his tree.

Marcus had cut the distance in half by the time the aches and pains in his body wore away. The only nuisances he had left to deal with were exhaustion and hunger. Stopping to survey his surroundings, he checked for more travelers in the area not wanting to make the same mistake as he had last evening. Certain there was no reason for concern, he took off a sprint making it home in record time.

As he laid down in the hollow trunk, he thought about how narrowly he had escaped. It was entirely his fault. He had grown complacent in this spot near the little village. Their routine was well known to him, and he could enjoy the area within several miles at a leisurely pace knowing he would not be seen. This reinforced that it was time to move on. He couldn't let a lapse like this happen again for he might not be as lucky. A new terrain with new people to study would sharpen his senses and keep him alert. It would be safest, but it would mean leaving Leena behind. The last thought he had before passing out into the longest sleep he'd had since arriving was that if he never attempted to go that far again, he would be safe amongst the small piece of land he knew.

Chapter Eight
Her Match

Lilah sat on the porch swing with her coffee and a blanket draped over her. It was still dark outside. In a few weeks, daylight savings would have the sun rising by now. She looked out over the horizon trying to figure out which way was east.

"Sunrise to your left," she heard a man say. She turned and saw her Uncle Todd step outside followed by her mom.

"Can't sleep?" her mom asked.

"I did for a bit, but when I woke up..." Lilah shook her head. "It's just so sad."

"What is?" Abby passed Todd a confusing look.

"The tsunami," she looked at them surprised they didn't know.

"There was a tsunami?" her Uncle Todd asked.

Lilah nodded.

"I haven't even turned the TV on yet to hear the news," he said, walking to the rail.

Lilah didn't say anything. She hadn't watched the news either.

"How did you hear about it then?" he asked.

Lilah just looked at him. She glanced at her mom then looked back at her cup hoping to find an answer inside.

"Lilah?" her mother said her name more as a question.

"I..." Lilah wasn't sure how to answer. "I heard it."

"You heard it?" her mom sat next to her, and her Uncle Todd knelt down next to the swing.

"You could hear the tsunami?" His interest seemed genuine, but it worried Lilah.

"No, not the tsunami."

"Then what did you hear?" He shifted around and sat on the porch in front of her with his back to the railing.

"The people," she answered as her mom took her hand.

"I woke up, and the voices..." Lilah trailed off again. Tears were in her eyes at the memory of the screams. The knowledge that her ability to hear them must be somehow unusual only added to her distress.

"I could hear all of these voices at once. It was like an extraordinarily loud hum. If I try now, I can hear it still. It's so loud like everyone is talking over everyone else, but some voices are louder or more frantic."

"And that's how you know about it? You heard," her mom paused, thinking of how to finish her question. "You heard the victims?"

"Yes."

Her mom squeezed her hand and put her other hand around her shoulders giving her a half hug. Todd wasn't saying anything, and Lilah couldn't hear his thoughts.

"Is this different too?" she finally asked them.

"No, not really," her uncle stood back up and walked to the steps of the porch looking around before coming back toward her.

"I can listen now and hear the people who are trapped, or the thoughts of those whose loved ones are missing. It's just that I usually don't try to hear their thoughts until after I hear about the disaster. Not the other way around."

Lilah leaned forward and looked back at her mom. "So this is different," she repeated, certain this time.

"You just have to learn to control it, Lilah. That's all," Abby tried to reassure her. "You were flipped like a switch, remember? Ours had to gradually warm up like an oven. We learned control as our powers grew. It is different, but it's not a difference to be concerned about."

Lilah couldn't be sure, but she thought she saw her mom and uncle exchange a fleeting worried look. She tried, but they definitely weren't allowing her access to their thoughts either. She headed back inside to her room not sure she wanted answers to the questions that plagued her.

She looked at her clothes from the night before tossed in a heap on the floor. There were dirt and grass stains and a few blades of grass still managed to cling tightly. Their lifestyle meant they always had to be ready to pack light which means clothes were limited.

'I guess its laundry day,' she sighed as she gathered the pile and the rest of her clothes. She walked down the back stairs to the utility room where the washer and dryer were hooked up. *'Good. No one else is using it.'*

Most of her family were still asleep, but a few had wandered down the stairs. She could hear them in the kitchen, but it was hard to tell if she was listening in on thoughts or conversation. The tsunami was the main topic of discussion this morning. Lilah was a close second. There seemed to be a lot of curiosity concerning how quickly her powers came flooding in last night. They had to be unaware she was close enough to hear them which means she managed to turn her thoughts off without intending to again.

She sighed and leaned onto the washing machine with her head hung down. This was too much for her to deal with right now. Between her powers, learning the truth about the Elementals, and the boy she quite literally couldn't get out of her head, she had enough going on without having to worry about if she was some kind of freak. More than she already was, given her family.

Lilah fumbled with her clothes turning them right-side out and checking pockets. That's when she found the paper she had tucked away the night before. She had forgotten all about Jackson's note. Lilah finished starting her wash then darted back upstairs. She laid on her bed and carefully unfolded it.

Jackson was in his garage working on his 1979 Firebird. Lilah knew this because she had been able to sense him all morning. It was almost impossible not to spy. She didn't have to try to have the images start playing in her mind. In fact, she had to force it to turn off with great difficulty, and even then, she still knew what he was doing. The only time it dulled was when she focused on something else, but that was hard too. Distractions kept interrupting her concentration bringing Jackson back to the forefront.

Written on the paper was his number. Lilah's heartrate quickened, and she felt her face flush. She had met many good looking guys in her life, but none of them had interested her. Her parents were okay with her socializing. She had attended school dances and had even dated. There just hadn't been anyone that really caught her eye regardless of how handsome, friendly or caring he was. One quality of Air is they mate for life.

'Is that why I feel this way? Could I have possibly found my match this young?' She knew her mom was over two hundred and fifty years old before she met her dad. Lilah shook off the thought. *'Unlikely. It's probably just nerves and stress from everything else I've dealt with in the last twenty four hours.'*

Lilah picked up her phone and added his number. She pulled up a new text screen and stared at the phone for several minutes. She didn't know what to say. She set the phone down thinking maybe this was a bad idea. It definitely was bad timing. She picked it back up immediately and typed, "Hey. It's Lilah...from the restaurant."

'Send,' she thought as she pushed the button and listened to the phone chime the notification. She kept the phone in her hands intent on the screen and was about to go find something distracting while she waited for a response when she saw the three dots.

'He's typing!' Lilah felt the nervous excitement grow.

"Hi. I wasn't sure if I would hear from you. How you feeling today?"

"Good. Better. Thanks for helping last night."

"It was nothing. Glad I was there."

Lilah felt a growing panic. She'd never been in this position before. She finally met someone she wanted to talk to, and she couldn't think of anything to say that didn't sound dumb. As hard as she tried to think of something, her mind kept going blank.

He texted again, "A bunch of us are going to a party tonight. It's an annual bonfire in the country in honor of Halloween coming up. Want to go?"

Lilah squealed then typed, "Sounds fun."

"So that's a yes?"

"Yes."

"I can pick you up at 7?"

More panic. Her mom would never agree to this. "7...at the restaurant. Meet you there."

"I'll see you then."

Lilah set the phone down and rolled over to stifle a scream into her pillow. She had a little over twelve hours to figure out how she was going to manage to get out of the house tonight to see Jackson.

"NO," ABBY'S VOICE WAS firm.

For a moment, Lilah regretted not choosing to sneak out again. "Mom," she began.

"Absolutely not, Lilah!" her mom's anger was growing.

Lilah glanced at her Uncle Todd who quickly shot her a look saying he was not getting into this conversation. "Wouldn't it be a good thing?' she asked.

Her mom looked at her like she had suddenly sprouted Spock ears and a Pinocchio nose. "After last night, you guys were worried about people talking. So let me stop the gossip, or at least put a spin on it."

Lilah could tell her uncle was processing the idea as a good proposal, but his words didn't match his thoughts. "I'm sorry, Lilah, but we have no idea what's going on or when we will be needed. We need to stay here, stay together until we know more."

"I'll have my phone, and you guys will know where I'm at if I'm needed," Lilah scoffed, thinking she probably won't even be a necessary part of anything that happens.

"We don't even know how long we'll be in this place, Lilah," her uncle finally voiced his opinion. "Now isn't the best time to make friends."

---

1. http://www.clker.com/cliparts/7/6/9/b/13309573511112670181decorative-lines-2_large-md.png

"I know that. I do. I can't help it. I like him."

Abby smiled, "He was cute, wasn't he? I can see why you'd like him."

"It's not that."

Lilah stared at her glass of water concentrating on keeping her thoughts turned off while images of Jackson kept floating through her mind. It was like an endless gallery of still frames from the restaurant, and Lilah couldn't figure out how to stop the slideshow.

"I know you're upset, but there will be other parties. Other boys," her mom added.

Lilah shook her head, "This one is different."

"What do you mean?'

Lilah looked at her mom and stopped concentrating. Her mom's expression slowly changed to surprise, and Todd sat down next to Abby on the couch. "Is that him?" her uncle asked. "In the garage?"

"Yes," Lilah answered.

"You're stalking him?" her mother teased.

Lilah felt her cheeks turn red. "I'm not trying to. I can't turn it off."

"You see him all the time?" she asked.

"Yes, even when I'm listening to others' thoughts or talking to you or going to the bathroom!" Lilah yelled out exasperated. "Once I learned to shut out the crowd of voices in my head this morning, he was still there, and I can't get him out of my mind no matter how hard I try."

Abby and Todd didn't say anything for several minutes. Lilah leaned back on the recliner with her eyes closed watching Jackson work on an old car with a friend. They were talking and laughing like what Lilah assumed normal people would do.

Her uncle interrupted her thoughts, "Do you think...?"

Lilah opened her eyes. Her mom looked at Todd and said, "It sounds like it."

"What?" Lilah asked.

Her uncle leaned forward and rested his elbows on his knees. "Last night at the restaurant, did you see Jackson before you passed out?"

"Yes."

"You heard his thoughts?" he pressed on.

"Yes," Lilah adjusted the recliner to sit up again trying to read the faces of her mom and uncle.

"Did you hear his thoughts first? Before you heard the other customers?"

"I don't know."

"Think," her mom prompted. "Just try to remember."

Lilah thought back to when she first entered the restaurant. She knew the waitress spoke to her. She had heard a few comments, but she wasn't yet trying to determine if they were thoughts or spoken words. "I really don't know for sure," she finally said. "Jackson was the first person I knew I could hear what they were thinking, and afterward, the thoughts of everyone became so loud and overwhelming. I just can't be sure if his were the first."

Silence. They were mulling over what Lilah had said.

"Well, that's it, then," Uncle Todd finally stated.

"Todd," her mother begged.

"It makes sense, Abby. Everything that has happened? We couldn't figure it out. We didn't know what was happening or if it was connected to why Marcus wanted us here. This... *This*... makes sense of it," he emphasized.

Her mom sighed.

"What makes sense?" Lilah asked. Then before either of them could answer, she asked, "He's my match, isn't he?"

Her mom collapsed into the back of the couch and some low moan escaped her lips.

"I think so," her uncle told her.

"I had wondered that. Earlier. I've never reacted to anyone this way before, but I thought it was just my nerves or something. I'm still so young."

"Yes, but everyone's-"

"Different," Lilah cut off her uncle. She took a sip from her glass and looked away out the window. "Jackson is my match, and that triggered everything?"

"Think of it like puberty," her mom explained.

Lilah shot her mom a look, "You're kidding."

Todd laughed hard and unexpectedly, causing him to cough several times to be able to regain control.

Her mom grinned and tried to choke back a laugh, "No, sweetheart, I'm not. It's a huge change. Normally, you go through it slowly. We all...," her mom motioned toward Todd and the other family gathered in the kitchen, "have compared it to puberty before. A second puberty. There are different signs that occur, different stages, and eventually, it's over. You're on the other side of it fully equipped."

"And, honestly, I think you're the first in the family to find their match before going through that process," her uncle added.

Abby thought about it for a moment then nodded, "You're right. Meeting Jackson...well, I think that triggered your Elemental puberty to commence at once."

"Can you please stop using the word puberty?" Lilah begged in frustration.

Todd and Abby laughed. "What?" her uncle asked. "Embarrassed?"

Lilah glared at him without answering.

They sat in silence for a few minutes more. Lilah was trying to process everything. Jackson. Her abilities. He was her match. She didn't know anything about him, but he would be the one by her side for eternity.

"Here, let me try to help," her mom offered an olive branch.

"How?" Lilah asked.

She thought for a moment before answering. "I had this problem before. We all have."

"Not all of us," Uncle Todd butted in.

If Jackson was her match, that meant there were only two in the family who had yet to find theirs. Maddie was one, and Uncle Todd was the other. Hard to believe that after almost a millennium he still hadn't found her. The story passed through the family was that he had been in love once and strongly believed the woman to be his match. He had been horribly wrong. Ever since, he had never even wanted to try to find his match and was probably quite thankful he hadn't.

"Most of us," her mom said. "This is what my mom taught me to do. Close your eyes."

Lilah listened to her mom's instructions and shut her eyes tightly.

"Don't try so hard. Relax."

She stretched her neck, leaned back and gently closed her eyes.

"Okay. Let the images come to you. Don't try to fight them."

"That won't be hard," Lilah scoffed.

"Shh. Focus."

Lilah let the image of Jackson bent under the hood enter her mind. "Okay. Done."

"Now, picture a door."

"A door?" Lilah's eyes shot open, and she looked at her mom questioningly.

"Yes. Any kind of door. A house door. Barn door. Your pick. Close your eyes," she insisted.

Lilah started over, picturing a large barn door this time. "What next?"

"Close the door over him like you're locking him in the room."

This was sounding stupid, but she did as she was told. The barn door slid to the side and shut in front of Jackson. Well, it almost worked she thought. I'm stuck with an image of a barn door in my head instead of a creepy stalker crush cam.

"Open your eyes," her mom told her.

Lilah looked at her mom, and then her uncle who appeared pretty curious about the process himself.

"Did it work?" he asked her.

She was about to remind him about the barn door that was stuck in her mind when she realized it was now gone too. The surprise must have shown in her face because her mom's laughter rang out shrilly.

"That's exactly how I reacted the first time I did it."

"Can I get him back?"

"Anytime you want. Just go back into your mind and open the door."

Lilah closed her eyes and tried it. Door open. There was Jackson wiping his greasy hands on a shop towel. Door closed and nothing.

"Well, have fun tonight," her mom drew her away from her thoughts.

Lilah looked at her surprised and unsure of how to respond.

"At your party," her uncle added.

Lilah looked back and forth between them her excitement growing. "Really?" she asked. "You mean I can go?"

"If he's your match," her mother began.

"He is her match," her uncle corrected.

Her mom shrugged and smiled, "He's your match. We can't stand in the way of that. We couldn't if we tried."

"Thank you!" Lilah squealed, jumping up from the recliner. She hugged and kissed them both then ran off to get ready for a date that wasn't going to happen for another eight hours.

2

LATER THAT EVENING, Lilah nervously paced the porch. She tried to calm herself sitting in the swing and breathing deep, but it was no use. Up she would go to pace to one end then the other. Back to the swing and repeat again. Her date with Jackson was an hour off, and her nerves were working overtime.

She continued this pattern for some time until Gene and Sara came out to join her. "I love you, doll," Sara said, "but your energy is setting the entire house on edge."

Lilah had been pacing, but immediately retreated to the swing. She took a couple deep breaths, and was about to get up and start walking again. She caught herself, slunk back, and groaned, "I can't help it."

Gene sat down next to her, "You know you have nothing to be nervous about."

Lilah's mouth dropped and her eyes opened wide, "How can you say that?"

"It's a done deal."

"I know, but I'm still nervous."

Sara looked up out of the corner of her eye like she was trying to see something inside her mind, "I remember being nervous like this over a first date once, but it was before Gene."

Gene raised his eyebrows with interest. "Before me? Who was this guy?" he asked as though he was upset, but it was obvious he was playing around.

"His name isn't important," Sara told him. She looked at Lilah, "when I think about it, the first thing that stands out is he wore a cream colored shirt on our first date. It's weird how your memory prioritizes what details to hold on to."

"Anyway, I was nervous. I knew he wasn't my match, but I worried about everything else. Would he be a gentleman? Would we have fun? Would everything go smoothly? And I could answer all those questions! I knew what was going to happen. It didn't matter. Still got my nerves going."

"So you weren't nervous with me?" Gene asked her.

"No, I was a little, but not like this," Sara told him pointing to Lilah.

"Is there anything we can do to help?" Gene asked Lilah.

"Like what?"

"I don't know. I would think knowing it's going to work out beforehand would eliminate the nerves."

"What are you nervous about exactly?" asked Sara.

"That's what I'm nervous about. I've met him. Briefly," Lilah added. "It's just...." she sighed.

Lilah shook her head and looked across the porch as if that's where she'd find the answer. In a hushed voice she finally manage to say, "I know that tonight I'm going to start getting to know the man I'll spend the rest of my life with, only the rest of my life means so much more for us than it does for others."

"I still think that should take the worry out of it," Gene told her.

Sara shot him a look that told him to be quiet. "Go on," Sara coaxed.

"I've never thought about it."

"Thought about what?"

"About who my match might be. Mom used to tell me stories of how she would daydream about who he was, his looks, interests, everything. Of course, dad wasn't anything like she had imagined, but he was also better than she had ever imagined. I've never given it any thought. I thought I had time. A lot of time!" Lilah's anxiety was growing again. "I mean how old were you when you found Gene?"

"I was one of the younger ones myself. I was seventy-seven."

"Now, she's an old lady of two hundred and twenty-six," Gene said and leaned toward Lilah mouthing the word, "Woah."

Sara rolled her eyes and crossed her arms over her chest. Gene winked at Lilah, "She likes 'em young too. I'm only one hundred and seventy-five."

Sara playfully kicked at him, "You hush."

Gene raised his hands. His eyes were sparkling, and said, "Hey, get mad all you want, but the numbers don't lie," before smiling at his wife.

"I'm only twenty-one."

Gene and Sara became serious again. "You're the youngest yet," Gene said and gave her leg a quick squeeze.

"Yeah," Sara inhaled deeply and let it out. "You be nervous all you want. You've had a lot thrown at you in the last day or two. It'll be over soon."

Lilah looked at her puzzled.

"It's about time for you to leave isn't it?"

Lilah glanced at her phone. It was twenty till seven. "Oh crap!" she jumped off the swing and ran into the house looking for her mom.

Sara sat on the swing next to Gene and lay her head on his shoulder. They leaned back, and he put his arm around her pulling her close. "Do you think this is a good idea?" he asked her softly.

"Lilah and Jackson?"

"Yes. The timing is off."

"The timing seems off to us," she told him. "The universe knows what it is doing."

"I suppose that's right," he said, kissing the top of her head softly.

³

LILAH CLIMBED UP INTO the cab of Jackson's truck, and he closed the door after her. Her nerves disappeared the moment she looked into his round sky blue eyes. Jackson walked around the front of the truck, and she studied his every movement. He got into the cab next to her, and put it in drive.

"I'm really glad you came," he said as he maneuvered through the busy parking lot.

Lilah smiled as if by instinct. She nodded, trying to find the words, "Me too. I'm glad you asked me."

"I actually wanted to talk to you last night. I just didn't work up my nerve before..." his voice trailed off. "Before you left."

Lilah remembered his internal struggle to approach her and said, "I know."

As soon as the words were out of her mouth, she realized her mistake.

"You know?" he asked more amused than anything. "How would you know?"

Lilah shook her head. "I meant, well," she struggled for an explanation. Lilah sighed, "I wanted to talk to you too. I was trying to say I know what you mean about working up the nerve. I just... It wasn't," Lilah flushed. "It came out wrong."

It was Jackson's turn to beam. He turned onto the main highway headed out of town the opposite direction of the farmhouse. "So you're new in town?"

---

3. http://www.clker.com/cliparts/7/6/9/b/13309573511112670181decorative-lines-2_large-md.png

"Yeah, visiting family," Lilah replied with the story her mom had her rehearse.

"Oh," Jackson seemed disappointed. "You're not going to be here long?"

"Not sure actually. There's talk. It's all kind of up in the air now."

He nodded and kept his eyes on the road.

Lilah knew he was thinking that it was just his luck to finally meet someone who wouldn't be sticking around. "But, I guess whatever happens, I can always visit awhile longer if I had a reason to stay," she shrugged.

She felt him relax. He turned his signal on and began to slow down. Jackson was about to start his turn when terror filled Lilah.

"Wait!" she yelled out and reached a hand toward the wheel.

A red sports car veered around the bend in the road just ahead careening fast. The driver almost lost control of his car. The car flew past them, and both Lilah and Jackson craned their necks to watch it as it disappeared behind them. If Jackson had made his turn, they would've been hit.

He flashed her a quick smile that was hiding his jitters, "I didn't even hear it. Thank god you did."

She simply smiled at him not sure what to say. He was extra cautious before turning on the country road this time. Lilah looked out the window at the sun that was setting, taking deep breaths and trying to ignore the images of the wrecked red metal and pained screams that were happening now not far from them. The sky was painted with shades of purple, orange and red. She found herself thinking about how sunsets never lost their appeal, and she hoped they never would, no matter how many hundreds of years she lived.

"It's only a few minutes out," he cut into her thoughts. She looked through the windshield again at the winding country road. "Where are you from?" he asked.

"Florida," she responded as it was the most recent place she had lived.

"Florida?" Jackson repeated. "This must be a big change then."

Lilah held up her gloved hands and said, "I bought these two days ago. I've never had to wear them before now."

Jackson laughed, "I bet not. So do they do bonfire parties in Florida?"

"Probably. They do parties, and there are bonfires. I've never been to one though."

Jackson stole another glance before directing his attention to driving again. "It's a lot of fun. You'll see."

Lilah just smiled at him. She already knew she'd enjoy the night.

He slowed down and peered forward to find his turn. The truck veered to the left and started down a long and winding lane. "This place is owned by my buddy Sam's dad. This is," he grinned and looked at her, "kind of like the back entrance to the property."

"No one's supposed to be here?"

He shook his head. "His dad knows we get together out here. He doesn't want Sam telling him about it, or rather asking him every time. As long as we don't cause trouble, Sam's dad doesn't care."

The tree lined lane opened into a large empty field. There were already about a half dozen cars and trucks parked along one side. Jackson turned around and parked along the lane facing the road. "We're a little early," he shrugged. "But once the sun sets, this place will be packed."

He unbuckled his seat belt, so Lilah did the same. They opened their doors and climbed out. She walked to the rear of the truck, and Jackson was already waiting on the other side. He held his hand out to her, "Ready?" he asked.

She smiled and nodded taking his hand. He led her off in the direction of the pile of wood that was starting to catch. "Is that a couch," Lilah asked.

Jackson stopped and tilted his head to the side for a moment before looking at her. A grin spread over his face, and he nodded slowly. "It is," he said with pride. He pulled her closer to him and started walking, "This is how we do it out in the hicks."

Lilah met a mirage of people over the next couple hours. She had promised herself she wouldn't veer into people's private thoughts tonight. She'd just be normal for a change. Her vow didn't last long. There were too many names to remember.

Jackson had been wonderful all night. He never left her side. He never introduced her as his girlfriend, but he made sure everyone knew they were there together by the way he would hold her hand or drape his arm over her shoulders and pull her close. He also never left her alone in a sea full of strangers.

The night wore on, and the bonfire was down to a normal blaze when Lilah first saw her. It was the witch she had noticed days before at the restaurant. She was with a group of friends. Lilah tried, but they were all blocked. No doubt under a protection spell. The witch veered off straight toward her and Jackson.

When Jackson saw her he whispered to Lilah, "I want you to meet someone. She's a witch."

Lilah was taken aback. Her thoughts raced. How did he know? She tried to read him for answers, but didn't have enough time.

He yelled out, "Lee-Lee!" and went to her. They hugged quickly, and Jackson made the introductions. "Lee-Lee this is Lilah, she's new in town. Lilah, this is my oldest and dearest friend."

"My name," she started to say while giving Jackson a stern look, "is Everleigh," she turned to Lilah and smiled. "This buffoon is the only one who gets away with calling me Lee-Lee."

"That's because you love me," Jackson grinned.

"Keep calling me Lee-Lee and see how long that lasts," Everleigh told him.

They laughed. Lilah smiled at them still intrigued by Jackson's comment. Everleigh studied her for a moment and Lilah briefly worried that maybe somehow she could make the connection. Air and Earth, face to face. They weren't enemies by any means, but the Elementals did tend to stick to themselves for the most part.

Everleigh nodded like she had just figured something out, and Lilah held her breath. "He's a good guy though. One of the best if you ask me," Everleigh told her.

"Aww, see? I knew you loved me," Jackson batted his eyelashes at her. Everleigh lightly punched his arm.

"I was beginning to think you weren't going to show," he said.

She shook her head. "Bad accident near my house,"

Jackson's face was filled with questions. "Car accident? Everyone okay?"

"Yeah, there were police and rescue vehicles all over the place. I waited to leave. Didn't need to be trying to get around all that."

"Wow. Who was it? Anyone local?"

"I don't think so, and I don't think whoever it was survived," Everleigh answered.

Lilah was aware that Everleigh knew more than she was saying just as she did. It was an out of towner driving a red sports car. One fatality.

"Man, that's horrible. What is with people driving crazy? Lilah and I were almost in an accident earlier ourselves."

Lilah nodded at Everleigh backing him up. He had no idea it was the same reckless driver.

"Well, I got to get back. My cousin is in town and doesn't know too many people. A little shy too. Can't leave her for long."

They said they're goodbyes to each other. "She seemed nice," Lilah told Jackson.

"Lee-Lee and I have known each other forever. Her grandma used to babysit me."

"Why do you call her Lee-Lee?"

Jackson shook his head. "You know, it's funny. For a long time, I actually thought that was her name."

Lilah bunched her eyebrows and looked at him questioningly.

"Yeah, I guess I couldn't say Everleigh correctly, so I started calling her Lee-Lee. It just stuck. I don't remember any of this. Her grandma tells the story every time I see her."

Lilah didn't say anything. She was trying to get a read on how he knew about Everleigh. She didn't have to.

"She's my oldest friend. The best kind of friend you could hope to find."

"Then why did you call her a witch?" Lilah asked.

"Because she is."

Lilah rolled her eyes and hoped it looked sincere.

"No, I mean it. She's a witch. Like spells and circles. And whatever witches do, witch."

Lilah was amused and shocked. Her family's secrets were never shared with anyone who wasn't in an Elemental family, and even then, rarely shared outside of Air. She had never given a thought to how other Elemental lines handled their secrets. Sure, people knew about witches, vampires and werewolves, but most of what people think they know wasn't real.

"Why do you say she's a witch?"

"She told me."

Lilah said almost mockingly, "So she just announced one day 'hey Jackson, guess what? I'm a witch.'"

He sighed, feeling made fun of, "Not exactly. She was always talking about it when we were growing up. Everleigh would say she came from a long line of witches. I didn't really believe it of course. It wasn't until high school when I realized she meant it."

Lilah stared at the fire and played with her lower lip. Everleigh confided in a friend. How many times had Lilah wanted a friend to talk to about her family?

Jackson saw her and assumed Lilah didn't believe in what he was saying. "It's true though."

She looked at him and asked, "Her being a witch?"

He nodded and looked off at his friend. "There has always been talk about her family being witches. It's really just mockery based on some of the weird things they do, but she really is a witch."

Lilah wondered why he would tell someone he barely knew about his friend's secret like this. "I believe you."

"You do?" Jackson looked surprised and pleased.

"Yeah, I mean why not? I think witches are real." Lilah shrugged, "I'm a psychic myself."

"You mock, but I'm telling the truth."

Lilah only flashed him a playful smile. In time, he would learn that she was being truthful as well.

4

THEY DROVE UP THE DRIVE to the farmhouse, and he came around to her door to let her out. It didn't comfort Lilah that no one was outside waiting because she knew they could see.

"I had a great time tonight. I'm really glad you came," he said, grabbing her hand to walk her to the steps.

"Me too," she smiled nervously.

"I hope you had fun."

"I did." She looked in his eyes which even in the darkness shone a brilliant shade of blue.

"I'll text you tomorrow, okay?"

She nodded. For a moment, he lingered, and Lilah thought he was about to move in for a kiss. Instead he smiled and walked back to the truck.

Lilah walked up the steps to the house giddy with excitement. Jackson was wonderful. She practically floated into the house. She didn't notice the tiny mud tracks that ran behind the swing showing evidence of the squirrel she'd begun to think of as a pet. She definitely didn't notice that there were two sets of tracks either indicating he'd ran across more than once since the light rain that morning, or he had a friend to keep him company during the long winter months.

She walked inside, and the house looked empty. Panic filled her for a moment. She had tried to have a normal evening and blocked all outside thoughts. What had happened while she was gone?

---

4. http://www.clker.com/cliparts/7/6/9/b/13309573511112670181decorative-lines-2_large-md.png

Just as the thought overtook her, a figure stepped out of the kitchen. "DADDY!" Lilah squealed and ran to him.

"When did you get here?" Lilah asked still hugging her dad tightly. "I didn't know you were coming today."

"I wanted to surprise you. Besides, I wanted you to have fun on your date," he winked.

She saw her mom emerge and realized others had already come into the living room. "So that's it then? Everyone is ready."

"Yes," he answered. "Everyone is either here or at the other house with Aunt Sophia."

Lilah looked around, "Where's Maddie?"

Myles and Abby exchanged glances.

"What happened?" Lilah asked, fearing the worst. It was true Maddie wasn't exactly her favorite cousin, but that didn't mean she ever wished her ill will.

"Nothing," her dad replied with an amused grin.

Lilah narrowed her eyes confused.

Her mom tried to hide her smile. "It seems she's decided to stay at Aunt Sophia's house instead.'"

That was the best news Lilah had received about their stay here since she'd first been filled in on what was going on. "That's too bad," she muttered with obvious sarcasm.

"Yeah," her dad tilted his head to the side. "It seems she's a bit upset about being bested in finding a match."

Lilah couldn't help the satisfactory grin that wouldn't stop growing. "What now?"

"Well," her dad began putting an arm around Abby who had walked over next to him, "now we wait."

"I can't believe no one has heard from Marcus yet," Lilah looked around at the other family members. "How long has it been?"

Her dad nodded. "It's worried me some, I admit. Marcus and Leena know what they're doing. We have to trust that."

"And while we wait," her mom grinned, "how about you tell us all about how things went?"

"Like you don't already know," Lilah rolled her eyes.

"We don't," said Todd from behind her parents.

Lilah looked around her dad, and her uncle was holding his hand over his heart like he was pledging the truth. "None of us spied. We gave you the privacy you've been wanting."

"In that case," Lilah looked around at everyone, "I met a witch!"

"A witch?" her dad asked.

"Yep," she looked at her mom. "The one from the restaurant a couple days ago. Her name is Everleigh."

"Oh," her mom nodded.

"It's weird. Jackson told me she was a witch," Lilah said, headed to the kitchen for a drink. She rummaged through the fridge until she found the juice and poured a glass. She was aware that she had been followed. Those who didn't come to the kitchen were hanging around in the other room listening. Lilah concentrated on keeping her mind shut off.

She turned and took her glass to the table and sat down. Her mom and dad and Sara joined her. Sara broke the silence first, "He just came right out and said witch?"

"Yeah."

"What did you do?" her dad asked.

"I tried to play it cool. Asked him questions. He's known since they were in high school."

"I'm not surprised. Witches have a long history of taking their friends to heart just like family. They protect their circle. Its common place nowadays for witches to be known," her mom explained.

"It just makes me wonder."

"Makes you wonder why we never tell anyone?" Her dad always understood her.

"Yeah. According to Jackson, the whole town knows her family has a witch history."

"We follow Marcus' rules, honey," Sara told her.

"I know. Just..." Lilah took a sip, "Do we still have to? I mean is the secrecy still necessary? Things have changed a lot since Marcus first arrived."

"The thing is," her dad looked off like the words he was searching for were across the room. "The Elementals. We're all..."

"Different," Lilah groaned and banged her head on the table. "I'm so sick of the answer to everything being that we're different."

"It's true," Sara reached out and patted Lilah's arm. "We can all have children, but only vampires and werewolves can create their kind from someone not born with their blood. We're immortal like the vampires. Witches and werewolves aren't."

"Exactly," said her mom. "We don't want to wind up being a test subject in some science lab while someone tries to bottle the mythical fountain of youth. If people learned you were psychic, you would be a novelty. If they learned of your immortality, it could be a danger to all of us."

"I'd hate to think about what would happen if humans learn how we can change our appearance," Todd said from the doorway.

Lilah stared at her glass from the side with her head on an outstretched arm. She knew they were right. "I suppose that makes sense," she finally agreed. "Except for one thing."

"What's that, Lilah?" Uncle Todd asked.

"Vampires can't have children."

Todd threw up his hands and with an amused look said, "Once again, I'm going to exit this conversation now, and leave you guys alone."

Sara jumped up after him, "Wait for me. You were going to uh...tell me...you know about the thing."

"Oh, yeah, the thing," Todd said. "Let's go."

They were out of the kitchen in a flash.

Lilah slowly sat upright without looking at either of her parents. "They're dead."

"Created vampires are," her dad told her.

Lilah pursed her lips, "So vampires can have children."

"Ye-"

"Nope," Lilah interrupted her dad. "I'm not asking. Vampires can have children. Witches are out of the closet. Werewolves are probably the only dog breed that doesn't know how to swim."

"Actually..." her mom began.

"Nope. I'm done for one night."

Lilah stood up and walked to the other side of the table. She gave her parents a hug saying, "I'm going to sleep. Don't worry. I'll check under my bed for zombies."

She walked through the doorway of the back stairs. "Oh look! A fairy."

Her parents smiled at each other amused by their daughter's humor.

Lilah's voice was still trickling down, "A leprechaun? You don't say? Maybe he will lead us to his pot of gold."

Abby and Myles started to chuckle. They leaned their heads to one another trying not to lose it listening to their daughter's sarcasm.

"Oh my God! Mom! Dad! Come quick! It's Bigfoot!"

Her parents were laughing so hard they couldn't hear the rest of the family joining in with them.

Todd wiped the tears from his eyes. That girl has been through and learned so much the last few days. It was good she could still laugh. It gave him hope that she would pull through whatever was coming without too much lasting damage.

Lilah lay back on her bed. She didn't even bother to undress. She had so many questions swarming, but she was too exhausted to pay them any attention right now. It could wait until tomorrow. She would learn the remaining truth about all the Elementals then. For now, she only wanted to rest.

The last thing she did before drifting off to sleep was look at her phone. She had one notification from Jackson that read, "Looking forward to seeing you again."

Chapter Nine
Visions of the Night

It was almost Halloween, but you couldn't tell it by the snow that blanketed the ground. Lilah sat in the front window with her coffee staring at the foreign white substance. Rarely had her family lived in a cold weather region and not since she was a young child. She was both fascinated by it and mad that she couldn't enjoy her coffee outside without altering the temperature around her to avoid freezing.

Slowly the others in the house began to wake and move about their morning. She barely paid them attention. She concentrated on the one small set of tracks that went through the snow to keep her thoughts blocked. She was so focused that she didn't hear her dad talking to her.

"Earth to Lilah!"

Lilah looked up and smiled, "Morning dad."

"Are you sure you're awake?"

Lilah looked puzzled. "I was up before anyone else."

"I've been trying to talk to you."

"Oh, I was lost in thought."

"I figured you might be today. I guessed you might have some questions."

"Yeah, I do. Well one anyway."

Her dad pulled a chair over by her and sat down. "Okay I'm ready. What's on your mind?"

"How did mom tell you about who she really was?"

"What?" Her dad was taken aback.

"You know, about being an Air."

"I know what you mean. That's your question?"

"Yeah."

"That's it? That's all your curious about?"

"Is there supposed to be something else?"

"I was prepared to talk to you about the other Elementals. I would've bet your first question would be how vampires can have children."

"That too."

Her dad laughed, and Lilah heard another voice joining them. She turned to see her Uncle Joseph leaning against the back of the sofa. Lilah smiled at him. He mostly kept to himself, so she hadn't been around him much growing up.

"Morning, Uncle Joseph."

"Good morning, Lilah," he looked around at the family. He looked almost out of place in his own house with the number of Air descendants packed in it. "I hope you don't mind if I join you and your father. You've been a bit overwhelmed the last few days. I want to try to help you make sense of it all."

"You can join us anytime, Uncle Joseph."

The noises in the living room grew louder as more people began to wake up and mill about. It was clearly making her uncle uncomfortable. "Should we go to the dining room? It might be quieter there."

"Absolutely," replied her dad.

Her uncle looked thankful for the suggestion.

They moved through the kitchen into the dining room and closed the door to decrease the conversation and television noises that would otherwise flood through. Closing if for privacy would be useless when everyone in the family would be able to follow the conversation whether or not they were present.

"So you really want to talk about Jackson?" Her dad asked still in disbelief that this was the most pressing question for her.

"I just...well," Lilah wasn't sure how to begin.

"He will handle the news fine when he learns of your ancestry," her uncle told her. "All matches do."

"I know this. I do. It's just that Everleigh messaged him last night about me. She couldn't get a read on me at the party."

"That's because you're an Air. You're naturally blocked to other Elementals. You'd have to willingly allow her to read you, but if you grant her access, she can see anything she wants," her uncle warned.

"Right. She told Jackson to be cautious with me. She didn't know what it meant that she couldn't read me, but it worried her."

Her dad smiled, "Now this makes sense. He's your match. Things will fall into place. You could drive yourself crazy watching it unfold in your mind, but you know the future is fickle. Freewill changes it constantly."

"Matches always work out," her uncle added. "All you have to do is let the pieces fall into place. Besides, there are more pressing matters at hand."

"Do you know why we've been summoned?" she asked.

"It's a matter of grave importance. That's all I know. That's enough," he answered her.

Lilah sipped her coffee. For a moment, she had hoped that the gathering might be explained.

"You can tell him, or choose for him to figure it out slowly," her dad interjected. "The ladies in the family have done both. Do whatever feels right as time moves along. He isn't going to ask you about his conversation with Everleigh, so you won't have to explain yourself so soon."

Lilah rubbed the back of her neck and thought it over. He was right. They both were. Her eyes popped open and she looked back and forth between her dad and uncle. "Alright then. Spill it."

Her dad laughed and slapped his knee. "I knew it. You want the birds and the bees of the vampires, don't you?"

Lilah rested her elbows on the table and slowly lifted her coffee to her lips without taking her eyes off her dad. "I want to know everything."

1

LILAH SAT IN HER ROOM alone. Her family were growing restless after several days without news from Marcus. They would continue to wait, but how long would it be and to what end? No one knew. People murmured. Tomorrow would be another attempt at the Return. The Elements had now been on Earth for a millennium.

Some had thought the Return would be successful this year, and Marcus gathered them to say goodbye. The window to do this was slowly closing which made everyone scramble for new hunches. Everyone but Lilah. She wanted to know and would probably be impatiently pacing the floors with the others if it weren't for Jackson.

He was texting her now. He had been since the party they had attended. Jackson invited her over for dinner with a couple of his friends. They were going to order out pizza and watch a horror movie. Lilah wanted to go and was sure she be allowed even though Marcus could appear at any moment. Jackson was her match which means no one would interfere.

There was only one reason Lilah was even considering not going. That reason was Everleigh. She would be there along with her cousin Amber. Lilah was unable to pick up on Amber's thoughts which could mean she was under a protection spell, but given the surge of newly called witches, it was likely Amber was a witch herself.

Everleigh was the main cause for concern. She was suspicious of Lilah and for good reason. The Elementals held a certain upper hand over humans,

---

1. http://www.clker.com/cliparts/7/6/9/b/13309573511112670181decorative-lines-2_large-md.png

but those tricks could not be used on other Elementals. Everleigh suspected her of being a witch or at least an acquaintance of one. But who would have cast the spell? It was actually her idea to do this with Jackson and Lilah just so she could try to learn more.

Lilah was torn. She wanted to spend time with Jackson regardless of who was around, but she knew if she went, there was a high chance of a scene being caused. Accusations would be flung. She needn't worry about making up with Jackson afterward, but she didn't want to go through it at all. She had been debating about it all day, internally using the excuse that she had a family matter she would have to try to get out of later. It was time for her to make up her mind.

She wandered downstairs silently asking her mom to meet her in the kitchen as she went. Lilah came off the bottom step and saw Uncle Liam rifling through the fridge for something to eat. Her mom walked in and sat at the table. Lilah walked to the cabinet and got a glass for tea. She was trying to kill a little time hoping for some privacy, but gave up when it occurred to her that with this many Air under one roof, privacy was a rare commodity. She should've asked her mom to come upstairs.

She sat down and sipped her tea. Lilah grimaced. It was bitter. She pushed the glass away and announced, "Jackson wants me to come over tonight. Pizza and a movie," she said nonchalantly.

Her mom's face softened. Abby had been worried that it might be something far more serious than this. "That's fine, sweetie. Have fun. You know we'll call for you if we need you."

"There's going to be witches," Uncle Liam said from the counter where he was spreading chicken salad on a bun.

Lilah hooked her thumb in his direction. "What he said."

Abby rubbed her hands in circles again as she always did when she was nervous or unsure. "How does it look?"

Uncle Liam then turned to them both, "She tries her best to dodge some questions which leads to one witch getting mad and the other warning her guy that Lilah's a liar." He lifted his sandwich and took a big bite holding the plate underneath to catch the dollops of chicken salad that fell out.

Abby and Lilah pierced their lips shut to keep their grins contained. "Would you like to join us?" Abby motioned to an empty chair.

"No. Not my business," he said and left the room.

Lilah and her mom giggled. "What do you want to do?" her mom asked. "What do you feel comfortable with?"

Lilah wasn't sure how to answer. She knew what she wanted to do, but she wasn't sure her mom would approve.

"I mean you can always stay home. I know how it feels when you find your match. I remember it like it was yesterday. That feeling," her mom took a deep breath like she was smelling something intoxicating, "it never goes away."

Lilah got up took her glass over to the counter. She added some sugar to her tea, stirred it and took a sip. *'Much better,'* she thought.

She had played tonight out in her mind in so many ways. None were that much different than the rest except for staying home. "I know it sounds selfish. I just really want to see him," she finally said as she sat back down.

"It may be selfish. I don't know. That connection is a force stronger than anything I've ever experienced. He's feeling it too, you know."

Lilah's eyes lit up, "Well now I really don't want to stay home."

"So what do you want to do then?" her mom asked.

Lilah knew then her mom wasn't asking if she wanted to go, but rather which possible outcome she was going to choose. "Honestly? I want to just tell Everleigh I'm an Air."

"I think that's the best course of action to take." Uncle Todd's voice startled Lilah. She hadn't seen or felt him sneak in.

"You do?" Lilah was surprised. All this talk about Air keeping themselves secret, but now she was just supposed to give the information to a complete stranger freely.

"For one, I wouldn't call her a complete stranger," Uncle Todd said reading her thoughts. "Well, her maybe, but not her family. But two, it's going to come out eventually no matter what you do tonight."

"How do you know that?" Abby asked.

"C'mon," he said, throwing up his hands. "Marcus gathered us here. Here. This town specifically. The same town where a familial order of witches are not only gathering, but spawning in record numbers. That can't be a coincidence."

"I've thought that, too." Abby agreed.

"So you know what's going on?" Lilah asked excitedly.

"You mean why we're here? No, but it has to be connected," he sat down next to Abby.

"Okay, then. I will tell Everleigh outright since her family will probably find out about us anyway when everything comes to a head." Lilah headed to her room to start thinking about outfits.

"I hope we're doing the right thing having Lilah come out with it." Abby said.

Uncle Todd looked up out of the corner of his eye and rocked his head back and forth. "Well, it's either that, or Meredith will tell her."

2

LILAH NERVOUSLY WAITED on Jackson's porch. It seemed like an eternity before he answered the door even though it was only mere moments. He smiled at her and she melted.

"Hi," she smiled back.

"Come in. It's freezing out."

Lilah walked in and unzipped her coat. "I knew it wouldn't be as warm up here, but I wasn't expecting this."

"It's normally not this cold yet, and it's definitely too early for all the snow we got today. We're having an unusual October."

---

2. http://www.clker.com/cliparts/7/6/9/b/

13309573511112670181decorative-lines-2_large-md.png

Jackson took the coat from her and hung it on the rack in the hall. When he turned back, he looked at her sweater with a weird look on his face.

"What?" Lilah looked down worried she had spilt something on it before leaving the farmhouse. She gripped the bottom hem and pulled the sweater out looking for stains or snags.

"It's nothing," he walked to the living room. "Just that earlier as I was making sure I had everything ready for tonight, I pictured you in a red sweater just like that."

She followed him to the couch. "Hmm, I guess maybe we're just really in tune with each other," she said, wagging a finger back and forth between them knowing there was more truth to that than jest.

He flashed another smile at her and a shiver ran down her spine. He didn't seem to notice, "Yeah, I guess."

Jackson had barely sat when the doorbell rang again. He jumped up and let Everleigh and her cousin Amber inside.

"Brrrr!" Everleigh cried out. "I need a few minutes before I part with my coat."

"Aw, come on. It's not that cold out, Lee-Lee."

"Mmm-hmm," she said. "You tell me that when you walk the eight blocks to my house in this weather."

"You walked?" he asked in surprise.

"Yeah, my aunt needed the car because hers is in the shop. Urgent business," she mimicked, making finger quotes in the air.

"More like a hot date," Amber chimed. They laughed.

"She couldn't drop you off?"

Everleigh shrugged and unzipped her coat. "She left a couple hours ago."

"Why didn't you text me? I'd have picked you up."

She reached up and pinched Jackson's cheek like he was a child and said in an overly sweet voice, "Because I knew you were getting ready for your big night. Besides, it's only eight blocks."

They hung their coats and joined Lilah in the living room. Jackson made the introductions. "You two have already met. Lilah, this is Everleigh's cousin Amber. Amber, this is Lilah."

Lilah stood up and said, "Nice to meet you."

Amber didn't say anything at first. Everleigh gave her a slight nudge in the side. "Good to meet you too, Lilah."

Everleigh and Amber sat on chairs opposite where Jackson and Lilah cozied up on the couch. The conversation was forced and awkward. The only person who didn't seem to notice was Jackson. He was blissfully unaware of the pointed questions aimed at Lilah, and the glances shot back and forth between the cousins.

Lilah was thankful when the pizza arrived, and they started the movie. No more questions to try to dodge. It was all for Jackson at this point. She knew what would happen when the movie ended, and she knew the girls would know the truth about her before the night was over.

The movie finished, and Amber was quick to make it known she was ready to leave. Lilah began to make her exit excuses too. Jackson was disappointed hoping to have more time alone with her. She would rather stay, but it had been agreed with her family she would confess her heritage tonight.

Lilah offered to give them a ride home, so they wouldn't have to walk in the cold. Amber looked eager to accept the ride, and Jackson thanked her.

Everleigh, however, was not a willing participant. "That's alright, Lilah. I don't want to be an inconvenience."

"It's no trouble," Lilah countered. She beeped the button for the remote start. "By the time we get our coats on, my car should be warmed up. No need to freeze if you don't have to."

Everleigh was going to refuse again, but Jackson's eyes pleaded with her. It was easy for all of them to see that the only thing this boy wanted in the world right now was for them to get along. "Okay," she said reluctantly. "Thanks."

Lilah and Jackson said their goodbyes then the three girls headed out to Lilah's car. They buckled in and Lilah put it in drive. "Turn left at the stop sign," Everleigh told her.

"I know where you live."

Lilah felt her stiffen up. She couldn't know for sure what Everleigh was thinking, but she was certain that it had something to do with wishing she wasn't in this car anymore.

Everleigh reached over and picked up a barrette out of the console tray. She rolled it over in her hands before commenting, "This is pretty. Where'd you get it?"

"You won't be able to sense anything, Everleigh."

A gasp as loud and clear as a gunshot came from the backseat, and Lilah knew both of them were probably contemplating a jump from the moving car. "The barrette is my mom's. I don't know where she got it. You won't be able to sense her either."

Lilah slowed as she approached Everleigh's house. She put the car in park, and the cousins sat frozen in place. She turned to the witch sitting in her passenger seat and introduced herself again, "My name is Lilah Thomas. I'm an Air. It's great to finally meet an Earth."

Everleigh's mouth dropped open. Then closed. Then dropped open again. "You're an Air?"

"Yes."

Amber started muttering in the backseat. "Girl, I wasn't sure if I was going to run away or come at you, but I was leaning heavy on coming at you when you started all of that you can't sense me talk."

"Me too, only I was ready to run for my house screaming 'FIRE' as I went!" Everleigh joked.

"Maybe it was a bit over the top. I just haven't exactly had this opportunity before, so I wanted to get the most out of it."

"My Aunt Meredith knows an Air. His name is Todd," Everleigh mentioned.

"Uncle Todd's friend Meredith? She's your aunt? How is that even possible? She can't be that old."

"Shouldn't you know that anything is possible?"

Lilah felt embarrassed. Of course her aunt used an aging spell to make herself look younger. She felt like an idiot.

Everleigh opened her mouth, but paused. She turned to face Lilah. "My aunt visited with Todd earlier today. You guys are nearby?"

"Yeah, out in the country."

"Your family?"

"Yes," Lilah wasn't sure why she was asking.

"Your *whole* family?"

Lilah was becoming uncomfortable. *How much would be too much information to give out?* she wondered. "Not my whole family. Not all of Air."

"Oh," Everleigh sounded disappointed. She looked down and fidgeted with the zipper on her coat.

"Wrong answer?" Lilah tilted her head and waited.

"Nah, girl. It's just that there are new witches like me are popping up left and right. More are spawning than ever before," Amber said.

"Amber!" Everleigh tried to quiet her.

"What? It's true. You were hoping the same thing was happening to Air, and you know it."

"It's not the same for Air," Lilah told them.

"We know," Everleigh said before Amber could have a chance to speak. "Your numbers are limited."

"I was still hoping that maybe something was happening round your way too," Amber spoke up from the back seat again.

"We were summoned." The words fell out of Lilah's mouth so easily she wasn't really aware of what she was saying until it was done.

"Summoned?" They asked in unison.

"By our Element. A lot of us are here, but the rest of us are about an hour away."

"So something is up with you too?" Amber wasn't afraid to say what was on her mind.

"We don't really know what's going on," Lilah told her.

The girl in the backseat piped up again. "You guys are psychic right?"

Everleigh shot Amber a look then turned her attention back to Lilah, "She's new."

"I already told her that," Amber was irritated.

"She's this past summer new," Everleigh added.

"It's okay. We are psychic, but our powers don't work on the other Elementals. Like how you guys couldn't get a read on me."

"You heard about the vampires though?" Everleigh asked her.

"Yeah. Do you know who's doing it?"

"No, not exactly." Everleigh put her hand on the door and asked almost too quietly for Lilah to hear, "You know about the werewolves and the witches?"

"I know something is going on with the werewolves, but nothing specific. Witches? Well, you guys are multiplying your numbers. That's it."

Everleigh looked at her house through the window. She knew her grandma would sense their arrival, and she would have some explaining to do later. "Do you have to go straight home, Lilah?"

"No."

She put her seat belt back on. "Do you know the coffee shop on Main Street?"

Lilah didn't, but she could find it in her mind. "Yes."

"Let's go there," Everleigh told her. "Before someone comes outside to see why we're just sitting here."

Lilah drove off. The coffee shop was only a few blocks away. It was almost empty no doubt due to the weird Midwest weather. She parked her car right out front, and the three of them went inside.

Everleigh excused herself to call her grandma, and let her know they'd be home a little later. Amber and Lilah ordered three hot chocolates and found a table. Everleigh joined them after the phone call.

Lilah stirred the whip cream into her hot cocoa letting it melt. No one said anything. She looked around. There was one other customer who was seated across the room. The barista was busy on her phone. "There's something else going on with the witches isn't there?"

"We're next," Everleigh answered.

"What do you mean you're next?"

"We're being hunted," Amber raised her eyebrows then blew on her cocoa.

"That's a little dramatic, but yes. And Air will be after us." Everleigh said.

"Wait," Lilah rubbed her temples. "Hold on. We're all going to be attacked. You're certain?"

"It makes sense doesn't it? The vampires are the most powerful. It's mainly the hereditary vamps that are being murdered. There's very few left we know about."

Lilah's eyes widened, and she glanced at Amber who nodded.

Everleigh leaned closer. "Did you hear about the concert in New York City last week? A lot of people died."

Lilah vaguely remembered something about it. She was too busy being mad over the move at the time. "I kind of remember it."

"Search for it," Everleigh told her. "There was a fire. It was blamed on some faulty pyrotechnics display. One hundred and twenty-two people died."

Lilah closed her eyes. She saw it. It was chaos. People were screaming and running. People were being trampled. She didn't see any pyrotechnics though. Then she found what she was looking for. In the back. There was a room piled high with bodies charred beyond recognition. It didn't look accidental. Firemen were there. They were talking to someone, but the image was blurred like censoring on a television show. The blur was giving them something. It was... Wait. It couldn't be. Her eyes shot open and fear shown on her face.

Amber was staring into her cocoa like she was reading tea leaves.

"Did you see it?" Everleigh's voice was weak.

"I couldn't see anything about the people who died. They were..."

"Vampires," Everleigh finished her sentence.

"But who was the other one?"

"Who?" Everleigh asked.

"The person talking to the firefighters. Staging the story," Lilah withheld part of what she saw.

"I don't know. Maybe it's the person who's behind all of this?'

"It would have to be a vampire then," Lilah stated.

"Or a werewolf," Amber suggested.

"We know werewolves are involved, but not how much," Everleigh told her. "It's the werewolves coming after the witches. After us, they'll go for Air. Take out the vampires especially the hereditary ones, then the witches, and that leaves a handful of you by comparison."

"How do you know it's the wolves?" Lilah asked.

"There's a tribe in Mississippi. Been there long before the settlers first explored the area. We got a coven of witches in that area too since a couple hundred years ago."

Everleigh stopped talking as two more customers walked in the door. They ordered they're drinks to go. "Anyway," she continued when she was sure the new customers weren't paying them any attention, "you know how we can't help each other?"

"What do you mean?" Lilah asked.

"They don't teach you anything, do they?" Amber sneered.

Everleigh shot Amber an angry look.

"It's okay," Lilah insisted. "They don't. We keep to ourselves. It's always been that way."

"Alright," Everleigh went on, "you can't use your psychic ability on me, right?"

"Right."

"Well, it's like that with our spells. I can't make someone fall in love with you because you only have one soulmate." A slow realization set in, and Everleigh straightened up looking at Lilah with eyes wide. "Jackson?" she asked.

Lilah didn't say anything, but she felt her face turn a deep shade of red.

"Oh, my. Jackson!" Everleigh repeated with a shocked smile. "Does he know?"

"No. I thought we'd get to know each other a little before I spring forever on him," Lilah joked.

"What about Jackson?" Amber was puzzled.

Everleigh cut her eyes to the ceiling. "Don't worry about it. I'll fill you in later."

Lilah's face was beginning to hurt from the wide smile she couldn't control, and she bit her lower lip trying to do her best to contain it.

"Wow," Everleigh shook her head and rubbed her hands on her jeans. After a few moments, she clasped her hands together on the table and asked, "Anyway, where were we? Oh yeah, I can't cast a spell that would stop a vampire from craving blood for example."

"I see what you mean now."

"But, the Mississippi witches could cast a spell that would make the transformation pain free for a werewolf."

Lilah's eyes widened. "You can do that?"

"Actually, no. I don't even know the spell. That's what the coven did in Mississippi and has done for generations. They did more than that. They figured out a way to stop them from transforming during the lunar cycle as well. That coven of witches and that tribe of wolves have been friends for centuries. Each new generation of witches will spell the younger wolves, so they don't feel pain."

Lilah was impressed. She knew witches had great power, but had no idea they were capable of anything like that.

"A few months ago, witches started receiving the calling all over. It doesn't matter if you're from a skipped generation, or if your family already had a witch from your generation. Siblings of witches were coming into powers. All of my cousins received the calling. We were panicked."

"I bet. What did you do? What did you think was going on?"

"I was afraid. I knew it had to be something big, but we didn't have to wonder long. Word spread fast."

"About the wolves?"

"Exactly. The tribe in Mississippi were told that there would be a move against witches. They told the coven that's been helping them about it and said they weren't going to fight. They would help them defend themselves instead."

"What happened?"

"Nothing yet. The wolves are still preparing. The ones from the north, from the Great Lake area, they're on the move. We can't track them. Our locator spells don't work on them no more than your psychic ability would."

Lilah let all this information sink in as she sipped her cocoa. It's the wolves. They're behind the attacks on the vampires, and after the witches, her family will be next. "Wait. This doesn't add up."

Everleigh sat silent.

Amber asked, "What doesn't?"

"The spell on the werewolves." Lilah noticed both of them smile.

"If our powers don't work on other Elementals, how could that one spell work?"

They didn't say anything for what felt like an eternity. They stared into their cups with the wickedest smiles at the corner of their mouths.

"You tell her, cousin. This is your show," Amber leaned back and waved her hands in front of her chest.

"There's a reason I don't think I can perform the spell," Everleigh hinted.

"What's that?"

"Let's just say the Mississippi covens might have a little werewolf blood in their heritage."

"Oh," Lilah said. "Oh!" she repeated as it sunk in what Everleigh meant. "I guess that would be how it works, huh?"

The three girls laughed. Their cocoas were finished, and it was almost time for the shop to close. Lilah knew she had been expected home a long time ago. They left and piled back into Lilah's car. She drove them the few blocks to Everleigh's house.

When she pulled up, Lilah said, "It's Water, then. That's who is behind everything," more to herself than the other two girls in her car.

"Not entirely. Someone else is pulling the strings. The wolves are carrying out orders."

"Orders? From who?" Lilah was baffled.

"We don't know, and neither do our allies in the south."

A few moments passed while Lilah tried to think of who else could even know about the Elementals true existence.

Putting her hand on the door, Everleigh told her, "I'm really glad you outed yourself tonight. We need to join together. It's the only way we have a chance."

Lilah agreed, but it was up to her family. Everleigh knew that too. Neither was sure what would happen now.

Another car drove past and pulled into Everleigh's drive. "Aunt Meredith is back," Amber noticed.

Meredith got out of her niece's car. She was exactly as Lilah had remembered her. "She uses an aging spell, doesn't she?" Lilah asked without taking her eyes off Meredith.

There was a gasp from the back seat. If Lilah had looked in her rearview mirror, she would have seen Amber shaking her head and mouthing words of pity for this poor child who knows nothing.

"An aging spell?" Everleigh was amused. She opened the passenger door of the car and said before she got out, "Things aren't always what they seem."

"What does that mean?" Lilah quickly asked, but it was too late. Everleigh had left with Amber right behind her. They hugged their aunt who turned to wave at Lilah. She waved back then headed home.

Lilah arrived at her house expecting a welcome wagon on the porch wondering where she had been. She was surprised to see no one. She walked inside, and saw the other nineteen members of her family who were gathered at the farmhouse in one room. They were everywhere. They squeezed together on the sofas and chairs, the arms of the furniture, the floor, and some had brought in chairs from the tables in the kitchen and dining room. The room was quiet, and the air was so thick it clung to Lilah like damp strings of hair.

She looked around the room. No one lifted their gaze to her. Lilah spied her mom and dad sitting side by side on the large recliner. Her mom finally looked her way.

"You guys know?"

Her mom nodded. "I'm sorry, Lilah. I only read your mind because I was worried you weren't home yet. I'm trying to give you your privacy like you've asked."

"I'm glad you did."

"What?" her mom was genuinely surprised.

"I'm glad I don't have to tell you."

Lilah moved through the room. There was barely a space anywhere. She found a spot on the floor between a couple cousins and sat down. "So what are we going to do?"

"What do you mean?"

Lilah turned to see who answered her. It was her Uncle James. "What's the plan?"

No one answered.

"We have to do something," Lilah insisted.

"What can we do?" Abby asked.

"Lilah," her Uncle Todd stood up, "I think its best you retain your friendship with Everleigh until Marcus arrives. We need to stay current on any new developments."

"That's it?" Lilah asked in disbelief. "That's all you got. That's all anyone can come up with?"

She stood up and walked toward the window then turned and faced the room. "You want me to spy on the witches? That's the plan. Well, I guess we're doomed then. It's been nice knowing all of you."

"Lilah!" her mom yelled through gritted teeth. "That's enough."

"No, mom, it's not enough. We have to be active in this. We can't just sit back and wait to see what happens with the witches or wait for Marcus."

"You know our ways," Uncle James told her.

"I do. I also know we haven't faced anything like this before, and Marcus isn't here to instruct us. So until he shows up, we need to do something to prepare ourselves for whatever comes our way." Lilah was practically yelling by the time she finished. She was angry at them, but mostly she was scared. She was afraid of losing her family or Jackson. Whoever was doing this had found a way to subdue vampires without fire. That frightened her most of all.

She waited, but no one responded to her outburst. She wasn't sure how she could get through to them. She sat back on the floor farther away than where she had been sitting. She didn't want to go to her room and isolate herself, but she still didn't feel like being too close to them.

Minutes ticked by. Lilah's mind jumped from one horrible outcome to another. She thought about Jackson. She might never have a life with him the way her family had with their matches. She worried about him getting hurt because of her. She had to shake those thoughts away because crying would do no one any good right now.

"Tell us, Lilah," she recognized her dad's voice without looking up. "What would you have us do?"

"Well," Lilah hadn't thought about it herself. She figured someone older and wiser than her would figure this out. "For starters, we should track the wolves. We need to know where they're headed and when to expect them here."

"You know we can't," her dad told her.

"They're Water, Lilah. You know this," her Uncle Todd spoke to her like she was a child again.

It hit Lilah suddenly in an instant. "We can't track them," she said eagerly, "but we can track the absence of them."

Murmurs went through the room. "Their absence?" Sara asked.

"Yes!" Lilah sprang up from the floor. "The tribe of wolves up north is the largest remaining tribe, right? If they're on the move, someone has noticed something."

Her family still seemed mostly confused, but Lilah saw a few sets of eyes light up as they figured it out.

"Like large groups traveling together?" her dad asked.

"Yes," Lilah's excitement was growing.

"Vacant properties," Gene added.

"Exactly like that!" Lilah told him. "If they all leave together or close together, that's going to raise some eyebrows. It has to. We just need to pick up their scent from the area where they lived, and follow the clues of the people they run into on their way."

"It's not... There's no guarantee," Todd sighed.

"It's a start," her mom told him.

"Okay, so where were they living?" Lilah asked.

"All I know is they were somewhere in the Great Lakes area," Uncle James answered.

"That's better than nothing," Lilah was trying to keep everyone encouraged. "How big is the tribe?"

"Multiple families." Her Uncle Todd sounded a bit more interested.

"Maybe fifty then? Like us?" she asked.

"It's possible, Lilah," Sara told her. "We really don't know for sure."

"With children?" The gears in Lilah's mind were spinning now.

"Schools," said her mom. "The kids would be pulled out of school, or would be considered truant."

"Yes!" Lilah pointed at her mom. "Concentrate on the school systems in that area."

She turned to the family and started grouping them off on areas to focus. Moving trucks. Rental properties suddenly emptied. Utilities shut off. Would they bother with it? She didn't know, but it was worth a shot.

"If you move, you get rid of a lot of unnecessary stuff, right?" Lilah was talking more to herself then to anyone in her family. "Sara and Gene, take the garbage routes. See if multiple homes had huge amounts out for trash like you'd leave behind in a move."

Sara and Gene nodded. They pulled out their phones and looked at a map of the area dividing up the towns each would focus on to see if they could come up with anything.

Uncle James asked, "What about me, Lilah?"

"Follow the money. Account closures. Out of state purchases or anything that might look suspicious on bank accounts or credit cards."

"I'll help him," her Uncle Todd offered.

Soon everyone was tasked with some small detail to examine that might bring them a clue. Lilah made her way to the kitchen. "What are you going to work on?" her dad asked.

"Coffee," she replied without stopping. "I think we're all going to need some."

Lilah went into the kitchen and turned on the light. She set about getting the coffee pot ready to brew. Her phone vibrated in her back pocket, and she pulled it out. It was a message from Everleigh.

"Grandma wants to meet you. Is that cool?"

"Yes, just tell me when."

"Okay. She wants to know if Air is willing to help."

Lilah replied with absolute certainty, "Yes."

She pulled up her message screen with Jackson. Nothing since she'd texted him from the driveway that she was home, and he had replied good night. She wanted to text him. He was awake. She could see him. He wasn't able to sleep because he was thinking about her.

Lilah knew it was the wrong time to start up a conversation with him, but the pull was so strong. She would give anything to be able to go to him again right now, but her family needed her. More than that, all of the Elementals needed their help. She watched him until the coffee brewed then rejoined her family.

They were just starting to map out the route they believed the wolves were on when there was a knock at the door. Todd jumped up to answer it.

It was definitely a witch. Lilah could sense it. She knew it wasn't Everleigh because she would've said she was coming over. It must be her aunt.

Todd opened the door. "Meredith!" he shouted happily.

"Can we come in?"

Lilah looked up. She could see Meredith from where she sat.

"We?" Todd asked.

A man stepped from the side. Lilah didn't recognize him and couldn't get a read on him. He wasn't a witch. He must be under a protection spell, but his energy was different.

"Hello, Luke," Todd said. "You are always welcome here. Please, come in."

The two of them walked inside where the family was busy tracking wolves. No one barely looked up except for Lilah who couldn't peel her eyes away.

"What brings you out so late?" Todd asked concerned.

"Eloise kicked us out," Meredith told him.

"What?" Todd's eyes lit up amused.

"Well, to be fair, I didn't exactly ask permission to stash a vampire in her attic."

Lilah gasped. Her mouth dropped open. She stared at him. She had never seen a vampire before that she was aware. He looked normal which was almost disappointing.

The three of them heard her, and they all turned to face her. "Luke, this is my niece Lilah. You have to forgive her. She didn't know vampires were real until a few days ago."

Lilah couldn't stop staring.

Meredith snapped her fingers in front of Lilah's face. "Aren't you going to say hi?"

It took another minute, but Lilah slowly turned her head away from him to look at Meredith. "Hey," she smiled then glanced back at Luke. "Are you really going to be staying here?"

"That's up to your uncle," Meredith answered.

"Well, not exactly," Todd said slowly. He looked at everyone gathered in the living room. "I think there's a few more who need to weigh in on this, too."

Luke and Meredith looked at all the faces who were beginning to take more notice of them. She was sure Todd would be okay with it, but convincing his family was an entirely different matter. They had always been so private. It worked though as they'd never suffered the same fates as the other Elementals.

Finally it was Sara who spoke up, "Why not?"

Even Todd looked surprised. "Really? Just like that?"

Sara shrugged, "I mean it seems we're breaking all the rules anyway."

The family muttered their agreements then went back to work. "I guess that's that," Todd told them still in disbelief.

Meredith continued to look at the large congregation of Air, but leaned toward Todd and whispered, "Are they feeling okay? Did something happen?"

"Yes," Todd answered. "The Elementals are being hunted."

Luke walked toward the coffee table where there was a notebook spread open with a rough map drawing that was spread out on two pages. "Is that Michigan?"

Abby looked up and grinned from ear to ear. "Thank you!" She turned to their cousin Lauren with her nose dramatically up in the air, and said, "Even someone who doesn't know what it's supposed to be can tell what it is."

"I still think it looks like a dog, Abby. Sorry, not sorry," Lauren told her.

"Michigan? As in the wolf tribes?" Meredith was intrigued.

"Yes. Lilah's idea," Todd motioned toward her. "We've been working pretty much since she got home tonight."

"Working on what? Can we help?" Luke was interested.

Todd smiled at Lilah and said, "Go ahead. This is all you."

Lilah looked at the three of them standing in front of her. It was a little intimidating. There weren't any comfortable places left for them to sit, so Lilah stood up. She walked to the side and started to explain her plan to track the wolves by using the blanks they came across when they were searching for information.

"Because you can't psychically pick up on other Elementals," Luke stated more than asked.

"Exactly," said Lilah.

"So you're tracking the void areas?" Meredith asked. "I understand what you're saying, but I'm not sure I understand how it works."

Lilah nodded. "Yeah, we have some students who suddenly stopped going to school, but we can't pick up anything on them or their families."

"Wolves," Luke said his voice filled with disgust.

"More than likely," Todd added.

"There are other clues too," Lilah continued. "Well, I call them clues. We're looking at rentals, movers, bank accounts, and so on."

Meredith looked at all the members of Air who sat with their notebooks, phones and laptops, looking at maps or taking notes. It showed on her face that the whole process was slowly beginning to make sense. She chuckled and smiled, "Genius, girl! This is great!"

"Can we help?" Luke asked.

"Slow down, honey, I need to get you spelled first."

Luke deflated. His shoulders slumped, and his head fell back. "Then no one can talk to me."

"Hon," Meredith said. "I had to hide you, so no one at the house found you. These people know you're here. You don't have to be hidden."

Luke breathed a sigh of relief. "Get started then."

Meredith stood in front of him and took his hands. She closed her eyes and quietly said a few lines. When she finished, she looked at him and smiled then gave him a quick kiss on the cheek.

"That's it?" he asked.

"That's it."

"And just like that, no one can find me?"

"Oh, ye of little faith," Meredith rolled her eyes and playfully swatted his chest. "I've kept you safe this long, haven't I?"

"Yes, love, you have."

"Alright," Meredith said loudly rubbing her hands together. "This is a game changer. We've been trying to figure out a way to get our magic to finally work on the other Elementals. Let me think about how to use our magic like you are using your psychic abilities by reverse engineering it." She set off to the back of the house to find a quiet place to think.

Luke stayed behind to talk to Todd and catch up. "I've been trying to reach you for weeks, and you've been in Eloise's attic this whole time?" Todd asked.

"Not the whole time. Meredith and I moved around quite a bit trying to make sure we weren't being followed. With Halloween approaching, she knew she needed to be home."

"How were you discovered?"

"I don't know. Eloise never came up there. Sensed it somehow I guess. Meredith insisted this spell was fool proof even from other witches."

"It is!" Meredith yelled from the back of the house.

Luke looked in her direction and smiled. "Eloise is pretty powerful. She might have sensed something. Hell, it could have been a lucky guess."

Todd agreed, "That makes sense. Meredith wouldn't leave you for long or venture far away."

"Wait a minute," Lilah interrupted them.

"What, little lady?" Luke asked. "You know how Eloise found out?"

"No. It's just... Um... I," Lilah looked back at the screen on her laptop and waved them off.

"Now, I'm curious. What's on your mind?"

"How do Meredith's spells work on you?"

Luke glanced at Todd for help like he didn't understand the question.

Todd just stood there with his mouth open unsure how to respond.

"Why haven't you taught this girl anything?"

Lilah turned to see Meredith had reappeared in the doorway sternly looking at her uncle.

Luke slowly started to understand. "Ah, it makes sense now."

"What makes sense?" Lilah asked.

"Just that I think I understand why you don't know how the spells work on me. The Elementals are protected from each other, but each Elemental can use their abilities on their own kind."

"Yeah, but Meredith is a witch," Lilah said plainly.

Meredith stood there smiling. "I was born into Earth, honey. I became a witch in my teens, but that was back before this country had its first president."

Lilah stared at the floor. She knew what Meredith was telling her. There was no ageing spell. Everleigh had told her that things weren't always what they appeared to be. Meredith was a vampire. That's why she always looked so young.

"I didn't know a witch could become a vampire," was all she could manage to say.

Abby leaned forward and put her hand on Lilah's shoulder. She hadn't expected her daughter to get a crash course on everything in a few days' time. She had thought she would have years to go over all the varied ins and outs of the Elementals. She started to doubt herself for not teaching Lilah more over the last few years.

Her mom reluctantly, and maybe even a little remorsefully, started to explain it. "Fire and Water can potentially turn anyone."

"With a bite?" Lilah asked.

"A werewolf bite works only when they are in wolf form to cause the transformation, but very few have ever survived a wolf attack."

"And vampires? Is it the bite or the blood?"

Luke stepped forward. "It's our blood. There's a process. You must have our blood in your system when you die. You'll awaken, and you must drink human blood to complete the transformation."

"If you don't drink the blood?" Lilah didn't blink captivated by the lesson she was learning.

"You die," Luke answered coldly.

Meredith clicked her teeth and glared at him. "You have a little time."

Luke nodded, "A day at the most, and it's not pleasant."

Lilah narrowed her eyes, and her face filled with questions.

"It's the same painful death that first killed them only it's prolonged until they drink or pass away." Meredith tried to explain it to her. "See, most of us know this is what we want before we ever drink the blood. My death was quick by a broken neck. When I resuscitated, my neck was pained and my head was sore."

"Y-You said most," Lilah uttered barely above a whisper.

Everyone looked at Luke who immediately became defensive. "I never participated in that nonsense!"

Lilah looked at him, then the others waiting, hoping someone would continue.

"There was a time," Luke hesitated, "when vampires messed with humans as if it were sport. But not me!" he growled.

It was hard to hear. She felt like she was going to be sick.

Uncle Todd bent over and checked on her reminding her to breathe. "That era is long over. There are still those who are fed the blood unknowingly as a precaution. Perhaps the blood was used to heal them, but it was too late. It's rare, but there are occasions when someone finds themselves unwittingly in the middle of the transformation."

"Did you turn Meredith," Lilah asked looking at Luke.

"I did not."

Lilah's eyes widened, and she gazed at Meredith surprised. She had just assumed Meredith turned to be with Luke.

"Slow down, Lilah. I see those wheels turning in your head," Meredith cautioned.

"It's different for the Elementals. Only Fire can turn a different Elemental," Luke explained.

"And you don't have to drink anyone's blood," Meredith happily pointed out.

"Then how did you become a vampire?"

Luke held up a hand indicating to the rest that he would take this one. "Really, she's not. She has immortality, and a touch of all Fire's abilities such as speed and strength. That is why she still practices witchcraft. Once she drinks Fire's blood, she will complete the change."

"That doesn't sound so bad," Lilah thought out loud.

Meredith knelt down in front of her. "You know, it was hard because my family did not approve. They liked Luke just fine, so long as he was only a friend. But I fell in love," she gazed wistfully up at Luke. "I still am. I fell in love with a vampire just like-"

"It's really late," Lilah's dad announced. "I think that's enough for one night. We should all turn in, and pick up on the tracking in the morning."

Meredith stood up and whistled. "Man, I always knew Air was funny about their ways and their secrets, but you guys should really be a little bit more inclusive with your own kind."

Todd shot Meredith a glance that told her she was treading water with the invite for the two of them to stay, and she should think twice before making any more revelations.

"What are you talking about?" Lilah asked.

Meredith had the eyes of everyone in the room on her as she answered, "Nothing, honey. It's just that in all the years I've known you, I didn't know no one had told you about me and Luke."

Lilah smiled at her. If only she knew the vast amount of information her family had kept from her, this wouldn't be a surprise. Not in the least.

Chapter Ten
The First Return

It's the last night before the Return, and Marcus was wrought with agony. His love for Leena had grown every day since his arrival, and it broke his heart to leave her even though he knew they can't be together. He had watched every heartache she's had to face in the last year helpless to do anything to comfort her.

He watched her lovingly care for her father during his illness and rejoice when he recovered, only to lose him during the last moon. Her father's illness took a toll on his health, and he degraded swiftly when the first signs of autumn appeared.

Marcus lingered on the edge of the forest as her family and the village mourned. He wanted to hold Leena, to comfort her, but he did his duty and stayed out of sight. Her father's death changed her. She had planned to run away from her upcoming marriage to Yaxkin, but she always felt she'd be unable to follow through. Her father's death meant there was nothing keeping her in the village any longer.

Her mother had died in childbirth, so her father married her mother's sister. She never treated Leena the same as she had her own children. It was she who had arranged the marriage to the warrior, and Leena felt no loyalty to this woman to carry out her wishes now that her father was gone. His death gave her the push she needed to leave.

"Leaving also means death," Marcus said to himself with sadness in his voice. He didn't know which was worse. Death alone in the wilderness that comes swift. Or dying slowly in a life that tortures you while surrounded by the people you've known and cared about your entire life.

He wanted for nothing more than to take her away, to save her. Doing so would anger the Divine Spirit, and Marcus didn't want to find out what the punishment would be. "Without the full use of our powers, we won't know what consequences our actions will have." He repeated again as he had hundreds of times as a reminder that no life was to be interfered.

Marcus began his preparations to leave knowing Leena was doing the same. He had cleared out all of his belongings from the hollowed trunk, save for the water bucket and a small amount of fruit to eat before his hike back to the cave in the morning. While he was getting rid of any evidence of his presence from the last year, Leena was hiding provisions to take with her.

She had gathered some of the harvest as well as a small store of seeds. Also in her cache were two spears, and flint rocks. She'd thrown everything into a fur and tied the ends to make it easy to carry.

Leena didn't yet know where she'd wind up or if she'd find a friendly tribe anywhere. She knew she'd need to be able to provide for herself. Not all tribes took kindly to strangers, so she risked being on her own permanently or being killed if she ran into a group that didn't want to risk their safety. Or worse. Leena felt in her heart that all options were better than life with Yaxkin.

Marcus lay down watching her in his mind. He knew she'd be on her way by the rise of the sun. She'd head west through the hills, and the village's search would begin shortly after dawn. He would have to leave before her to make it back to his cave for the Return without being spotted. He knew tonight would be the last time he'd be able to watch her. This time tomorrow, she'd be dead.

He drifted off to sleep as she lay in bed barely able to close her eyes. She was both excited and frightened for what her future held.

Marcus woke with a start, afraid he had slept too long. It was still dark, and Leena had not yet made her move. He knew he had a little time left before he had to make his way back.

Marcus opened a coconut and drank while eating the last papaya he had. He tried to savor the flavors, so that he'd never forget their tastes. The remains of his breakfast he placed in the tiny hole he dug inside the tree and covered it with dirt. Marcus surveyed the area one last time hoping he hadn't forgotten anything.

He cupped his hands into the water bucket and took a drink. He stood and slowly poured the water out. Carrying the bucket, he emerged from his tiny home and looked toward the village. Marcus knew Leena was awake now and would soon be on her way. He had to hurry.

Marcus quickly walked to the stream where the rock bridge was that he had crossed many times during his stay. He set the bucket on the surface of the water and let it drift. He watched it bounce and spin around in the stream until it was out of sight. Now all he had were the robes he arrived in and a large walking stick to help him scale the hillside.

He entered the tree cover about the time Leena was sneaking out of her hut. She would move fast, and he needed to stay ahead of her. Marcus closed his eyes and took off running across the forest floor expertly dodging fallen trees and exposed roots as he used his inner sight to guide him.

Before long, Marcus was climbing up the hill toward the cave as fast as he could. He reached the cave just as light started to creep in from the east and just as Leena finished crossing the stream. He approached the spot where he had stood on his first day waiting for his eyes to adjust to the brightness of the midday sun. *'Not yet,'* he thought.

He walked further into the cave and into the darkness. There he crouched down and waited. He stayed perfectly still, eyeing the dim light from the opening that was slowly growing brighter. He stayed still even as his knees begged for him to show mercy and change positions. He stayed still, waiting to see her when she passed by. It would be the closest he had ever been to her.

It seemed like an eternity had passed before he felt her climbing the hillside near the cave. Then suddenly, there she was. She stood at the cave opening not ten feet from where Marcus was kneeling with his back flush to the cave wall. For a moment, she looked right at him without seeing him then moved on.

Marcus let out his breath not realizing he had been holding it. A few more moments passed before he stood up. He felt his knees pop, and the sounds echoed through the cave. Marcus jumped then laughed at himself. "I'll have to tell the others about that one," he mused.

He walked forward and looked at the spot again. He could feel the energy pulsating from it. Marcus took a deep breath before taking a step into the cave wall.

On the other side, he was back on the flat rock. He was the first to arrive. He had no choice but to leave early if he wanted to remain undetected, and he knew the others all had plenty of time left.

Marcus turned slowly and looked around. It was no wonder why the Divine Spirit chose this location. No one lived anywhere close to this rock. Marcus wanted to step off the rock to explore the land, but knew he was not able to. "You had a year to explore, Marcus," he told himself. "You chose not to."

He sat down on his corner and waited for the others. He couldn't wait to begin to share their experiences, to learn from each other's journeys as well as their own. Marcus had missed them many times over the last year. He knew now they were like a family, and a twinge of sadness brushed over him because he knew once they crossed the veil all human emotion would leave them, including thoughts like this.

As the sun passed overhead, shade slowly inched its way across the rock, and Marcus spread out. He lay in the center with his fingers clasped behind his head. His thoughts drifted back to Leena. He could still spy on her. She had found a cave where she thought she was safe to wait out the party searching for her. It wouldn't be long now before she'd be forced to run in the dark. It wouldn't be long until she met her end.

Marcus sat up and pulled his knees to his chest. For a moment, he rested his head on his legs as he thought of her. "Soon," he whispered. "Soon you will be home, and your attachment to her will be as if it never existed."

Marcus wondered if that was what he even wanted. He knew it was only the human condition that made him feel how he did, but did he really want to give it up?

He stood up and rocked back and forth on his feet for a moment before steadying himself. The heat from the sun was starting to affect him. He reached down and brushed the dirt from his robes. Marcus was looking down when Earth emerged from her corner with such force that she almost knocked him over, not that it would have taken much effort.

Their hands grasped each other's arms, and they looked at each other as loud smiles spread across their faces. He pulled Earth to him and hugged her. His excitement was so deafening to his senses that he didn't pick up on Earth's shattered heart. Finally, he relaxed his embrace and looked at her. That's when Marcus saw it. The hurt. The pain. The sheer and utter agony that Earth wore in her eyes.

"What's the matter?"

Before she could answer, another presence had joined them. Marcus stood on tip toe to look over Earth, but no one else had arrived. That's when he felt it. The peaceful calm of the Divine Spirit. He looked back into Earth's eyes which were filled with tears. Marcus was plagued with questions about what had happened. There was no chance to find out.

Immediately they knew they were the only ones who made the Return. Marcus saw the terror in Earth's eyes the moment he felt it encroach upon him. What could this possibly mean for them?

Neither had a chance to say a word. Marcus was back in the cave. Alone, but only for a moment before the presence of the Divine Spirit surrounded him.

He communicated with Marcus through thought. *"Those who leave together must return together. Balance must be acquired and is of the utmost importance."*

Marcus' head spun as he learned he was the only one who followed orders and didn't interact with anyone. His rewards would be great.

"What do I do now?" Marcus asked the quiet darkness of the cave.

"Live your life," was the answer placed in his mind. *"The Return can only be achieved on this night each year. You must attempt it every year no matter how long it takes."*

"No matter how long it takes! What does that mean?"

His question was ignored. *"Go to her. There isn't much time."*

Marcus opened his mouth to speak again, but the presence was gone. He had so many unanswered questions, but only one mattered now. Did he have enough time to save Leena?

Chapter Eleven
Halloween

It was Halloween. Earth would be gathering to celebrate their new year. The preparation had been in the works for days, and Everleigh had even invited Lilah to the celebration much to her Grandma Eloise's disapproval. Lilah had turned down the offer to be with her family who were growing more and more concerned at Marcus' absence.

They still hadn't heard a word from him or Leena since they called the family together. It weighed on everybody's mind differently. Some like Abby were finding little things to do to keep their hands and minds busy like cleaning an already clean home for the sixth time in a matter of days. Others like her Uncle Joseph were trying desperately to search for them somehow and becoming highly irritated by anyone's unwillingness to help.

Lilah spent her day talking to Jackson. He was going to be home that night handing out candy to the trick or treaters then possibly going out afterward. He had asked Lilah to spend the evening with him, but she knew better than to even give the idea weight in her mind. It was a very important day for everyone, and not hearing from Marcus only made the day that much more solemn.

It was the day of the Return. It would be the thousandth attempt. The Elements had been down here for a full millennium. No one breathed easy on this day until after the attempt was made because no one knew what would happen when the four Elements finally made it home. Even being unsure of their future, her family always hoped for a completed Return. Balance was steadily growing out of control. They needed to complete the Return before too much more damage was done here.

This year, it was worse for everyone. Usually Marcus communicated some form of well wishes to his family in the event they were successful. Every year when the Return attempt failed, he would let them know he was back for another round. There was nothing from him. No one could be sure if anything had happened to him or even what could have possibly occurred that would keep him silent.

The possibilities were as endless as their imaginations, and their imaginations were rich and colorful. Distraction was the best route to take in Lilah's mind. She felt bad for those who joined her uncle in trying to find news on Marcus' whereabouts. She understood, of course, why they had to try, but she would drive herself crazy with worry if she thought about it for too long.

It wasn't easy trying to come up with a good excuse to not hang out with Jackson tonight. She could only use family matters so many times before she would have to start answering questions about her family that she wasn't ready to face. She told him she wasn't feeling well and should stay home and rest.

This made Jackson want to change his plans to care for her. She knew that he often worried he was coming on too strong. Their connection was definite only he didn't know the reason behind why he had such strong feelings for her from the start. She wanted to come out with the truth to him like she had with Everleigh, but whenever she saw it happening in her mind, the reaction wasn't clear enough to risk. He was her match, so they would work out in the end. She just didn't need to bring on any more trouble or stress right now than she already had until after the Return and after news from Marcus.

Eventually Jackson became more preoccupied as little children dressed as ghouls and princesses started steadily knocking on his door. Lilah used this as her chance to take a break from texting him by saying she was going to lay down on the couch and hang out with her family. She told him to text her before he went out to see if she was feeling better.

Lilah headed downstairs to join her family in the wait. They faced this year after year. The Return could be over at any time. The Divine Spirit always knew who would and would not show. Once everyone that would arrive was there, they would be told immediately that the opportunity had passed again for this year. Air and Earth were the only two Elements who made the Return attempt every single year. Fire came about as often as he didn't show, but Water had never made the attempt once.

Her mom tried to make the wait a little less tense by asking how Jackson was doing and if he had any plans for Halloween.

Lilah didn't answer her.

Her mom waved her hand in front of Lilah and said, "Hello? Are you there?"

"Yes, mom. I just don't think anyone else here cares about what Jackson is up to right now. Besides, you can find out for yourself if you really wanted to know."

"No, I can't." Abby told her then sucked in a breath like she regretted the words as soon as she said them.

"What do you mean you can't?" Honestly Lilah probably wouldn't have paid any attention to what her mom said if it hadn't been for her reaction afterward.

"You must have blocked him at some point without realizing you were doing it," Todd came to Abby's rescue.

"I can do that?" Lilah hadn't known it was possible. He was her match, so in a way, it made sense. Her mom had been able to block her before under certain situations. "How?"

"You were right, dear. Maybe now isn't the time," Abby answered not wanting to delve into it right now.

The minutes ticked by and no one said another word. Lilah felt her phone vibrate and checked the notification. It was from Everleigh telling her that she was missing a great party. She replied asking if Everleigh had heard anything about the attempt yet, but the answer was no.

She looked up and her family was staring at her. They couldn't read Everleigh, but they could clearly read Lilah's thoughts. It made her feel uncomfortable the way they were staring. It's not like she had to tell them what had been said. They already knew.

"It's alright, little one," her dad told her. "They're staring because they're hoping for news soon. I think we all are willing your phone to receive another update from Everleigh."

The wait was agonizing for her as well. She went out on the porch for some air. It was freezing outside, and it was enough that she wished she'd brought a jacket. She rubbed her hands together and concentrated on the air around her like a bubble. She had never tried to change the temperature near her before because she hadn't had the ability to do it until a few days ago. It took her several attempts, but finally she felt the warmth starting to grow. Pleased with herself, she sat on the swing and looked out on the snow that was starting to melt.

She was lost in her thoughts for a while when it dawned on her that there were no new tracks in the white blanket that covered the ground. She hadn't seen her squirrel friend for at least a day. She tried to remember when exactly it was that he last was around. It was possible that the cold front that came through made him hibernate a little early, but it was supposed to warm up for the next few days.

An idea hit her. She went inside to the kitchen on a mission and searched through every cabinet until she found what she was looking for, a bag of unsalted peanuts in their shells. Her mother had almost quite literally bought at least two of everything when they shopped to stock the house. She knew there had to be peanuts or some kind of nut somewhere. Heading back to the front door, she felt all eyes on her as she passed. She ignored them. They could find out what she was up to if they wanted.

Lilah walked back outside and opened the bag. She through a handful off to the side of the porch in the area she saw the white squirrel the most then left a few scattered about the porch as well. Hoping it was enough to attract him, she turned to head back to the swing surprised to see her Uncle Brian sitting on it. She had been so caught up in her white squirrel mission that she hadn't noticed anyone else coming outside.

He nodded toward the open part of the swing next to him, and Lilah walked over and sat down. She didn't know her Uncle Brian as well as some of the other family and was a bit surprised that he was interested in spending time with her at all. A thought she didn't bother trying to block from him either.

Uncle Brian picked up on it quickly, "I know Maria and I tend to be more loners than part of the group. I just thought I'd join you as the tension in the house is becoming unbearable."

Lilah tilted her head to the side and smiled. She never thought of him as a loner. Whenever he was around, he had always been very friendly. They were mostly private which isn't saying a lot coming from this family, but it's also the life they'd always known. Keep to yourself at all costs.

The peanut bag was still in her hands and she opened and refolded it shut nervously.

'*You know, the squirrels and other animals can find food on their own,*' he thought openly, '*but I get it. It's busy work. You need to keep your mind occupied.*'

She hadn't thought of it like that before, but maybe that's exactly why she did it. She had thought she was trying to draw the white squirrel out of hiding because she missed seeing him. '*Was that all there was to it?*' she wondered. Maybe she was subconsciously trying to find ways to keep her mind off the wait and stay distracted. She wouldn't have to speculate much longer.

Her phone vibrated in her pocket, and Lilah took it out slowly. Uncle Brian had immediately stopped swinging and sat forward waiting to see if it was Everleigh who had texted her.

The screen showed one text from Jackson. Lilah looked at her uncle and shook her head. His disappointment was obvious. She clicked on it. He was telling her it was starting to slow down, and the hours for the kids to be out were almost over. He wanted to know if she felt well enough to go out.

Before she could answer, another notification covered the top of her phone screen. It was from Everleigh. The attempt had failed. Immediately, Lilah was hit with a dizzying array of thoughts and worry from her family. They had been following her every move waiting on news. Now they had more questions than answers.

Lilah started to reply and deleted the text several times. She struggled to word a message that wouldn't give away the position they were in with their own Element missing. She settled on simply asking if Everleigh knew yet who didn't make the attempt. She didn't, but said she would try to find out. She asked Lilah to let her know if she learned who it was first, and she agreed.

Uncle Brian stood up and went inside with Lilah following him. She knew her family didn't need her to tell them what was said or update them if Everleigh messaged again, but she felt like she should be with them now. They all had the same fear. Everyone worried that Marcus hadn't been there.

She was so focused on waiting for Everleigh to reply that she almost forgot about the text from Jackson. She could feel her mom telling her with absolute certainty that she was not going anywhere. She looked at her mom and was about to tell her she knew better when she received the answer everyone was waiting on. Fire was the only one who didn't attempt the Return.

The room instantaneously burst into commotion. Some of it was spoken, but some people's thoughts were louder than others' voices. This meant Marcus made the attempt. Regardless of the reasons behind his lack of communication, he must be okay if he made the attempt. More than that, Water actually showed up for it.

Not once had Water attempted a Return. Water was the entire reason why the Elements had been trapped in this plane of existence for so long. There was so much on everyone's minds now. Is this why Marcus had been so secretive? Had he planned this somehow? Maybe he and Leena had reasoned with Water to finally attempt the Return only to have Fire fail to show this time.

Everyone was talking or thinking over everybody else. Only two things they knew for certain. One, Marcus was well. Two, they would have another year wait before they would possibly learn what would befall them if the Return was completed.

Another message came through Lilah's phone. It was again from Everleigh telling her that she should come with Jackson to her party tonight. Lilah didn't know that was what Jackson had planned when he said he was going out after giving candy to trick or treaters. She had barely finished her thought when her dad told her to go.

She looked up at him, but he only sat there nodding at her. She was surprised with all the relieved excitement running through the room that anyone was paying attention to her anymore.

Her Uncle Brian added, "Perhaps you can learn more while you are there."

Lilah smiled and ran upstairs to get ready before anyone could change their minds. She finally replied to Jackson telling him to come get her. She changed and touched up her makeup as quickly as possible. She bounded back down the stairs and into the front room just as Jackson pulled in the driveway.

Her family didn't have to tell her to be safe. They didn't have to tell her what they hoped she would find out while she was gone. Their thoughts yelled at her as she headed out the door. She smiled when Jackson saw her. He was almost to the porch.

"You look like you're feeling a lot better," he told her.

"Sometimes all it takes is a little down time with family," she said as a joke to herself.

He leaned in and just before he kissed her, she blocked her family from her mind. She knew they would be mad, but they didn't need to know everything. The kiss was slow and gentle. Lilah felt her body's response begin in her chest and spread warmly out till every part of her body was alive with excitement. She pulled her head back and knew without a doubt that while so much was still up in the air in her family and in her life, right now in this moment was the happiest she'd ever been.

Chapter Twelve
Getting Serious

They climbed into his pickup and headed down the drive. Jackson made the turn toward town. Lilah was trying to keep a promise she'd made to herself days ago that she wouldn't dive into his mind when they were together, but she could tell something was wrong. It was taking all of her self-control to keep that promise now.

Jackson sighed and looked almost embarrassed when he said, "Before I say anything, I promised Everleigh I'd ask if your family could hear us first."

Lilah was mortified. She couldn't believe Everleigh had told him to ask that. She wasn't ready to tell Jackson anything about her family, and here Everleigh was about to leak it all out. She wasn't sure what to do or how to answer him.

"I know," he said, shaking his head and slowing down as they approached the town's limits. "I know it sounds crazy. I feel crazy saying it. But she made me vow on my life that I would ask you that first. It must be a witch thing."

She relaxed the tiniest bit and smiled playfully at him. She crossed the area over her heart with her finger and said, "I promise my family did not put a wire on me."

It was enough. He laughed. "Well, alright then, we're not going to Everleigh's."

"We're not?" Lilah asked curiously. Everleigh herself was the one who sent the text about coming over.

"Oh no! Are you kidding? Her family takes today very seriously. She just thought your family wouldn't give you a hard time about skipping out on them if you were going over there."

Lilah mulled it over. *'Why would Everleigh think that? How much did she know about what their family was going through right now with their Element unaccounted for?'*

"I don't know why Everleigh thinks they would," he continued when Lilah didn't say anything. "Her aunt is a friend of your family's apparently, so maybe she said something."

That's when it hit her. Of course! Today is the Return. She has to know it's important to us as well as all the Elementals. Even if we aren't celebrating our New Year, she would probably think we have our own traditions.

"Yeah, her Aunt Meredith," Lilah stopped herself before mentioning her uncle. Jackson had already met him, and if he remembered Todd's name, he might question how young he looked.

"Meredith is a riot," he lowered his voice as though he thought someone might be able to hear him. "You know she's a lot older than she looks. She uses an aging spell or something."

"You don't say," Lilah knew the truth, but only flashed him a smile and let him believe, as she used to, that it was magic.

He lifted his right hand off the steering wheel and held up his three middle fingers. "I'm telling you. Their family really is steeped in magic. They're witches. Scout's honor."

Lilah laughed. She knew he was telling the truth, but how could she possibly let him know that she truly believed it. "Where are we going then?" Lilah changed the subject.

Jackson flashed her a grin that sent the butterflies in her abdomen into over drive. "My house. My dad's still on his hunting trip. I have a ton of chocolate left over from tonight, and two of the best horror movies ever made are waiting for us."

They arrived at Jackson's house, and Lilah's butterflies were getting a workout. This was the longest they would be alone together since they met. Even the night of the bonfire they were only completely alone when they were in his truck.

She checked her phone when she was hanging up her coat expecting an angry text from her mom. Her only message was from Everleigh which said, "You're welcome!!!!"

Lilah got a kick out of that and replied, "Yes, thank you!"

Later she would see that Everleigh messaged again asking her to text when she was home because they needed to talk. Lilah left her phone in her coat pocket, so there would be no distractions tonight. She knew it was a risk as her family might need her, but they did know where he lived. They could always come get her once they found out from Everleigh where she was. It gnawed at her that what she was doing was selfish, but she wanted this time with him tonight.

Jackson got them some soda while Lilah got situated on the couch. She sat in the middle, planning to curl up into him whichever side he chose to sit on. He set everything on the coffee table in front of them and started the movie. He quickly turned off the lights before finally sitting down.

Lilah felt like he took forever to get seated, but once she snuggled up next to him, and he put his arm around her, everything melted away. She felt like she was exactly where she was supposed to be and nothing else mattered. Not her family. Not the Return. Not even Marcus.

It was a movie that Lilah had seen many times before - a classic werewolf movie. It was different watching it now after learning the truth. This movie actually didn't get the details too wrong compared to other forms of pop culture. In the past, when something was accurate about witches, she had always wondered if the author was someone who was in the know. Maybe not an Earth themselves, but someone who knew one personally. She started to wonder that about the person who wrote this script. It wouldn't be a stretch to think that the writer knew his work was fiction based on fact.

Jackson leaned forward to get a drink from his glass. Lilah moved to make it easy on him. When she leaned back into him, he turned his head to her, and their eyes met. Lilah held her breath. She knew he was going to kiss her, but if she was wrong, she'd make the move for him.

He leaned in, and their lips touched. It was gentle and slow. He pulled back, and Lilah smiled. Her eyes were closed, and she was remembering the feel of his mouth on hers when he kissed her again unexpectedly. This time the kiss was harder and with more passion.

Lilah's eyes flew open for a moment at the shock of it. She quickly closed them again and ceded to him. Her passion quickly rising to meet his. The next few minutes raced by in a blur. Jackson pulled her closer to him, and a moan escaped her lips. That was all the encouragement he needed. His hands roamed across her body over her shirt, and she reached underneath his as she tried to pull him even closer to her.

In one swift move, he put an arm around her waist and used his other hand to move her leg as he came down on top of her, laying her on the couch beneath him. Lilah arched her back up and pressed her hips into him urging him on. She wanted nothing more in that moment than to give herself to him completely.

Jackson lifted her shirt up to her neck and ran a trail of slow kisses over the top of her breasts that were exposed around the edge of her bra. She moaned seductively and pressed her hips into him again letting him know she wanted more. She needed more. He leaned back and tore his shirt off. Lilah would have been mesmerized by his chiseled physique, but something flashed across his face that caught her attention instead. She didn't know what it was, but it scared her.

She lifted herself up on her elbows causing him to lean back. She didn't say a word because she didn't know what to say. Whatever it was she saw had terrified her, and that's not the type of thing you want to tell a guy when you're in this position.

After a minute, Jackson fully sat back and put his face in his hands which were covered by his shirt. He took a couple deep breaths then looked up again across the room where the movie was still playing. He put his shirt back on and leaned back into the couch. Lilah slowly brought herself up sitting cross legged facing him.

He reached out his hand, and Lilah eagerly took it. She pulled his hand down into her lap and held it. She couldn't take her eyes off his fingers wrapped around hers. She was still at a loss for words.

Luckily, he wasn't. "Hey, look at me," he told her softly.

She hesitantly looked up at him. She had been avoiding looking directly at his face since whatever it was she saw flashed across his features minutes before. When she lifted her eyes, she saw the same handsome man she longed to be with.

"It's okay," he told her.

She searched his face for clues. Did he know what she saw? Could he tell her what it was? She didn't fully know what had happened. It could've been a reflection from the television or maybe even her own imagination. That made the most sense.

"It got pretty intense really fast. I," he paused and looked away for a second, "I hadn't planned on this... When I invited you over... I wasn't trying anything."

"I know," she reassured him. "It just happened. Like you said. It happened fast."

"I'm glad you stopped. I'm not sure I would've," he looked at her with his face filled with guilt. "That sounded bad."

Lilah shook her head and leaned forward until her forehead touched his. "No, it sounded honest."

"Yeah, but it makes me sound like some kind of animal or something."

That was it. That was the clue Lilah needed. The flash on his face was more the look of a wild animal than anything else. She had never seen anything like it before. "Not an animal," she told him, thankful he was unable to read her mind. Yet. "An animal wouldn't have stopped."

He lifted his head up and kissed her forehead then pulled back. "What now? Finish the movie, or..." His voice trailed off. He was looking at her to make the decision.

As much as she wanted to stay, she knew she should probably head home. Her family would be very upset with her as it was, and if she stayed, they might not stop the next time. She had an eternity to spend with Jackson. There was no need to rush anything now.

"I should probably head home. We should-"

"Take a little break and cool off," Jackson finished her sentence with a twinkle in his eye.

"Maybe a cold shower?"

He threw his head back and laughed. "I may need two," he joked.

They drove back to the farmhouse in silence, but it was a comfortable quiet not the awkward kind that usually occurs when people are still getting to know each other. Lilah sat next to him in the middle of the truck's bench seat with his arm around her the entire drive. She barely knew him, but already couldn't imagine her life without him anymore. She had the insight to know they'd never part, but that was something she would have to keep from him for a little longer. They shared many glances and smiles along the short trip. Lilah had been feeling like she had ruined the evening by causing it to be cut so short, but he made sure that she knew she hadn't.

When they reached the end of her drive, he put the truck in park and pulled her close for one last kiss. She didn't want to leave him, but she had to. Their time would come, and she would have to wait patiently for it to arrive.

After she shut the door behind her, reality quickly set in as she saw the look on her mom's face. She had temporarily forgotten how angry her family would be over her shutting them out.

"I've been texting you," her mom's voice was sharp as knives.

Lilah took her coat off to hang by the door, and in doing so, she brushed her hand across the top of her shirt. Images of Jackson's body on top of hers, and his mouth roaming over her chest filled her mind. A heat began to spread through her again, and her cheeks flushed. She couldn't stop the smile that formed thinking about it.

"You think it's funny? What you did?" her mom was infuriated even more.

"No, mom, I don't. I wasn't smiling because of you."

"You had us so worried when you didn't answer," her dad joined in.

Lilah sighed. There were eight people in the living room beside herself, and only two of them needed to be present for this conversation. She walked into the kitchen knowing her parents would follow.

"I left my phone in my coat, so I could enjoy the evening," she said without turning around.

She heard her mom sigh. "Lilah, I know it's unfair to you. There's just so much going on right now."

"It's not that. I don't need an audience for this."

Her mom nodded in understanding. "Okay, maybe we can work something out in the future then like if you promise to check in? At least until we hear from Marcus."

It sounded reasonable, so Lilah agreed.

"Now the real question on everyone's mind is did you learn anything?" her dad asked.

Lilah was lifting the glass to her mouth when she heard her father's question. She stopped and set it back down. "About that," she said.

"What is it?" her dad sounded worried.

She turned to look at her parents knowing the reactions she was about to receive. "I wasn't at Everleigh's."

They didn't say anything. She could tell by the looks on their faces they were waiting for her to explain. Lilah shifted her weight uncomfortably and quickly said, "She sent the text to get me out of the house, so I could hang out with Jackson. But I swear I didn't know anything about it until after I left."

Her parents weren't nearly as mad as she expected them to be. Lilah wasn't sure if she should feel relieved, or brace herself for it to hit when what she said sunk in for them.

Her dad shrugged and left the room. Abby told her, "Yeah, we know."

"You know? How?"

"Meredith is here visiting Luke. She showed up not long before you did."

Lilah had been so caught up in what she was feeling toward Jackson that she paid no attention to the cars parked outside, or if any of them were different than the ones that were normally there. Now that she thought about it, Meredith's little red car was parked on the side near the barn.

"So how was your night? You're home earlier than I expected."

She thought about what to say. She knew better to lie. Everyone in her family could spot a lie before it was even spoken. She also wasn't sure how much she wanted her mom to know.

"It couldn't have been that bad," her mom was picking up on her hesitation.

'Maybe her mom could tell her why she saw what she did,' she thought. She told her mom about what happened leaving out some of the details, but she described what she saw flash across Jackson's face. "I don't know what it was, mom, but it scared me."

Just then she could hear her Uncle Joseph in the next room say as clearly as she could hear her mom, "Tell her."

"Tell me what?"

"All men are animals," her mom answered.

Lilah raised an eyebrow at her mom. She knew that wasn't what her uncle was talking about.

"I'm not sure what you saw, honey, but think about what you've been through the last few days. It's a lot to take in at once, and you've had plenty of emotions to deal with as well," her mom shrugged and shook her head as though she wasn't sure how to explain it better.

"I thought that too."

Her mom smiled and held her arms out for a hug.

Lilah accepted and while they were hugging, she asked, "What did Uncle Joseph mean when he said to tell me?"

She could feel her mom tense up. Abby backed away. "I, well, we were hoping you'd have news that could clear things up for us when you got home."

"What happened?"

"Meredith. She told us something when she arrived."

"Mom? What? Happened?" Lilah wanted her to just spit it out already.

"That's the thing. We don't know what it was exactly. We only know that something happened at the Return."

Abby repeated the story that Meredith had told everyone. Eloise has an antique locket that once belonged to Anya. It's how Everleigh's family learns the news about the Return year after year. Eloise holds the locket to get an impression of the events that happened on the rock. It's a type of psychometry.

Lilah was fairly familiar with psychometry. Her family used it themselves quite often and without always meaning to do it. If they pick up an object, any object that belongs to someone else, they could get some form of vision. It's usually a memory related to the object itself, but not always.

"That's how they knew it was Fire who was a no show?"

Abby didn't respond. She rubbed her palms together in the same fashion she always did when she was nervous or upset. It was a tell of hers. Lilah learned at a young age that something was up when her mom did it.

Her mom went on to say that Meredith had been curious. Water has been a mystery to everyone for so long. She picked up the locket herself to take a look. She only had it in her hand for a second before Eloise yanked it away from her in anger and kicked her out of the house.

"What did she see?"

"A struggle."

Lilah looked at her mom wanting her to continue, but her mom said nothing. "With Marcus? What struggle?"

"That's all we know. Meredith said there was some kind of struggle. She said it was a fleeting image, too quick to really see it."

She turned her back to the counter and looked out the kitchen window on the far side of the room. She could see nothing except the darkness that draped over everything. It always unsettled her how easy it would be for someone to spy on her in the dark. You can't see out, but they can see you. Jackson's changed animal like face flashed in front of her on the window for a fleeting second. She closed her eyes and turned away. It was only her imagination.

"This is why you were disappointed I wasn't with Everleigh? Not because my plans changed, but because you wanted news?"

"Yes, but if Eloise didn't like Meredith finding out, she surely wouldn't want Everleigh to know either. We knew it was a long shot."

"I'll text her."

Lilah grabbed her glass and headed up to the privacy of her room. It was late, and she had a lot on her mind before she had even come home. Now, there was even more weighing on her. She didn't need her entire family gathered round waiting for her phone to chime.

Chapter Thirteen
Saving Leena

Marcus ran as fast as he could through the growth on the hillside. His side was screaming at him with sharp pains that told him he needed to rest, but he couldn't. There was barely enough time to make it to her. Marcus had to keep going.

His breath was heavy and labored. He could feel the burn throughout the muscles in his legs. Marcus would be sore later, but all he could focus on now was getting to Leena in time.

He still had a long way to go, but he could see everything playing out ahead of him. Leena had found a cave to make camp for the evening. She left to fetch water, but the search party from her village had found her cave while she was gone.

Leena had taken off with the men from her village close behind her. She almost lost them several times, but they always managed to find her trail again. She ventured off the path to try to make some time on the cliff when she lost her footing.

The search was now over. Her people were returning to the village where it would be decided to not look for her again. She would be disgraced from her people which was worse than death, but death was what was in her future now.

Leena clung to the side of the cliff not knowing how much longer she could last. Her fingertips gripped to a crack in the rock and her right foot was resting on something unseen in the dark, cloaking the rocky wall below. She couldn't move.

Tears stung her eyes. She wanted to scream out, to cry for help, but she couldn't. Even in what was sure to be the last moments of her life, she couldn't call out to the men she was running from. Not only would her insolence be punished with a public lashing, but it would send her back to Yaxkin. Leena found herself making the decision to let go and end her life quickly rather than the agony of a lifetime as one of Yaxkin's wives.

As she prepared to push back off the cliff, something brushed past her face. Even in the darkness, Leena could tell it was some sort of garment like a dress, but she didn't recognize the material. She grabbed hold, and the feel of it in her fists was new. Leena did not know who was on the other end pulling her out of danger, but it was not anyone from her village. She was afraid of who may be on the other end, but at least it was not Yaxkin or one of the other men who had been chasing her.

Marcus pulled Leena from the side of the cliff using his robes. His bronze skin nude against the light of the moon, he strained down until he could reach her arm. Effortlessly, he grabbed her, and with one sturdy yank, she was safe beside him. His heart raced to finally be next to the woman he had longed to be with for an entire year. He stared at her not knowing what to do next until he remembered his robes were on the ground and not on his body.

He scrambled to gather the robes and drape them over his body again. This was no way to meet the woman he had pined for the last year. He could only hope that the darkness protected most of his physique from her eyes.

Leena quickly sat up without taking her eyes off of him. As she pulled her legs close to her, she winced. She reached out for her ankle which throbbed hot beneath her hand.

Marcus eyed her ankle carefully. He knew her language, all languages for that matter, but he was afraid if he spoke to her in her native tongue, it may scare her away. He didn't want Leena to think he was in any way associated with those who had chased her to what should have been her death.

Instead he motioned to her ankle trying to tell her he wanted to take a closer look. Leena nodded. Marcus carefully examined it. Nothing was broken. Marcus breathed a sigh of relief. He looked at Leena and smiled. It was only twisted. He motioned again for her to stay where she was.

Marcus left to find sticks sturdy enough to make a brace for her. He smiled the entire way. He was with her at last. He was with Leena. After an entire year of wishing his circumstances were different, he had his chance.

Marcus stayed focused on her mind, so he knew that she was not scared of him and welcomed having a companion right now.

He made a makeshift brace for her ankle, and helped her to her feet. She winced again and cried out. Marcus pulled her to him preparing to carry her. Before he did, he motioned again with his hands asking her where to go.

Leena looked around unsure. This territory was new to her and in her hurry to lose the men following her, she got turned around. Perhaps if it were light out, she could find her cave. She needed to find her cave. All of her provisions were tucked safely away inside of it.

Marcus nodded at her and smiled. He carefully swooped her up into his arms and began walking. He pretended to look this way and that to give the impression he wasn't sure where to go. Marcus even checked a cave he knew wouldn't be accommodating. He set Leena down outside and went in to investigate. He emerged moments later shaking his head then carried her off again.

Finally, Marcus neared Leena's cave, and she recognized the area. She started pointing to show Marcus where to go. He brought her inside the cave and set her down gently. Leena was scared that her people might come back. Marcus knew they wouldn't return, but she did not. There was no way Marcus could explain to her how he knew this either.

He looked around and motioned to himself and then a spot on the other side of the cave nearer to the entrance asking if it was okay to stay. He knew her answer would be yes. She didn't know him, but something drew her to him just as he felt drawn to her. She wanted Marcus there. She felt safe with him.

Marcus helped ready the cave with her. They would have to move on soon, but not before her ankle had healed. He started a fire and looked around for the water bucket. She had dropped it in the chase. Using hand motions, he asked her about a drink. She looked around frantic then upon remembering what had happened, tears fell from her eyes.

He ran to her and took her in his arms without a moment's thought. She welcomed his embrace. She cried and cried. No doubt the sadness, fear and anger of her father's death, and her unwanted engagement that had been building up were finally being released.

Marcus just held her and let her cry. He stroked her hair and rocked her softly. When she had calmed herself, he looked deep in her eyes and smiled. He knew their future together would be long. It was hard to know for sure because the future changes every second, but he knew Leena's heart would belong to him just as his heart had always been hers.

He communicated as best he could that he would go find water. He made a torch from the fire and left. Marcus walked straight to the dropped bucket then the nearest stream to fill it. All the while he kept his mind on her thoughts.

Leena was thankful he had saved her. She was mad at herself for deciding to give up in a moment of weakness. She was glad Marcus stayed with her and somehow she knew he could be trusted. She also liked how it felt when he held her. Leena grew flustered wondering if he would try to do more partly because the thought scared her and partly because she wanted him which scared her even more.

That thought made Marcus happy. He had spent an entire year longing to know how it felt to be near her, to touch her. He could wait for as long as it takes for them to become one. When she started to worry about how long he was taking, Marcus made his way back.

He entered the cave holding up the water bucket and smiling at her. Leena knew it was the one she dropped. She didn't know how he had found it when she wouldn't have been able to find it herself. She knew there was much more to this chance encounter than purely luck, but something told her he could be trusted. She hoped to one day find out the truth, but it wouldn't weigh on her mind for long.

She watched the light bronze skinned man who saved her life stoke the fire and prepare her water. Leena knew she would be eternally grateful to him. It would take a lifetime for her to repay him. Somehow she also knew he would gladly spend his lifetime with her for her to do so. As she thought this, she could see him smile from across the cave where he was preparing a makeshift bed of leaves to sleep on.

In the morning, Marcus opened his eyes and immediately turned to her. She was sitting by the fire. She must have woke some time before and brought the fire back to life. He sat up and looked around. They would need more wood. He rose and dusted off his garments. She smiled at him and lifted something toward him. He motioned to her to wait, and he left the cave.

Marcus gathered what firewood he could nearby as quickly as possible and carried it back to the cave. He stacked it along one wall and brought a couple pieces over to add to the fire. Leena smiled at him and held up her offering again.

It was pemmican. This had been his staple for months during last winter. He took it from Leena and sat down near her to eat. It tasted considerably better than what he had managed to make. They stayed there for a while both enjoying the nearness of the other and the warmth of the fire. They would occasionally steal glances or smile. Marcus kept reading the signs from her to know what to do next. He knew theirs would be a blissful love story, and he would spend all of his time following her lead to get it to play out.

Chapter Fourteen
Spell Casting

Lilah sat on her bed and pressed the home button on her phone. There was a text from Everleigh asking her to let her know when she got home. She checked the time stamp on it. It must have been sent while she was still at Jackson's house.

"Home," she sent back.

The dots appeared so fast Lilah thought Everleigh must have been staring at their message thread waiting for a response. She wondered if Everleigh actually had more news of the Return to share.

"Can you leave again?"

Lilah wasn't sure. She knew her family would not argue with it as they wanted information, but she also knew there was no way she would get away with blocking them again if she left. She had been pressing her luck enough the last several days. She replied and told Everleigh she didn't think she could.

Whatever was going on, Everleigh wanted to talk to her in person. She asked Lilah to sneak out. She practically begged her to.

That was something Lilah could do easily. After texting instructions to her house to Everleigh, she left as quickly as she could. She closed her bedroom door to keep the cool air from blowing out into the hall as much as possible, opened the window, and in minutes was on the roof of the back porch trying to inch the window shut from the outside. Soon she was running alongside the drive down to the road. She didn't have to wait long until headlights were blinding her. Everleigh only lived a few minutes away.

Lilah opened the door.

"You live here?" Everleigh asked, looking through the trees toward the house on the hill.

"Yeah, it belongs to my uncle," she said, climbing in the front seat of the car and buckling her seat belt.

Everleigh didn't wait. She had already made a U-turn and was speeding back toward town before the lock clicked.

Neither said a word the entire drive. Lilah was curious about the way Everleigh asked about the farmhouse. There had been something in her tone that made Lilah suspicious that once again, Everleigh knew something she didn't. This wasn't the right time to ask.

Lilah stayed quiet and held on tight. Everleigh was already driving too fast, and she didn't want to distract her by asking questions. They approached the street where she should have turned to go to her house, but she didn't. Still Lilah didn't say anything. When Everleigh made the turn that would take them straight to Jackson's house, Lilah's interest piqued. She wondered why they would be going there. She had thought Everleigh wanted to talk to her about the Return or something to do with the Elementals, but that couldn't be the case if they were going to see Jackson.

Everleigh squealed to a stop out front. Lilah could tell something was really bothering her. Her hand was shaking when she lifted it off the wheel.

"What're we doing here?"

"I'll explain everything inside."

"I thought what you wanted to see me about had something to do with the Return."

Everleigh looked at her with sheer fright in her eyes, "It does."

"Then why are we here? We can't discuss this in front of Jackson."

The look on Everleigh's face slowly changed from fear to a completely blank stare. "I knew your family was secretive, but..." She didn't finish her thought. She grabbed her phone and started typing a message.

"But what?" Lilah grew impatient waiting on Everleigh to finish typing. "Sorry, had to let my grandma know where I was or else she'd worry."

"But what?" Lilah repeated with a harshness to her tone. She might not be able to read Everleigh, but she could tell she had lied about the text she sent. She just didn't know why.

"But I didn't realize how secretive they were. Jackson's your match. You haven't talked him about anything yet?"

"No," Lilah answered. She felt like she was being put on the defensive. Her decision not to tell him had more to do with wanting them to get to know each other as individuals first then it did anything else.

"Well, I do," Everleigh announced. "I tell him almost everything. That's why we're here. He knows about the Elements and the Return."

Lilah gasped. She couldn't imagine sharing that information with just anyone. They had always moved so much that it made creating strong friendships difficult, but it never crossed her mind to tell even the closest friends she had ever had.

"Yeah, I thought it might freak you out a bit."

"Did you tell him about me?"

"No, I didn't," Everleigh answered checking her phone, and Lilah could tell she was being honest. "There he is. Let's go."

Lilah saw him standing just inside the front door waiting for them to come up. They got out and made their way through the slush of the melting snow. She was starting to feel more comfortable with the idea of discussing this with him. It would make it easier when she decided to let him know about her heritage and tell him that he was her match.

He swung the door open when they reached the porch and held it wide for them. They walked inside and took off their coats. He greeted them both, but he wrapped his arm around Lilah's waist and kissed her on the cheek when he said hello.

Everleigh rolled her eyes and made a retching sound, "Get a room."

"If you insist," Jackson told her taking Lilah's hand and pulling her toward the stairs.

He stopped before going up, and they all laughed. They followed him into the kitchen where he had a pot of coffee brewing. Lilah had never been more thankful for small miracles like caffeine. "I thought we might need some help if this takes a while," he said, pulling mugs from the cabinet.

"If what takes a while?" Lilah asked.

Everleigh glanced at Jackson, but he still had his back turned.

Lilah was frustrated. She hated being kept in the dark. It's all she had known her whole life. Secrets kept from her. Secrets that she had to keep. She was growing tired of the shroud of mystery that seemed to overcast her life every second of every day. "Someone please tell me what's going on," she said angrily.

"You are going to get a crash course in spelling tonight," Everleigh said while poking her head into the dining room. "Now help me get started before Meredith and Luke arrive."

Lilah followed her through the downstairs. It appeared as though Everleigh were looking for something, but she didn't know what it could be.

"This will have to do," Everleigh said, looking at the living room.

She instructed Lilah to help her rearrange the furniture. They moved the coffee table and rug exposing a bare hardwood floor underneath. The couch wasn't easy. They tried to lift it, but they weren't going to get far. It was too heavy. They lifted one end at a time shuffling the rug underneath the legs to prevent scratching the floor. Then it was dragged back until it was practically in the dining room. It's a good thing there's an open floor plan here she thought, but she was doubtful the two of them could have lifted it through a doorway.

Lilah had asked her about the spell they were going to perform. It was a locater spell meant to find Fire. That is why Meredith was coming. With vampire blood running through her veins, she was the only known witch who could successfully try to find him.

Jackson had walked in once to set down three mugs of coffee and barely took notice of the work they were doing. He had obviously been well informed of plans unlike Lilah. He quickly dashed back into the kitchen. Lilah followed him with her eyes until Everleigh snapped her fingers to get her attention.

"None of that goo-goo eyed puppy love stuff now. We have to get moving. Come with me."

They went into the kitchen where Jackson was searching for something in the pantry. "We got this," Everleigh told him. "Be a dear and move the rest of it, will you? The couch wore me out."

He stood up straight like he was taking orders with a haphazard salute and marched out of the room. Everleigh rolled her eyes behind him. "Okay, where are the candles? Candles...candles..." she repeated, turning around in a circle trying to think of where to look.

"Here!" Lilah blurted and turned to a drawer near the closet. She opened it, and there was a box of long white taper candles in it along with flashlights and cords.

"These will do," Everleigh said from behind her and reached in to grab the box. "Now can you find the candle holders?"

Lilah closed her eyes and concentrated. "There's some in the top drawer of the hutch in the dining room. How many do you need?"

"Nine," Everleigh answered as she left the room. She returned quickly with her hands full. There were four identical taper candle holders and two pillar plates. She handed the four to Lilah to get ready while she melted some wax on the pillar plates to hold the candles in place.

"It's not pretty, but it will do."

"Is this enough?" Lilah asked.

Everleigh retrieved her bag she dropped by the front door and pulled out a large book. She flipped through it until she found the page she was looking for. Lilah walked closer trying to peek. "It's a grimoire. It's ancient. It belonged to an ancestor of mine."

Lilah looked at the page filled with drawings, chants and ingredients. "May I?"

Everleigh nodded. She flipped a few pages at a time before stopping to glance. It didn't make much sense to her. One of the pages had feathers pressed in the bend and another had herbs in some old wax like paper. "It's like a scrapbook."

"In a way," Everleigh agreed. "It's a scrapbook of spells. Sometimes we do keep little bits in the pages. It could be remnants of the spell cast, or if it's a hard to come by ingredient, a witch may store some here."

She closed the book and slid it toward her bag. "But look, don't tell my aunt I let you do that. I'm modern in every way, but the older witches take their grimoires quite seriously."

Lilah reached out and touched her arm. "Wait. Is that the Star of David?" she asked pointing to the cover.

"*Now* it's the Star of David," Everleigh stressed. "It wasn't always the main symbol of the Jewish religion. There's many old Christian churches, paintings and you name it that use it too."

"I didn't know that."

"It's true, and when this grimoire was created, it wasn't known as the Star of David. There are alchemy symbols that make up the six point star." Everleigh ran her fingers over the image naming each one.

"We are inversed," she told Lilah. "Air is a triangle with the tip at the top and a line. Earth has the tip and line at the bottom. There's Fire, Water, and one more. Balance."

"And since witches call on all the elements for their spells, it makes sense for a grimoire to embrace that." Lilah thought out loud.

"Exactly," Everleigh was happy that Lilah understood. "Anyway, back to business," she said, tucking the book away.

"Where were we?" Everleigh looked at Lilah.

"Candle holders. How many do you need?"

"Ideally, we need nine, but six is...," Everleigh let out a long exhale. "Meredith will insist on nine. She might have some with her."

"Does she usually just walk around with candle holders on her?"

Everleigh gave Lilah a look that asked if she was joking and told her, "Don't let that vampire blood fool you. She is a witch. She's always prepared. If she meets you on the street, she could easily help you get pregnant or give you bunions depending on how you treat her."

A slow grin spread on Lilah's face as she tried to stay collected.

"You think I'm joking?" Everleigh crossed her arms and raised her eyebrows.

"Nah," Lilah drew her lower lip between her teeth to hold in her laughter. "I was just thinking the pregnancy bit could work if you made her mad too."

It took a second for it to register, but then Everleigh leaned back and clapped her hands. She walked a feet away shaking her head and placed both hands on her hips. "You're right. Either way, you're going to have a baby aren't you?"

They both started laughing. Jackson walked in and announced, "You might want to get it under control. They're here."

Lilah picked up the candle box and holders near her and hurried into the living room with Everleigh close behind. The living room was practically bare except for the television on the wall and a plant in the corner. Jackson had drawn a large circle on the floor with a five point star in the middle.

"Chalk?" Lilah asked.

"You know we don't have to have a star, right? That's just movie effects."

"You said you needed the five points, and yes, its chalk. I have to clean all this up before my dad gets home," Jackson answered them both.

"I said we needed room for five points for the spell, not that we needed it drawn out."

There was a knock at the door, and Jackson hurried to answer it. Luke walked in with Meredith at his heels already unwrapping her scarf. They wasted no time. They threw their coats on the floor, and Meredith immediately started barking out instructions to everyone in the room, including Lilah, but she was too distracted by the two strangers that had followed them inside the house.

Everleigh saw her stare, and introduced them. Matt and Rita had just arrived from the south and not a moment too soon either as Meredith could use them tonight. "Rita is one of the witches from Mississippi I told you about, and Matt is..."

"A wolf," Lilah finished without taking her eyes off of them.

"I prefer lycan, but if you must," his expression hardened.

She had never seen a wolf before. Hell, she didn't know they were real until a few days ago. She knew she needed to stop staring. She tried to will herself to look away. She couldn't break her gaze away no matter how hard she tried.

"You have to forgive her. Lilah is an, um, well she's new here and getting a crash course in our history," Everleigh caught herself before spilling the information Lilah didn't want Jackson to hear.

That snapped Lilah out of it. The almost slip up gave her a momentary scare as she flashed Everleigh a look of fear. If she hadn't been so focused on what Everleigh almost said, she might have caught what Jackson mouthed to him.

"We've heard," Matt walked over to Lilah. He took her in from head to toe. It made her nervous because she was afraid he would be able to sense what she was or at the very least that she was different and say something. He didn't. After checking her out, he extended his hand to her and said, "Pleasure to meet you, Lilah."

They finished setting up the area for the spell with Lilah following orders and doing as she was told. Meredith pulled so much out of the large tote she carried as a purse that Lilah wondered if the room inside was spelled to be endless. She had several very large rolled maps, more candles, and vial after vial containing who knows what, and she was still reaching in for more. The three witches worked together to set up the floor. Candles were placed along the circle, and a map was laid out. A vial of ash was used as an indicator.

Lilah didn't know she would be a part of it. Meredith needed an Air, so when she told Lilah to stand at a point, her heart sank. She quickly covered it by placing a feather in Lilah's hands, and she told her to close her eyes and imagine a cool breeze blowing to create the effect once she was ready to begin. Jackson was needed too. He stood on the point for Fire holding a vial containing Luke's blood.

Having her eyes closed, Lilah missed a lot. She didn't see the secretive telling glances between those gathered. Mostly, she didn't see it when her Uncle Todd appeared briefly. He snuck in from the back of the house where he had been hiding since Jackson opened the door for him while the girls were moving the couch. He stood silently with Luke, Matt, and Rita while Meredith cast the spell. Once the answer was visible, he was gone heading back home to meet with the family.

When it was over, Lilah opened her eyes at the map spread out on the floor over the five point star. A dark line ran over it from New York where Meredith poured the ashes to somewhere in the middle of the states. She had to walk around to the other side to see it better. Everyone was looking at it. Everyone except Todd who had disappeared out the back as quickly as he had come. The seven people left in the room looked at the map without saying a word. They could all see where it led, but no one wanted to be the one to speak it out loud.

Fire was here. He was in Fairview. Lilah didn't know what it meant, but it couldn't be good. She needed to get home and fast. She needed to talk to her family.

Chapter Fifteen
Uncontrolled Power

Panic was setting in, and Lilah could feel the room spinning. Stumbling backwards, she fell into Jackson who caught her right before she lost her balance. Tilting her jaw slightly, but without taking her eyes off the map, she whispered, "I need to go home."

"Alright, I'll take you."

Meredith approached, "Jackson, honey. I can take her. I need to talk to her uncle anyway."

"No, I can do it," he told her.

With her eyes on the map, Lilah couldn't see the concern on Meredith and Luke's faces as they tried to reason with him without saying too much.

"It'd be no trouble for us," Luke insisted.

He drew his lips back into a snarl before hissing, "I want to drive Lilah home."

Meredith held up her hands in defeat and backed away. "Sure thing. We'll be here when you return."

Lilah collected her purse and put her coat back on. They walked out to the truck with her still reeling, trying to figure out what this could mean. Three Elemental factions in one town was definitely not a coincidence. Whatever was coming for them started to loom bigger and more menacing with every passing moment.

"Is everything alright?" he asked her.

"Yeah," she mumbled softly not sure what to say to him. It would be hard to tell him anything without giving away the truth about her family.

"Not feeling well again?" He gave her the perfect excuse.

She shook her head and climbed into the cab of the truck. If he believed she was ill, it not only provided a reason for her to need to go home, but also a reason for her silence on the drive. There was so much going through her mind about the significance of this new information that she forgot she should be trying to sneak back into her bedroom.

Jackson drove Lilah home and made good time taking her the short trek to the farmhouse. It still wasn't fast enough for her. The sense of urgency to get this news to her family was strong, but she couldn't tell them over the phone. He flew up the driveway, and she gave him a quick kiss goodbye before bounding up the steps.

Her family were all gathered in the living room, and she could tell what was on their minds. The moment she saw them she knew they had already learned the news she was about to give them herself. She looked from face to somber face. They were still reeling, trying to figure out what this could mean themselves.

Abby waved her over and patted the couch next to her for Lilah to sit.

She did as her mother asked thankful no one was bringing up what she had been doing away from home where she was supposed to be. She was confused who could have possibly told her family about the spell and what was discovered. "How do you know?" she broke the silence.

Todd and Abby exchanged glances. She couldn't see it, but behind her several cousins were sharing shifty looks with her dad.

"Meredith told me. She called right after you left," her Uncle Todd explained.

Lilah had no reason not to believe him. Todd and Meredith had been friends for a lot longer than she had originally been led to believe. Of course Meredith would give her old friend the heads up about what had been learned from the spell.

"So what's it mean?" Lilah asked no one in particular. Nobody answered.

"It means something though, right?" she tried again.

"But of course. What do you mean? Everything means something," her Uncle Joseph replied, waving off the nonsensical musings of a child.

"It doesn't sit well with any of us if that's what you mean," her Uncle Brian added.

"Yeah, that's it. I had been told that Fire was adamant about making the Return this year. Wasn't that the plan? Marcus or someone must have located Water. It was going to work," Lilah grew more upset as she spoke.

Her mom patted her leg and grabbed her hand trying to center her hoping it would help her calm down. "We all believed this would be the year, Lilah. It was supposed to be."

"So if he didn't show tonight, and he's here in Fairview where apparently every supernatural being who has ever been in existence is headed, then that has to mean something," her mom's attempts had no effect on her. She was working herself up even more.

Myles knelt in front of her and took both of her hands in his, instructing her to breathe in and out, slowly. She found the exercise absolutely ridiculous. "Why are you trying to calm me down?" she blurted out. "Why aren't the rest of you upset?"

"We are," her mom told her. "We're all upset, Lilah. We've been in the dark for weeks now, and instead of answers, we only ever discover more questions."

"We need for you to calm down because your powers are new. You're unstable," her dad told her and immediately regretted his poor word choice.

"Unstable?"

He shook his head. "Listen to the wind."

Lilah had noticed the wind picking up outside, it and was howling like another early winter storm was about to hit. "Yeah, so?"

"You're causing it," her mom said.

"Me?" Lilah looked around the room. Some of her family nodded when she looked their way, but most wouldn't meet her eyes.

"Please, Lilah, you could rip this house apart if your anger continues to rise like this. Breathe with me," her dad pleaded. He took deep breaths in and out, and Lilah followed his lead. In no time, the winds had died down again.

Once she had regained control of her emotions, she sat in an awkward silence. No one's thoughts were open. No one was talking. "Does anyone have any ideas?"

Her mom gave her a look that said don't start this again and waved her off.

"I'm calm. Look at me," she took a couple deep breaths in and out. "There's no wind. I just need to know... We need to know what's going on."

"I think it's safe to assume he's with the wolves," Uncle Joseph shared his opinion.

"The wolves are already here?" Lilah took the deep breaths for real this time knowing the winds would soon howl if she didn't.

"No, I mean he is obviously working with them."

"To kill his own kind?" Myles wasn't buying the theory.

"It's not entirely impossible. We shouldn't rule it out," Uncle Joseph was sticking to his idea.

Abby joined in, "I don't think Fire would do that. It would serve him no purpose. Plus, it was resolute in his mind to complete the Return. What if he's with the wolves because they are keeping him?"

"You mean what if they are holding him?" Uncle Todd asked. "That would mean they would be able to hold Marcus and Earth as well. We'd just be repeating our argument from the other night."

"Maybe he's here because he knows the wolves are coming, and he's trying to defend what's left of his clan?" Myles' thoughts received approving murmurs from the room.

"His clan?" Uncle Joseph cried out in surprise. "There are only three natural vampires left including Fire! What clan?"

"That we know about," Myles reminded him.

This conversation was being lost on Lilah. She could hear the words, but was not fully following along. If she had been paying better attention, she would've questioned the identity of the third natural vampire. The only two remaining were Luke and Fire as far as she knew.

Lilah's head was spinning. The reality of everything was starting to take root, and she had never felt more afraid. The wolves were attacking vampires. The witches were next which would leave only her family. They would be greatly outnumbered. All of the times she insisted on being treated like an adult, getting angry for not having enough privacy or freedom seemed like mere child's play to her now. She was much too young for this. She wasn't remotely capable of fighting off an Elemental faction, and she most assuredly wasn't ready to die.

She was snapped from her thoughts by a loud bang as the wind outside whipped the porch swing back, hitting the outside wall of the house. Her family looked at her with worry, but mostly fear. Not fear of the wolves, but fear of her. She hadn't come into her powers slowly over the course of years or even a decade allowing her to fully develop each one. They were thrown on her like a food court slushy by a bully at the mall, and she hadn't had any time to clean up the mess. She was a loose cannon who could fire off unpredictably for any reason.

"It's been a long day. Why don't you go upstairs and rest?" her mom asked her sweetly.

Reason was lost on her. She was far too upset. Being asked to leave was only received as being left out of family business as she had always been. The anger continued to build as she thought of the embarrassment she felt when learning the truth about Fire and Water. It was because she was always treated as a child and never given the chance to prove herself.

A loud crack outside sent a branch from a tree falling to the ground nearly missing the house. Several of them rushed to her trying to help, but she was too far gone. Lilah stood up with her arms bent up in front of her. Her hands in fists looking like she was preparing to fight. She pulled her arms to each side as if she was breaking free from some form of restraints, and it sent out a powerful surge that knocked everyone near her to the floor. They watched terrified as she walked to the door of the house and went outside.

Later she would not remember doing any of this. All she would know is what was recounted to her, but she would never know everything. Her family had only seen one other with as much power as she exhibited, and he was their Element Marcus. They feared if she knew how vast her potential was she may use it purposely.

Lilah walked across the porch with the wind fiercely howling all around except near her. One side of the swing had fallen loose from the joist that held it when it hit the house and was hanging at an angle downward. She walked to the top step and sat down. The wind was picking up. It was no longer isolated to the farm, but was spreading out in all directions. Anyone in its path was now feeling the effects, and it would consume the entire town in minutes. Tomorrow the news would cover the strange weather phenomenon that caused tornado strength damage to some property in and around Fairview.

The only place safe was where Lilah sat. Like the eye of a hurricane, it was calm and peaceful. Her family were still inside. Some were looking out the windows horrified of what would happen next. The rest were trying desperately to come up with a way to subdue her.

No one would have ever believed what happened next if they hadn't seen it for themselves. They didn't notice the creature approaching until he was climbing the steps because he blended well in the snow. They would later question how he managed to move in the storm without being quite literally blown away with his small size and came up with no logical explanation. As the family worked hurriedly to devise a plan, a small white squirrel appeared on the step next to Lilah.

It showed no fear of her or the wind. It was perhaps because it was calm there. This was the only detail that made sense to anyone. In that moment, Lilah was less a threat to the small animal than the wind. That is why he showed no distress being that close, but how it was even possible that he finessed his way through the gales to get there was the riddle they couldn't solve.

After several minutes, the winds died down and only a gentle breeze remained. Her parents watched baffled by what was unfolding in front of them. Lilah seemed to be getting her emotions under control completely on her own which was a blessing, but also raised questions as to how. She continued to sit on the porch facing out toward the road. She hadn't moved once.

Her dad was the one who mustered enough courage to step outside to talk. He walked to the rail several feet on the side of Lilah not wanting to get too close in case she reacted badly. She didn't even acknowledge him.

"Feeling better?" He was almost too afraid to speak.

Lilah cocked her head to the side then turned to face him. Confusion cloaked over her, and she continued to look around wondering how she came to be outdoors. She saw the squirrel sitting so near to her side, but it quickly scurried off away from her as soon as she noticed it.

"What happened?" she asked, standing up.

"You don't remember?"

"No, I," Lilah stopped and tried to think about it. "We were talking about why Fire was in Fairview."

"That's all you remember?"

"I think I was scared wondering what the big picture was going to turn out to be."

He reached out and put his arm around her to guide her back inside. "No more of that tonight, Lilah. We're all tired and stressed. I want you to rest."

She didn't argue. Exhaustion was creeping in every pore of her body, and each step became heavier and more difficult. They walked in the house and all eyes were on them. She wanted to stay with the family and find out what was happening, but she was too drained. It would take everything she had to make it upstairs to bed right now.

Her dad walked her to the base of the main staircase and told her good night. Lilah went up and glanced back from the landing. They were still watching her. She would have to wait until morning to find out what went on tonight. She continued up the stairs and down the hall to her room. She laid down and was thrown into a disruptive sleep filled with vivid dreams almost as soon as she closed her eyes.

Downstairs, her family watched the ceiling as her footsteps echoed down the hall. They waited not wanting to draw her attention back to the living room. Once they were confident she was in bed, they began murmuring in hushed voices about the events that unfolded in front of them.

"I've never seen anything like it," Brian told the group.

"Of course not," Abby was in defense mode. "Have you ever tried? Have any of us? We've all been taught since day one to keep a tight rein on our abilities." She was taking a page from Lilah's playbook about the code Marcus created.

"I can move things. We all can," Brian continued. "I don't think I'm capable of knocking five strong people to the floor like your daughter apparently can."

"She was upset!" Myles cried out then glanced upwards hoping he hadn't been too loud.

"She was upset," he repeated much lower when he was sure the coast was clear. "Emotions heighten our powers. It's Air 101 only she has never taken the course."

Myles sat back and rubbed his wife's shoulders. They were certainly feeling the weight of this. Not only was it their daughter, but it had been their decision to introduce Lilah to their world and the world of all the Elementals slowly. The world had changed so much they believed they needed to adapt a little bit too. It would appear they had made the wrong choice.

"I'll be more than happy to stand here let you give it a try," Todd told his brother.

Brian scowled at him. "You won't be laughing when something happens, and that girl exposes us for who we really are."

Myles jumped to his feet, but Todd beat him to the punch. "That girl is one of us. You chose to distance yourself after Martin died, and we have all respected that. You chose to not create bonds with the newer members amongst us, and we respected that too. You need to choose now whether you are here to help, or if you are simply present because Father demands it. If that's the case, go join our sister Chloe in Trinity."

No one moved after his outburst. They barely breathed. The tension filled the room sucking the air out. Someone near the wall cracked open a window because real or not, even the illusion of suffocation would make any of those who were gathered uncomfortable and nervous.

Chloe's name was never mentioned in front of Brian. It was an unspoken rule. Todd could have just as easily told his brother to go to Sophia's house, but he didn't. He mentioned the name of the woman Brian held responsible for Martin's death as a jagged edged spoken sword.

"I think we should all call it a night before our emotions get the best of us too," Joseph told his brothers, trying to avoid having their fight escalate until a repeat of what had just happened with Lilah was on their hands.

Several people agreed and hurried off to bed thankful someone gave them a golden paved path to leave. The rest of them slowly began turning in until only the three brothers and Lilah's parents were left in the room. Joseph would've happily been in bed hours ago, but as Marcus and Leena's firstborn, he always felt compelled to handle family matters in his father's absence.

"Shall we agree to put this behind us and begin afresh tomorrow, or must we discuss it first?" he asked them.

"I like Lilah," Brian's voice surprised everyone. "I spent time with her this week. I mean no offense to her, but it is worrisome how strong she appears to be."

Abby understood and knew he was not the only one worried by Lilah's outburst. Abby was deeply concerned herself. "I have a suspicion about it if you're interested."

"Go on," Brian urged.

"The witches are spawning in record numbers."

"Yes," Joseph interrupted. "It's happened many times in the past when there was some form of enemy or danger facing them."

"This is the first time we've been in the position where we had an enemy to face. Our numbers are quite limited, and we can't create new members quickly to help aide us against an imminent threat."

"You're saying maybe this is why her powers are so great?" Todd asked.

"I'm saying maybe it's increased for us all. I've felt it. Haven't you?"

The tense quiet that followed was enough for Abby to know she was right. They didn't want to admit it. Maybe they didn't agree with her entirely, but they had noticed a difference.

"I originally thought it was due to a hive mind," she added.

"Me too." Sara had been lurking in the kitchen. She stayed out of the conversations all evening, but she could see Abby was in need of support.

Others muttered their agreements. "Hive mind," Joseph repeated. "I had believed this as well. Our powers strengthen if we work together."

"We've never had such a large group gathered at once," Todd joined his brothers.

"We haven't had any need to use our powers, but I believe we are all just as strong as Lilah," Abby finished up.

Everyone looked at each other. Myles blurted out, "Well I don't think we should attempt anything tonight."

"No," Brian agreed.

"Perhaps in the morning we can devise a test. Something we can do outside," Joseph said more to himself than the rest of the group.

"Yes." Brian was still uncertain this was the reason behind Lilah's strength and was devising a plan of his own. "Let us all turn in now. We will need to be rested."

Everyone made their way to their rooms except for Brian who hung back to prepare for the morning.

Chapter Sixteen
Chloe's Mistake

Marcus and Leena were enjoying the summer breeze while working their crops. Their younger children had helped them most of the morning, but after lunch, they turned them loose to play and explore with the other children in the village. Life was much different now than it had been for them the first few years after they were finally able to meet.

Four long years had been spent living in cave after cave as they tried to find a community somewhere who would welcome them. Leena had never questioned Marcus when he repeatedly refused to make the slightest approach to anyone they found as they traveled. He never explained to her his gift and what he was capable of doing. He didn't have to. They learned shortly after the first night when he saved her life that she was able to read his mind just as clearly as he could read hers.

For many years, he believed it was merely a gift the Divine Spirit bestowed for his success in doing as ordered. It would be learned in time the way all of the Elements were punished and what gifts each of them retained. The Air faction would have almost unlimited psychic power and immortality. They also had the ability to painlessly change their appearance to any form they chose to take on. The only thing they couldn't do was age themselves. This meant when a peaceful people were found, they couldn't stay long. There would be questions regarding their youthful looks and would become the hunted as anything that is unknown has always been perceived as a threat.

Leena never balked at any of it even as Marcus began sharing details of who he was with her, she only ever listened. It was almost like she already knew in some way. She told him once that she knew he was different the

169

moment she set her eyes on him. She knew he was unlike any person she had known or heard tales of before. Somehow she also felt a stillness that told her she was safe with him.

Their first child, Joseph, came quietly. Leena was blessed with an easy birth. Her recovery from which was fast as all healing is for them. The pending arrival of their second child made Marcus feel pressured to find them a home, and he did days before Chloe was born.

That was three villages ago. They were now blessed with twelve children, and they would never have to move again. The Shaman of this people was expecting their arrival. He told tales of the visions he had received that remarkable visitors would be arriving and should be treated with the utmost respect. No one in the village questioned why they didn't age or how they healed so quickly. They also refused the use of Marcus' gifts.

When their chief suffered a terrible accident that resulted in a painful death, Marcus offered to try to heal him. He had no idea at the time if it would work, but he wanted to do something for them after all the help they'd extended to his young family when they arrived. The chief refused. His death was a part of a greater design that no one had the right to interfere with even if they held the power.

They would learn from the Shaman that their blood did in fact carry healing properties which is why they were so healthy and suffered pain briefly as their injuries healed at an amazing rate of speed. Their blood would also turn back the wheel of the sun for anyone who consumed it. To heal the chief would have also meant rewinding his years. Marcus had been warned that there were those who would always seek to find this magical fountain of youth. If they were ever discovered, it would prove a tragic outcome for all of them.

So the chief's spirit was sent to the sky, and his son took over leading the village. Marcus, Leena and their children found other ways to contribute and helped as much and as often as they could. Leena shared the knowledge of irrigation she brought from her home, and Marcus predicted the hunts.

It had been over twenty years they had lived in peace with them. Some of their own children were now adults still living in the same village, but in separate huts. They had all been blessed with the gifts as well that Marcus received. Now that they had sent the younger children on their way, there was no doubt they were pestering their older siblings who were trying to work themselves. Marcus laughed at the thought, but knew they would either wind up helping out or be sent back home quick enough.

Marcus and Leena enjoyed the peace while they worked the land. Time passed quickly when it was just the two of them working efficiently without interruption. A cry for help shot through Marcus' thoughts like a spear had been aimed carefully at the middle of his forehead tunneling through to the other side. Leena had already dropped her tools and was running through the field. She'd received the same alarm.

He quickly followed his wife into the nearby village, following the cries that came faster and more urgent. The children were at the stream, and Martin was in trouble. As fast as their unnatural speed was, Marcus feared they wouldn't make it in time.

[1]

MARTIN COULDN'T WAIT to be done in the fields for the day. He ran as fast as his legs could carry him to find his brother Brian. They were only three years apart, but they were as close as twins. Inseparable since the day Martin was born, Brian had always looked after him. His brother was an aide to the chief, being groomed to have a larger role in the tribal council one day, but the chief never minded having Martin around so long as he behaved.

Today, he couldn't find him, and it upset him immensely. At the wise old age of fifteen, Brian could do no wrong in his eyes. He walked through the

---

1. http://www.clker.com/cliparts/7/6/9/b/13309573511112670181decorative-lines-2_large-md.png

huts of the village moping and hoping he would find him somewhere, but he knew that most likely he was on a hunt or out scouting.

That's when he ran into Chloe. She was much older and had long ago started to develop her powers. Something she loved to dangle in front of the younger ones who hadn't yet come into theirs.

"Why are you running about instead of helping mom and dad?" she asked him sternly.

"They told us we could have the remains of the day."

"Oh, and you came running to find Brian," she laughed.

"No!" he shot back. "I walked... Mostly."

That only made her laugh harder. "They're checking traps. You can go if you want, but they've been at it since dawn. They'll be back soon."

That filled him with hope that he'd still have some time to spend with Brian before the day grew old, and he would have to return home for supper.

"What are you going to do?"

"What?" Martin asked her.

"Are you going after him or not?"

"No, I'll wait."

She walked in the doorway of her hut and looked back to ask, "Want to help me a minute? I might be able to find something to give you if you do."

"Like what?"

Chloe looked out of the corner of her eyes in thought. "How about some beads for mom?"

"That's for mom not for me."

"Yes, but the anniversary of her birth will soon be here."

Martin thought it over. It wasn't too exciting, but it was better than doing nothing while he waited. "What do I have to do?"

"Help me carry a basket to the stream."

"That's all?"

"Yes, that's it, and help me carry it back."

Martin groaned. He knew there would be more to it.

"I'll be back long before Brian. I promise."

"Fine," he said in a huff. "I guess I'll help."

She went inside and carried out two baskets then made another trip in for a third which she handed to Martin to carry. Soon they were off on a well walked path through the trees to the nearby stream.

"You don't have to be his shadow," she told him as they walked.

"I'm not!" Martin objected.

Chloe's light laughter filled the woods and sent birds to flight. "You are, dear brother. Why do you think the chief calls you Shadow Bear? The names we are given have meaning. Yours is no different."

"Because I'm strong and mighty like a bear!" Martin insisted. That's what father had always told him. "And our skin is darker than the people of the tribe. Shadow Bear."

"Unh-huh," she eyed him. "Think about it a little bit harder than that."

Martin still didn't understand what she was trying to imply. Suddenly he stopped in the middle of the trail and almost dropped the basket of hides and other garments he carried.

Not hearing his footfall behind her anymore, Chloe turned around. The expression on his face indicated he had figured it out. "What's on your mind, brother?"

"Brian," he said.

"Yes?"

"The chief calls him Fighting Bear."

"And you, dear one, you are the Shadow of Fighting Bear. Shadow Bear for short."

He knew it should make him mad. Rather, he knew she was trying to make him mad, but it didn't work. It was a good thing to be named off his brother he thought. Wasn't it?

They made it to the stream, and Chloe wandered in to start her washing. Martin was headed in right after her when she stopped him.

"Take the bottom basket I brought. The empty one. Gather some blackberries in it."

"That wasn't part of the deal," Martin whined.

"True. I'll add some of the dried venison you love to your payment, and you can eat as many blackberries as you'd like."

It sounded like a good deal to Martin's ears. Taking the basket with him, he headed to the brush along the bank about fifty yards down where the berries grew wild. Even popping one in his mouth for about every ten berries that he picked, it didn't take long to fill the basket over halfway full. There was no need in overfilling it only to spill them on the walk back. Besides, Chloe never said how many he needed to gather.

He walked back to where he had left her, but she wasn't there. The baskets were still sitting on the bank as well as all the garments they had brought. It was evident she had finished her chore, but he didn't know where she might have gone. As he looked around in a circle, he heard her call his name.

"Martin!"

It sounded a little ways off. Looking down the bank of the stream to see if that's where she went, he caught movement from the corner of his eye. He was dumbfounded. "How did you get over there?" he yelled out.

Chloe stood on the far side of the stream. She must've gone for a swim which made Martin jealous since he had been doing her work while she was having fun.

"Watch this!" she yelled out to him.

Martin watched, but Chloe didn't do anything except stand there. It looked like she was staring at the middle of the stream. He kept waiting for something, but nothing ever happened. Right as he was going to yell out to her, he saw it.

Slowly the water in the stream stopped running along its natural course. The water rose up high in the air and arced over about ten feet before curving back down to where the stream flowed. It looked like a water bridge in midair. Under the bridge, there was nothing except the muddy stream bed. Somehow his sister had managed to alter the course of the water leaving an opening like a tunnel.

Chloe formed a circle with her lips and blew hard. The wind traveled across drying out the mud as it went until it reached Martin on the other side knocking him down. There was still water traveling on either side of the dry open path which seemed to defy the laws of how a stream flows.

He watched as his sister carefully walked down the far stream bank into the cleared out area then walked across to reach him on the other side. The water level on either side of her was easily up to her waist most of the way, but in the middle of the stream, it was almost to the top of her head not including the wet bridge that circled over her. Once she climbed up the bank using the roots from a nearby tree close to Martin, she flashed him a bright smile. "What do you think?"

"How did you do that?"

"You know how, little brother," she scoffed.

"But how did you know you could do that?"

Chloe sat on the ground and got a handful of berries from the basket to snack on. "I didn't. I dropped something in the stream one day. While I was looking for it, I somehow dispersed the water around me. Like a much smaller version of what I just did."

"You can move water," he blankly said, looking at her in amazement.

"Not exactly."

"But you did! I saw it!"

Chloe pulled her knees to her chest and tugged on Martin's arm to pull him down next to her. "Watch," she instructed. Taking a deep breath, she formed her lips into a circle and blew out hard. The water in front of them dented in like an obstacle had suddenly appeared in its path.

"Oh," Martin said not entirely sure he understood.

"It's quite difficult, you know. It takes a lot of wind to do what I just did, and I have to force the hot air to dry the bed. I could get stuck in the mud if I didn't."

Martin rolled his eyes at her not believing it.

"It's true. Especially nearer the middle of the bed. The muddy slop there could come up to my knees easily."

He played with a twig near his feet drawing lines in the dirt. It had been the most amazing thing he'd ever seen someone in the family do with their powers, but he couldn't admit that. Not to Chloe. There was a discord creeping in his mind torn between knowing one day he would have the abilities and wishing he had them now.

"I've just been trying every time I come down to the stream ever since to do it again and to do it better." Chloe continued.

"This was better," he told her enthusiastically.

She laughed. "Yes, this was definitely better."

"Can I try?"

"Martin, you haven't come into your abilities yet. You know that."

He put his hands on his hips. "No, can I walk across the bottom of the stream like you did?"

"You want me to clear it for you?"

"Yes!" he cried happy she understood. "I want to do it too."

Chloe shook her head and ate some more berries.

"Why not?"

"Father and mother don't like for us to play with our abilities for one. I'm taking a chance just doing it for me. Plus, if anything happened to you," she looked him in the eye and softened her tone, "I would never forgive myself."

"Nothing's going to happen."

She stood up and brushed the dirt off. "You don't know that."

"The worst that can happen is I get in the water and float downstream a bit. I'll get wet. It's not like I can die from it."

Chloe thought it over. There was a part of her who wished she had come into the ability to see the future already. Then she would know for sure if it was safe to let him do it. He did have a point. The worst thing that could happen was he'd get wet. She knew there was a lot more that could go wrong. Martin could get injured, washed a long way down, or many other possibilities, but nothing that couldn't be fixed easily enough.

"Alright, but you have to promise not to say a word about this."

"I promise," Martin happily agreed, jumping to his feet.

"I mean it. Not just that I let you do it, but father and mother can't find out what I'm doing at all."

"I promise!" he cried out with a huge smile plastered on his face unable to contain his excitement.

Chloe laughed and stood next to him. "Pay attention. I have to focus, so I need you to remember and do exactly what I say."

"I will," Martin promised.

She explained that first she would clear the water making a path across the stream. Next, she had to send the hot wind to dry the bed. "The mud in the middle of the stream is unforgiving. If you tried to walk in it, you'd probably sink like quicksand."

"No, I wouldn't," he still didn't believe her.

"You wouldn't sink completely, Martin, but you'd probably get stuck in it."

He shrugged which was the closest to an agreement she would get from him.

"I need you to wait until I tell you it's time to cross, understand?"

Martin jumped up and down eagerly waiting for his chance to run across the bottom of the stream with the water towering over his head.

"Do you understand?" Chloe repeated sharply.

"Yes," Martin groaned. "Wait for your signal. I got it. Do it already!"

She chuckled at his enthusiasm then turned to focus on the water flowing in front of her. She had to start over twice after scolding Martin to be still both times. The constant movement he was making was distracting her and breaking her concentration.

He took a couple steps back to be behind her, so she couldn't see him jump and dance with delight. This was by far the most fun he had with his family's abilities. Normally, no one wanted to use them for anything except to practice when they first developed. Practice was boring, and there was nothing he could do to participate in it in any way except watch.

The water of the stream parted, and Martin couldn't stand still. He bounced up and down behind his sister trying to wait for the signal telling him to go.

Chloe began blowing the hot wind along the bed floor, and in doing so, brought her arms forward to guide it through the divide. From the corner of her eye, she saw the low hanging dead branch of the tree near the bank swaying violently in the wind and start to crack. It had been too far away to notice when she did this from the far side of the stream.

Martin saw her raise her arms and mistook it as the signal to go ahead. He shot out from behind her and jumped to the stream bed below without looking to see how muddy it remained. Both of his feet sunk into the wet ground, and he struggled to lift them out of the muck.

She didn't see Martin take off in time to pull him back before he sprang off the bank, but she turned her head to follow him with her eyes just long enough to divert the direction of the wind onto the old oak tree which cracked in two from the pressure. Half of it fell sideways into the stream below heading straight toward her brother.

In that moment, Chloe's only concern was him, and she lost all control of everything she had been doing. The wind which would've carried the side of the tree farther out stopped causing it to fall straight down, and the water she'd been holding back came crashing in to fill the void. The last thing she saw of Martin before the water covered him completely were his feet still buried in the mud, and the bones of his legs stuck straight out through the back of his ankles where they found no give from his stuck feet as the tree crashed down on top of him.

Desperately she tried to free her brother. Using all of her power she cleared the middle of the stream, but the tree proved too much for her. Every time she saw Martin's legs lying so still barely visible as his body sunk into the mud, her concentration would break, and the water would start to rush at them again. Attempt after attempt was unsuccessful, and the longer it took the more emotional she became. As her sobs wrenched from her chest and she became blinded by tears, it proved more and more difficult just to keep the water off of them.

There were shouts in the distance, and she recognized the voices of her parents. Help was coming. That calmed her significantly, and she parted the water again as she had several times now. Marcus reached the bank first and lifting one arm toward the tree, he was able to move it off of Martin. He threw his arm to the side, and the tree was sent over Chloe's head and crashed down in the stream behind her.

Leena scrambled down to the bed of the stream with Marcus on her heels. They managed to remove Martin from the murky trap that held him and carry him to the dry ground along the bank. There was nothing discernable about him. All you could see was a large band of mud in the shape of a person.

Chloe followed her parents with her eyes letting the water come crashing down around her almost knocking her off balance, but she fought to stand where she was. Martin was going to be fine she told herself. It would be painful, but he would heal. They always did, and they did so quickly. None of them were able to die she told herself.

The village shaman appeared having heard the cries of Marcus and Leena, eager to help. One look at Martin, and he knew the sad fate the boy had suffered. There was nothing he could do except try to console them.

Marcus clawed at Martin's face trying to remove the mud from around his mouth and nose, so he could breathe again. It wasn't enough. The mud filled his mouth, nose and throat. It had seeped into his lungs as well. There was no way he could reach it all by hand. With no other options available, Marcus placed his mouth over his son's and sucked all of the watery mud and gunk from his throat and lungs. He repeated the act over and over again until he was certain no more remained. Then he did the same thing covering Martin's nose with his mouth. When he finished, Martin still didn't move. His body lay lifeless in Marcus' arms.

Leena wept loudly, and the shaman placed his hand on her shoulder.

'*This isn't right*,' Chloe's thoughts raged. Martin should be coming around by now. He should be yelling at her for not being more careful. She walked to the edge of the stream and clambered up the bank. The sight of Martin's still body became worse the closer she got. Beneath the traces of mud that covered his face, his skin was a deep blue and growing darker as her eyes lingered on him.

"Why isn't he awake yet?" she muttered aloud.

None of them answered her. The sobs from mother only increased, and her father sat as still as the totem in the village center.

"Father?" she pleaded. This can't be happening. We are immortal. Martin has to wake up.

When her father didn't say a word, she turned to the shaman begging him with her eyes. It made no sense. It was like they had given up.

The shaman walked over to Chloe and placed both hands on her shoulder looking her in the eyes. "Air is what brought your life, and in turn, air is what can take your life away. Young Martin has been without air for too long. I'm afraid his journey has come to an end."

Chloe began to hyperventilate. "No!" she screamed between gasps for breath. "No!"

A blood curdling scream came from the direction of the village, and she turned to see Brian who had stopped on the path taking in the scene. In an instant, he was sprinting toward them. He fell to his knees next to Martin and lifted him into his arms. His tears fell like rain.

Disbelief was the only hope Chloe had to hang onto. This could not happen. It wasn't supposed to happen. It had to be a punishment being doled out by her parents for playing with her powers. Any minute now Martin would open his eyes. She collapsed to the ground and wept. The tears wouldn't stop. Long after she had accepted that Martin was gone forever, the tears continued. After her parents had carried his body to the village to be prepared for the funeral pyre, she remained on the bank crying rivers into the earth. Even after the shaman left her side, she remained choking on her sobs. And after Brian had cursed her and swore he would never again view her as a sister, vowing she was as dead to him as his dear brother Martin, she sat along the stream drowning in her own tears.

Martin was dead. The words kept screaming through her head in her own voice. Martin was dead, and she had killed him.

Chapter Seventeen
Saved by a Witch

Monday morning, Lilah woke up feeling restless and tired. She still had questions about what had happened the night before and how did she lose time like she had. She slowly got out of bed and dressed. Jackson and Everleigh had both messaged her asking if she would be able to get together today. She was still much too tired to talk to anyone yet.

She came down into the kitchen. Some of the family were already up and starting their day, but many were absent. Her parents were seated in the kitchen having coffee. She walked to the counter to get a cup when her Uncle Brian handed her a glass of tea. It wasn't what she had in mind, but she didn't want to turn up her nose at the gesture.

Abby and Myles were discussing how to test something when she sat down. "How are you feeling?" her dad asked.

"Exhausted," she said after taking a long drink from her glass.

Lilah sensed that she had interrupted something. "What are you guys up to today?"

"We are going to test our strength," her mom declared.

She gave her mom a sideways glance. "What does that mean?"

"We're stronger together, and my theory is that maybe we are all stronger now. Like how the witches are spawning to prepare for what's to come."

"Count me out," Lilah told her.

Abby was surprised her daughter didn't want to be a part of it, but happy too. The family would probably be uncomfortable if Lilah were outside with the rest of them testing her strength. "Why is that?"

"I don't have the energy. I feel like I ran a marathon then worked out for six hours afterward."

"There's nothing wrong with taking time for yourself," Uncle Brian told her. "We all need downtime now and then."

"Yeah, I just don't know why I feel like this."

There had been an earlier argument regarding what to tell Lilah if she asked. Her dad's opinion was in the minority, but she was his daughter and would tell her what he thought was best. He quickly started talking before Brian could say anything different. "You got upset last night, dear. You affected the winds. I'm sure it drained you especially since you've had no practice."

Brian stormed from the room angrily. Abby ran after him hoping to talk to him, but he stormed out of the house ignoring her. She came back to the table and told Myles, "You knew he would be upset."

"I knew. I also don't care."

"We should get outside with the others. They'll begin soon." Abby walked over to her daughter and kissed the top of her head. "If you need anything, we'll be by the barn."

They headed out the back door leaving Lilah alone in the kitchen. The front door opened several times, and by the time she decided to go in there, the house was empty except for her. She walked to the back where the porch was empty and sat down to watch.

They were taking turns lifting logs and hay bales with their minds. Some managed to accomplish it easier than others. They even tried to move Abby's car. Working together, the car moved with ease, but not individually.

Lilah was wore out just watching them work. She went back upstairs and napped until the vibrating of her phone woke her up. It was Jackson. She let the call go to voice mail, and sent him a text. "Just woke up. Give me a few minutes."

He replied, "About time sleepy head. It's 4 in the afternoon."

She hadn't paid attention to the time. *How did it get so late already?* She didn't expect to nap for almost six hours. She scurried downstairs and found the family gathered again.

News of the Mississippi wolves and witches arrival had been given to them by Todd through his friend Meredith. They were spread out in Fairview and other small towns nearby. Apparently, the southern wolves wanted to open lines of communication with all the Elementals in the area. Lilah knew this would not go over well, and her family would discuss it well into the night. She also knew it made the odds of her being able to leave slim because her parents would want her to be a part of the discussion.

She rinsed out the glass from the morning that she brought down with her and poured a fresh glass of tea. She left the room for a minute to grab the jacket she had left on the back porch. When she returned, her Uncle Brian was sitting at the table.

"How are you feeling?" Uncle Brian asked her.

"Good. I can't believe I slept through most of the day."

He nodded. "Sometimes our body gets worn out. Emotional toll can do that as well. It's been a rough week for all of us, but most of all you."

Lilah sat down to be friendly, but she wasn't sure what to say. She didn't want to admit that the last few days had been rough. It was just one more way for her family to treat her like a child. It had been hard on her trying to deal with everything that was thrown at her at once, but she didn't like owning that to her family.

"What's on the agenda for tonight?" she asked, knowing the answer was the wolves.

"Agenda?"

"The family discussion."

"Oh, that," he waved it off like it was not something he was interested in. "They will eventually agree all the Elementals need to come together, but not until they've argued for several hours."

Lilah snickered. It was true. Her family would ultimately come to the right decision, but not before every one of them had an opportunity to voice their objections no matter how trivial.

She yawned. "I don't know why I'm still so tired. Maybe I should switch to coffee," she said finishing her tea.

"I can make a pot if you would like," her Uncle Brian offered. He got up and set about doing so before she answered.

Tidbits of the conversation would reach her ears from the other room, and it made her smile. The biggest point being made was how anyone could trust them. They could be secretly working with the much larger tribe from the north. Maybe they're just a Trojan horse so to speak. The witches vouch for this tribe, but how can we be sure we can trust the witches?

Centuries of peace between the two Elemental factions, and still her family couldn't trust them to work with them. They would argue it out until it had been analyzed a dozen times then argue it again for good measure. Part of her wanted to defend the two groups, but she knew she didn't have the energy for it.

She listened in until her uncle brought her a cup of coffee and set it before her. "I didn't realize it was ready. I could've got it."

"It's no trouble," he smiled.

"I think I'm going to take it to my room and sit for a while." Really she only wanted to get ahold of Jackson before she fell asleep again.

Upstairs, she called him. She was leaned against the wall because she knew if she sat on the bed, she would instantly fall asleep. "Hey, sorry. I'm just so tired today."

"Because you slept so long. Everyone knows sleeping too much makes you sleepier."

"Maybe."

"You should come out with me and Everleigh."

"I don't think the family would approve. There's a big meeting downstairs right now that I'm skipping out on, but to actually leave the house would probably make them mad."

"Sneak out then."

"I would fall and break my neck," she told him, knowing that even if she did, she would heal. It may take some time, and it would hurt of course. Still, she didn't want to explain that to Jackson just yet.

There was murmuring on the other end of the line. He was talking to someone. "Okay, Everleigh is going to come get you. She will help you."

Lilah got off the phone and changed. It was one of those times where she wished there were cameras in the house so she could watch the footage later and have a laugh. She was determined to avoid sitting down as she grew more and more tired, so she kept falling into the wall and doorframes as she struggled to pull on her clothes. At least she could laugh at herself she thought as she banged her arm on the door again.

She downed her coffee which had cooled when she was finally ready and made a mental note to have Everleigh stop for some once they left. She was going to need it.

Perfect timing. Everleigh called as soon as she finished. "I'm here. I left the car on the road, and I walked up."

"Okay. I'm ready."

"Where are you coming out? The back door?"

"My window like always."

"Jackson didn't tell you?"

"Tell me what?"

"Open your window. I'm under it."

Lilah went to her window. It was old and cloudy from years of moisture caught between the two panes. She couldn't see Everleigh, but trusted she was there. She budged it open and gasped.

"Bars," she said more to herself than to Everleigh.

"Yeah, bars. They don't want you sneaking out anymore."

"But when? Who?"

"This morning. Luke saw it and told my aunt. I don't know who."

The window was only open a few inches, but it was enough for Lilah to stick her hand through and feel the iron that was on the outside. Her window opened to the back porch roof which is why she could easily climb out. She tried to think about other options, but she didn't think any other window would work as easily. None that she could get to anyway. If only she weren't so tired, maybe then her mind would be clearer.

She shut the window and sat down on her bed wondering if it would be easy enough to walk out the back door while the family was distracted. It could work, but only if there were no stragglers in the kitchen or anywhere else. She could always go down there and wait for her chance to escape, but that could take hours. It could also be clear to make a getaway as soon as she made it down the stairs. It was impossible to know without seeing to the future. Even if her abilities were sharpened, she was in no condition to try.

Everleigh had other plans, "Listen. Meredith is on her way with Matt and Rita. She will help us. Just sit tight until then."

Lilah agreed and hung up the phone. Their arrival would provide the cover she needed. Once she knew Meredith was here, she would leave. The bed was so comfortable beneath her, and she thought she would be okay to lay down and rest for a minute. Sleep took her until she was harshly shaken awake.

It was hard to keep her eyes open long enough to focus. Meredith was shaking her arm trying to wake her as quietly as possible. Lilah kept falling back asleep as soon as she would open her eyes.

Then she was choking. Meredith was pouring something down her throat. Lilah tried to fight her off, but she had no energy. The witch clamped her hand over Lilah's mouth when she started coughing. She was frightened. She didn't know why Meredith would try to harm her. She lay still with wide eyes franticly trying to figure out how to get away. *'Maybe if I stop fighting, Meredith will loosen her grip,'* she thought. *'But to what end?'* Even if she gambled to run, she would surely be caught. It was still hard to keep her eyelids from closing even with the attack against her.

"I've only got a minute, girl. They'll notice I'm gone soon. I need you to listen to me," Meredith instructed.

Lilah tried to nod as best she could, but it was difficult.

"Alright then, I don't know what they got in your system, but it's a miracle I got anything down your throat at all. The medicine I gave you will counter most of the common sleeping pills and other nervous system suppressants, but without knowing what you took, I can't be sure it will work."

Her eyes widened in shock. *'Sleeping pills?'* No wonder she couldn't stay awake. There was a heavy haze lingering on her brain when she tried to think. She couldn't remember what she had for lunch, or even what day it was.

"I've got to get back. Lay here and be quiet," she ordered. "I'll let Everleigh know how to come in to get you." She lifted her hand away from Lilah's mouth slowly.

Lilah didn't move or make a sound. Meredith nodded at her like she took the silence for agreement. Then she was gone.

She struggled to stay awake by blinking repeatedly and moving around. Sitting up didn't work either. She was asleep again within minutes.

"Hey...Hey!" it was Everleigh.

It took Lilah time to adjust. She couldn't remember Meredith visiting her room until right before they left. "What are you doing here?"

"I'm helping you sneak out. Remember?" she asked, pulling Lilah up to a sitting position.

She didn't remember. She couldn't think. Her mind was a void wasteland. It was like nothing had survived. The last thing she remembered was watching her family outside. She didn't even know when that happened. It could've been days ago.

"Man, they really messed you up. Someone in your family obviously doesn't want you going anywhere."

"What do you mean?"

Everleigh was cautious. She didn't want to tip her hand, but she saved herself. "The bars on your window! Do you remember your name?"

"Yeah, it's Kara."

Everleigh's eyes widened and her grip loosened.

Lilah fell back on the bed with a smile on her face.

"Oh, that's how you're playing this? Alright... Alright. Least I know you're coming around."

She pulled Lilah up again and helped her swing her legs to the floor. The room started to spin, and Lilah grabbed the edge of the mattress as though she might fall off. "Aunt Meredith said this might happen. It's an effect of the medicine she gave you."

"Your aunt gave me medicine?" Lilah was serious this time.

"Oh, Lord. We need to get you out of here."

Everleigh kept an arm around Lilah while reaching for everything she might need. She draped a coat over Lilah's shoulders and tried helping her put the arms in the sleeves, but soon gave up. Phone and shoes were all that's left, and Lilah would just have to put those on later.

She knelt in front of Lilah trying to keep her focused. "We have to go down these stairs as quietly as possible. My aunt is going to make a scene to help us out, but we still have to be careful. The last few feet from the stairs to the porch is the trickiest because we will be in view if anyone looks that way."

Lilah nodded. She didn't think they would make it and wasn't entirely sure why Everleigh was acting like it was a jailbreak. There was no way they could come around the corner in the hall without being seen especially with everyone gathered downstairs.

They made it out of the bedroom with Lilah leaning on Everleigh for support. Whatever it was that Meredith poured down her throat was starting to work. She could remember it now, but only bits that came in flashes. Her legs still felt like jelly, but she could tell even that was slowly improving. If they could only wait a little longer, but Everleigh insisted they not wait.

The stairs were much trickier. They had to take them one at a time. Once Lilah had both feet on a step, she needed a moment before moving to the next one. It always felt like she was about to fall and would give themselves away with the commotion.

It took forever, but they made it to the bottom. There wasn't much room, but Everleigh bent down and looked through the keyhole. She didn't see anyone in the kitchen.

"Doing okay?" she asked Lilah quietly.

"Yeah, I think."

"We have to wait. I'm going to text my aunt."

Everleigh sent a message on her phone then stood with one arm around Lilah and the other hand on the doorknob. The seconds dragged by like minutes. Lilah could hear her heartbeat as well as Everleigh's while they waited in the dark for the signal, only she didn't know what the signal would be.

It was unmistakable. Meredith's voice shouted something, and the fight was in full swing. Everyone was yelling. Everleigh pushed opened the stairway door cautiously at first, but seeing the room deserted, she grabbed Lilah and headed toward the hall. They paused in the doorway to peek out. Lilah's heart dropped. Not two feet from them was her Uncle Todd, and he was looking straight at them.

Lilah's mouth fell open. She didn't know what to say or how to try to explain how Everleigh had got inside. She wouldn't have to.

Uncle Todd winked at her. He then turned toward the chaos in the living room and leaned against the wall providing them a little more protection against prying eyes.

The two young women hurried down the hall to the porch as quietly as possible. With every step, Lilah was feeling better. She was still weak and at times woozy, but she was more awake. Safe on the porch, Lilah finished putting on her coat and shoes then followed Everleigh outside.

They rounded the house on the kitchen side keeping low to avoid being seen through the windows. There were heavy curtains draped in the front room, so it was smooth sailing from that point. They ran along the drive to where Everleigh's car was parked on the road.

It might have been the sudden movements that Lilah wasn't used to after almost the whole day spent in bed. It could have been the medicine Meredith had forced down her throat, or whatever else she had been slipped to ingest. There were also her nerves to take in effect as sneaking out was relatively new to her, and trying to get away so near to everyone had her adrenaline pumping even harder.

Whatever it was, Lilah felt her stomach churn as soon as she opened the door of the car. There was barely enough time for her to turn away before her stomach emptied on the ground. Coffee and the white milky liquid was all she had in her.

She could hear Everleigh making gagging noises from the other side of the car. It only made things worse. When there was nothing left to come up and feeling like it was over, she finally sat in the seat.

"Better?" Everleigh asked, handing her a fast food napkin from the glove compartment.

"I think so."

"Well, if we had been seen, we would have been caught by now."

"I'm sorry," Lilah really did feel awful.

"That's a good thing," Everleigh reassured her. "I can take it slow to Jackson's house. Let me know if I need to stop for you."

Lilah gave a quick nod. She did feel awful still, but she didn't feel like she would be sick again.

Everleigh had her phone out. "I'm letting my aunt know what happened. I might have to get you something else since what she gave you is in the ditch."

The thought of having to drink anymore of it made Lilah's insides do a somersault. Instinctively, she reached for the door, but it passed.

"We good?" Everleigh put the car into drive.

"Yeah."

She stayed true to her word and took it slow. Well, she kept to the speed limit anyway. They pulled up to Jackson's, and he was already outside waiting for them.

"Nothing yet," Everleigh said, looking at her phone screen. "They're probably still fighting."

"How did she start the fight anyway?" Lilah asked curiously.

Everleigh knew she couldn't tell her honestly what bomb her aunt had dropped in the house that night. "Oh, my aunt can get under your skin when she wants," she tried to play it off like it wasn't anything real important.

Jackson rushed to put his arms around Lilah as soon as she stepped from the car.

"You may want to rethink that approach," Everleigh warned him.

"Why? What's going on?" he asked nervously, looking back and forth between the two of them.

Lilah could tell he was extremely worried. "I don't feel well," she explained.

"I bet not! I'd be sick too if my family was drugging me!" He went from worried to being pissed off in an instant.

"Wait. No one tried to drug me." As soon as the words came out of her mouth, Lilah had a hint of a memory play hide and seek in her mind. It was almost there. She could almost grasp it, but she couldn't get the whole picture.

She looked at her friends confused, and they both looked like they didn't want to be the messenger.

"Let's get inside," Everleigh shivered. "It's pretty cold."

They headed to the house as Lilah toyed with the broken fragments of the day. Her family was outside, she was in the kitchen, and then she thought Meredith was attacking her. That was basically it. She couldn't remember much before leaving with Everleigh except for a few picture like flashes that didn't make sense.

Inside, they took off their coats and headed to the kitchen. "Anyone hungry?" Jackson had his head in the refrigerator.

"I'm good," Everleigh was still waiting for a response from her aunt.

Lilah didn't answer because she hadn't heard them. All of her attention was spent on figuring out what happened during this day that was almost over.

"What Meredith gave me," Lilah didn't finish the thought.

"It's a counter medicine used in overdose situations, whether they be accidental or otherwise."

"And it worked." She was thinking out loud now.

"Yeah, well, I mean you're awake at least."

Jackson set some leftovers on the counter and walked over to Lilah. He put his hands on her shoulders gently rubbing them.

"It wouldn't have worked if I," her voice cracked and tears were stinging to break free. She pulled away from him and wiped the corners of her eyes with the back of her hands. It was too painful to finish the sentence.

"My aunt text back and said not to give you anything. Just keep you awake, and let her know if you get worse."

Lilah sat at the kitchen table and slumped over. *It couldn't be true, could it? Why would anyone want to harm her especially in her own family?*

"Listen. I can't imagine how you feel, and I don't want to make you feel worse. But there's only one reason the counter meds worked," Everleigh laid it all out in the open.

"But why would they do this to me?"

"I thought the bars were to keep you inside, but this...I don't know." Jackson was struggling to figure it out too.

"Are you sure it was a family decision?" Everleigh asked.

"What do you mean?"

"Who could have done it? Luke saw a man installing the bars while your family was busy with something near the barn." Everleigh had to catch herself from saying anything specific about what her family had been up to in front of Jackson while Lilah was around.

"It doesn't mean they didn't know."

"You're right," Everleigh agreed. "Do you remember anything at all? Who could it have been?"

Lilah tried to remember. She wanted this more than anything at that moment, but she couldn't. She shook her head and put her head back down.

"You're still a little out of it. Maybe when you feel better," Jackson was doing his best to be positive. "Anyone hungry?" he asked again.

Both women shook their heads. Lilah was feeling famished, but was still afraid she may get sick again. Jackson set to work heating up enough food for everyone at the table which he piled high on a plate in front of him. It was filled with remnants of a couple dinners and breakfast meat too.

"You're really going to eat all that?" Everleigh was disgusted.

"I'm a growing boy," Jackson replied, imitating a little child's voice.

It was enough to make Lilah want to smile at least. She sat up straight still trying to make heads or tails of what happened. "Let's say it was one person, or even one person who had the go ahead from the rest of them. Why?"

Everleigh looked at her friend with sympathy. It had to be a hard blow to take. Her own family had some issues, but they would never do this secretly. If someone did anything against another in her coven, you knew what was going on and the reasons for it.

"What happened after you went home last night?"

Lilah looked away shrugging. "What if I told you I don't remember?"

"It started then!" Jackson said with a mouth full of meatloaf.

Everleigh held up her hand. "What are you? Two years old? Mouth closed."

He swallowed. "I'm sorry, but it's just that you were fine last night when you were here."

"Yeah, but then she went home and doesn't remember now," Everleigh pointed out blankly.

"No, I remember being here. It's just I blacked out a little before I went to bed."

"Could anyone have slipped something in your drink?" Jackson asked.

"I didn't have anything."

"And you still blacked out?" It didn't make sense to Everleigh. Everything pointed to Lilah being drugged, but this could mean it was something else entirely.

"Only for a little bit. We were fighting," she glanced at Jackson. "I mean my parents and I were." She wondered how long it would be until she slipped up and said something she shouldn't. "And I was really upset."

That was all the information Everleigh needed. It all clicked now. The whole charade of keeping things from the boy who already knew was becoming tiresome, but that was Lilah's call. And Jackson's. They both had secrets. It would be so much easier to talk to them both at once, but she was going to have to do it the hard way again.

"Jackson," Everleigh's voice was as sweet as possible. "Would you be a dear and run to the coffee shop to get us girls some hot cocoa."

Jackson waited till he swallowed his mouth full of food. "There's cocoa in the pantry."

"You know the coffee shop has the best cocoa in the world."

He had stabbed a fork into a sausage link. "I'm eating," he shoved the entire link in his mouth.

"You're always eating," she was getting annoyed. "Now, scoot."

He continued with another bite then said, "When I'm done."

Everleigh reached under the table and pinched his leg. Hard. He dropped his fork and jumped up. "Or maybe I'll go now," he said, glaring at her.

It was easy to tell Everleigh just wanted him gone. As soon as the door closed behind him, Lilah asked, "What is it?"

"There was a storm last night."

"Yeah."

"A wicked storm."

Lilah continued to sit with a blank stare on her face.

"An unexpected storm," Everleigh's voice was growing louder and more pointed.

"Fine. I caused the storm. Happy now?"

"You did all of that? There was damage for miles."

It was something she hated owning up to, but it was true. She reached for the last sausage link off of Jackson's plate, feeling brave enough to attempt to eat when he wasn't around to see her if she got sick. "I didn't meant to," she said before nibbling.

"Wow. I'm impressed. I never knew you could do that."

"Me either. I don't remember doing it, but I know they were upset about it."

"Your family?"

Lilah's head snapped up, and she looked at Everleigh. A saddened comprehension set in her eyes.

"Took you long enough," Everleigh raised an eyebrow.

"I guess they would have reason then. They didn't want me out of control again."

The sausage went down easy, and her stomach didn't protest. Lilah pulled Jackson's plate to her and began munching on what he had left. "What do we tell him?"

"Tell him your parents fought with you about sneaking out, and they probably just gave you a bit too much to knock you out until you calmed down."

Lilah continued to eat without responding. She didn't want to lie to him, but she wasn't ready to come clean either.

"I just heard a door. He's here. I'll tell him," Everleigh could easily see Lilah wasn't up to carrying out a convincing lie right yet.

Jackson carried a drink tray filled with hot cocoa to the table before taking off his coat.

"Four?" Everleigh eyed the cups.

"Yes," Jackson called from the front hall.

"Why did you get four? Someone joining us?" She took two of the cups from the carrier and handed one to Lilah.

Lilah took it and slid the plate back to where Jackson had been. She had absent mindedly munched on most of it until only the green beans remained. Luckily her stomach was back to normal because she had been hungrier than she thought.

He appeared from the hall and crossed his arms. "I told you," his voice filled with an irritable tone from having to repeat himself.

Everleigh said nothing. She watched as Jackson removed the last two cups and sat down.

"I'm a growing boy," he repeated in his little kid voice grabbing the cups in each hand.

The girls laughed at him. "Goofball," Everleigh called him while giving Lilah a look that said this is who you're stuck with for eternity.

Jackson took the lids off both cups to help them cool quicker. "Hey!" he cried out. "Where's my food?"

There was a knock at the door, and everyone jumped. They hadn't been expecting company.

Everleigh looked at Lilah worried that her family realized she had gone and had come to get her.

Lilah knew the people on the porch were Elementals only because she couldn't get a fix on their energy. She wouldn't be able to tell who or what they were. There was nothing she could say in front of Jackson that would make sense, so she quickly shook her head to answer Everleigh's concerned look.

A second knock followed even louder this time. Jackson slowly stood up, and Lilah reached out and grabbed his arm. She was afraid not knowing who might be outside.

"I'm just going to look," he told her gently, trying to soothe her mind.

Just then, the door swung open, and Meredith stepped inside. "Honey, I'm home!" she called out.

The others were with her. Luke, Matt, and Rita all followed her inside.

"What? How? I know I locked that door," Jackson looked like he thought he was going crazy.

"You did," Luke said as the corner of his mouth quirked up.

Jackson put his hands on his head and his eyes widened. "Don't tell me you busted the lock. I'll have to fix it before my dad gets back."

Meredith walked into the kitchen looking at him like he was a child which he was in comparison to her years. She gently patted the side of his face like she was talking to a five year old. "Oh come now, sweetie. I've been doing unlocking chants since before this country had its first war."

Relief filled Jackson's face instantly, but he lay his hand over his chest pretending he was in pain. "You can't do this to me," he said, leaning on the counter for support.

He fell down to the floor continuing his charade. Gasping for air, he reached out to those closest to him for help before turning his head to the side to feign death.

"Well," Meredith stepped over his outstretched legs, "with him out of the picture, there's enough room for all of us to sit."

"Hey!" Jackson shouted back, getting up from the floor.

By the time he stood, all the chairs had filled, and Meredith had helped herself to one of his hot cocoas. Rita was reaching for the other one, but Jackson grabbed it first. He looked at her then handed it over with a sigh.

"You're such a good boy," Rita continued the ruse Meredith had started.

"You see how they treat me?" he asked Lilah and picked up his plate. He went to the counter and began piling it high again.

"If you ever do have a heart attack, it won't be from anything I do. It will be all that crap you're constantly putting in your system." Meredith watched him disgusted.

"A boy's got to eat," he said, sticking the plate in the microwave.

They all laughed. Jackson ate more like a teenager than other guys his age.

"What happened at the house?" Lilah asked without looking at anyone specifically and not sure if she wanted to know.

Meredith reached out and touched her arm gently. "It's going to be fine," she said reassuringly.

It did nothing to soothe her nerves. There were too many questions about why this was done to her.

"But what happened?" she repeated.

It was clear to everyone Lilah wasn't just talking about what went on when her and Everleigh snuck out. She wanted to know why she was drugged and who did it. No one knew how to answer her without saying something Lilah wouldn't want to hear. "Meredith just started a fight. That's all," Rita finally spoke.

Lilah looked at her with evident annoyance. She already knew that. The shouts could be heard long after they were out the door. The anger was rising up within her, and she feared a repeat of the storms if she got too mad, but she didn't understand why everyone was acting so ignorant.

"Jackson, honey, be a dear and make a pot of coffee," Meredith's voice interrupted her growing rage.

Jackson, she thought. *That's why no one is talking.* The calm that came over her was immediate. She had been so consumed with her desire to know the truth that she overlooked the one obvious reason for people to play dumb.

The conversation picked up after that. Everyone was keeping it light with a lot of teasing directed at Jackson. He took it well and dished it back at every turn. It started to feel normal to her which she realized was a crazy thought the second it popped into her head since she'd never had normal, but it did start to feel more relaxed.

Lilah couldn't completely relax as much as she longed for it. She sat tense amongst new friends joining in the conversation, trying to hide how she really felt from the others.

It wasn't unnoticed. It was something she couldn't hide no matter what she did. As much as she tried to pretend everything was good, the strengthening winds outside told all of them the truth.

Meredith knew she had to do something to get her under control. "Are you feeling okay?" she asked Lilah.

"I'm fine. Feeling better actually. Thank you for whatever that was you gave me."

"Are you sure? You look a little pale. Maybe you should lie down a while."

Lilah was about to object again when Meredith gave her a wink. "That probably wouldn't be a bad thing."

She went into the living room to lay on the couch with Meredith close behind.

"We only have a minute until lover boy comes in here." Meredith told her. "It wasn't your whole family. It was one person. I don't know his name. As soon as I hear from your Uncle Todd, I'll let you know."

The mention of her uncle's name stirred some memory she couldn't quite grasp. Her brows furrowed together in thought.

"What is it?" Meredith asked.

"Nothing. Well, I can't remember."

Meredith started to stand when it hit her.

"Wait. Uncle Todd...he helped me get out didn't he?"

A smile slowly spread over Meredith's face. "I don't know how much he helped, but he provided a little cover for the two of you."

"So he knew?"

"No," Meredith said firmly. "He knew nothing about any of this until I said something."

"Then why did he help?"

"Because he trusts me."

That was good enough for Lilah, but there was still something knocking on the back of her mind, hoping she'd find the door to let it out. Something about her uncle that was lost at least for now.

Jackson's head popped in the doorway. "Everything okay?"

"Yeah," Meredith said, standing and walking to him. "She just needs to rest a bit. She's been through quite an ordeal."

He came over to the couch and lifted Lilah's legs. He sat down and laid her legs over his lap. There was a blanket over the back of the couch that he pulled down to use to cover her. "Movie?" he asked, picking up the remote.

Lilah nodded pulling the blanket snugly up to her chin.

"What are you in the mood to see?"

"You pick." Lilah could already tell she would probably be asleep again soon. It bothered her losing a whole day like this, but there was nothing she could do except hope she would be better tomorrow.

Jackson scrolled through the available titles and settled on another werewolf movie.

'If only he knew the truth,' she thought before closing her eyes and drifting off to sleep. He may not be so quick to watch movies about form changing wolves if he knew the danger they posed to most of his friends. A danger that was already on its way to Fairview and getting closer by the hour.

Chapter Eighteen
Telling Jackson

Lilah woke abruptly, and it wasn't immediately defined why. The room was dark, and she could tell she was now alone on the couch. She wiped her eyes and forced herself up afraid of what it was that woke her. It wasn't a dream. She was almost certain. A loud noise perhaps or maybe her parents calling to her. All she knew was that she was not going back to sleep now.

There was a faint light coming from the kitchen, so Lilah wandered in hoping someone else was awake. The room was empty. The time on the microwave read 4:42 am. She went to the front hall to dig through her purse hoping in the daring rescue last night someone grabbed her phone. It was there. The time was the same, so the microwave wasn't wrong like she wished.

She went back to the kitchen and started a pot of coffee. She was feeling wide awake which was no surprise given how much she had slept the day before, but coffee was still a must to be able to function. Waiting for it to brew, she scanned through her phone logs. There was a number of calls and text messages that she couldn't remember, but she had answered them all.

A few were new ones. They were mainly from her parents hoping she was fine and apologizing for not realizing what was going on right in front of them. Uncle Todd had left a voice mail urging her to call as soon as she could. Lilah figured it could wait until later as he was probably sleeping. Then she saw where the call came through less than an hour ago.

This doesn't bode well she thought getting up to get a cup of coffee that had just finished brewing. It sounded urgent, and she figured she would call him in a couple minutes hoping he would still be awake. She sat the cup down on the table.

"Morning, early bird."

Everleigh's voice startled Lilah and she jumped knocking her chair over. She managed to catch it, but not before it hit the table leg creating a loud bang.

"Easy. You'll wake everyone with all that noise."

Lilah held her hand to her chest and could feel the rapid heartbeat underneath it. "You took a year off my life with that scare."

Everleigh poured a cup and joined her at the table. "You do know I know, right? Can't nobody take a year off of your life."

It was a saying she had picked up from some kids at one of her old schools. She had used it herself trying to blend in, and it became habit. It didn't even occur to her when she said it just now how ridiculous it might sound to someone who knew she was immortal.

"Everyone? The others stayed here as well?"

"Yeah, it got to be really late, so we all just crashed here."

"I'm surprised Jackson's dad has no problem with people always over like they live here."

Everleigh had a secretive look in her eye and pressed her lips tight before looking away from Lilah. She explained, "Ah, he's used to it from our high school days. Besides, he works a lot when he is around, and he's still on that hunting trip."

"I have to call my uncle," she said, picking up her phone.

"Todd?"

"Yeah, he left a message not long ago."

Everleigh waved her hand at the phone. "Don't worry about it. He'll be here soon."

"Here? Why?"

"The wolves have arrived."

For a moment, terror struck her hard, but then she understood, "From the south?"

"Yeah, they arrived overnight."

"How many are there?"

Everleigh's eyes narrowed, and she shook her head. "I really don't know for sure. I'd say around a hundred total counting the witches with them."

Lilah sipped her coffee. It was far too early to process all of this, and she was far too low on caffeine. "Coming here?"

"Not here," Everleigh replied dramatically.

"I don't mean Jackson's. I meant Fairview."

"Yeah or nearby. Listen, about your boy."

"What?" Lilah's eyes grew round worried something had happened after she fell asleep.

"He's fine. It's just...well, you need to tell him."

"I will."

"When? Someday?"

"It's just that who we are has always been something that came out naturally in my family."

"Lilah, it's not going to happen like that. Either you tell him or he finds out on his own, and it won't be something that comes out naturally."

There was a part of her that knew Everleigh was right, but she wasn't sure she was ready for it. So much had happened since arriving in town a week ago. There had been little time to adjust to anything much less plan how to let someone know that they were the true definition of soul mates, and he would now live forever.

While Lilah stayed quiet, Everleigh had a lot more to say. "Something else for you to think on over there. My aunt and the others have been kind for your sake trying not to slip up and say anything. Do you think these newcomers will?"

Everleigh was right, and Lilah knew it. Jackson had to be told, and the sooner the better.

"Why don't you look ahead and see if it works out?"

Utter fear poured down Lilah's face like someone pulling down a projector screen. "I can't."

"I thought you grew into your powers?" Everleigh joked.

"I did, but it's too risky."

"How?"

"Too many possible outcomes. If we look too far into the future," Lilah paused trying to find the right words, but came up empty. "It can be bad."

"So don't look that far. Take him in another room later and only look ahead as far as the conversation is concerned."

It made sense. Actually, it was brilliant. All she had to do was think of how she would put it into words when she started to talk to him, and she'd only have to look ahead a few minutes.

Lilah's eyes sparkled, and she smiled at Everleigh. "I'm going to do it. I'm going to tell him."

"Tell him what," Luke asked as he entered the room.

"You didn't go back to the farm?"

"Not a chance. It was pretty chaotic over there when I left," he looked through the pantry and carried out a box of breakfast rolls and place them on the table. "So what is it you're telling me then?" Luke sat down and glanced back and forth between the ladies.

"Not you, dork," Eveleigh's eyes rolled.

"I'm going to tell Jackson," Lilah started to say.

"About you?" Luke sat back in his chair so fast Lilah thought he might topple over.

"Yeah, about me," she said, smiling at how much it surprised him.

"About damn time," he said, hopping up to grab a cup.

"Luke!" Everleigh yelled, turning to keep him in sight.

"What? It's the truth. It's been a pain always having to watch what I say. Not my style."

"I'm sorry," Lilah didn't realize it had been so bothersome for anyone to keep her secret.

"You don't need to apologize to him," Everleigh said disdainfully.

"It sounded better in my head. I didn't mean to make it out to be this big ordeal. Friends?" Luke seemed remorseful.

"Yeah, friends." The words struck Lilah as being odd since she had never had real friends before anyway. She could only be friendly with people, but never have a deeper connection than that.

"Good," Luke walked over. "Because I'm famished. I tapped Everleigh twice yesterday, so she needs a rest. Want me to go for the wrist or the neck?"

Lilah jumped back in her chair so forcefully it fell over underneath her sending her sprawling to the floor. She composed herself quickly and jumped up lifting both arms in front of her similar to that of a boxer. It wouldn't be her fists she hit him with, but her mind. There was no time to think about whether she was strong enough. She was going to fight as hard as she could.

A small branch from a nearby tree hit the window, and Everleigh jumped between them. "What the hell, Luke?" she yelled out.

"I had no idea," he stared out the window at the tornado strength winds that had suddenly formed outside.

"Lilah!" Everleigh was trying to get her focused. "Lilah! It was a joke. A stupid joke," Everleigh glared at Luke. "But still a joke nonetheless. Luke doesn't want your blood."

Nothing changed. She didn't move a muscle, and her stare practically cut through Everleigh to the counter behind where she stood.

Luke walked to the window and said over his shoulder, "It's dying down. Keep going."

"Lilah," Everleigh started again much calmer. "It's me. You're fine. Luke is an idiot. Everything is going to be fine."

For a second, Lilah's eyes met Everleigh's then the blank stare returned. It didn't appear as though Lilah would be alright at first, but the winds had died down drastically.

"That's it," Everleigh comforted her. "Just breathe and relax."

Lilah's arms started to lower and were soon back at her sides with her fists still clenched.

Everleigh stood in front of her breathing in lifting her hands with the palms up in front of her chest. Then breathing out while flipping her hands over and pushing down.

Eventually Lilah started mirroring the breathing techniques. She looked around lost for a brief moment before landing her eyes on Luke. The chair was still on the floor, and she knelt to set it upright without removing her eyes from his back.

"Damn it, Luke!" Everleigh yelled at him. "What were you thinking?"

"I was thinking it'd be funny. I didn't expect all this." He continued to watch out the window until everything returned to normal.

Lilah was feeling more like herself and sat back down. It was a little bit funny now that she was aware it had been only a joke. Vampires were still a relatively new concept as far as she was concerned. There was a lot about them she didn't fully understand yet including their feeding habits.

"Man, just wait till the others get up." Luke clapped his hands and turned to face the ladies. His eyes were dancing with delight.

"You are not going to tell them about this," Everleigh ordered.

"Tell them? Hell, no! I'm going to show them!" Luke ran out of the room and back upstairs to where he and Meredith had spent the night.

There was no time for Lilah to dwell on his words. She put her palms flat on the table and concentrated on the space between them. Breathe in. Slowly blow out. Repeat. She knew someone would stop him if he seriously wanted to try to upset her again for sport. Breathe in. They would do it for their own benefit to not draw suspicion if nothing else. Breathe out.

"You're doing great, Lilah," Everleigh encouraged. "Can I do anything to help?"

With one hand, Lilah slowly pushed her coffee cup toward Everleigh.

Laughing, she stood up. "No problem. More caffeine coming up."

Lilah was still focused on her breathing when she heard her Uncle Todd, "How are you feeling?"

Her head cranked up so fast it almost hurt. "Uncle Todd!" she yelled and ran to give him a hug. "How did you get in?"

"Back door. Seems to be the way we're all getting around, isn't it?"

Lilah glanced at Everleigh, but chose to ignore the comment. "I'm feeling much better. Thank you," she smarted off at his lack of concern over why she had to sneak out in the first place.

"I'm not buying it," he snorted. "My car was almost blown off the road twice on the way here."

Everleigh sat Lilah's cup on the table and softly touched her shoulder to get her attention. "Come sit and relax."

Lilah sat down and held the cup in front of her. She didn't want to admit to anyone least of all her uncle that her power was out of her control. It would rationalize the use of medication to tame her. "I thought you were asking if I was recovering from what happened at the house."

"It is apparent you're feeling better if you're stirring up storms, and I'm glad you are well," Todd opened a cabinet and found the one with the mugs on his first try.

"Luke was being a trickster this morning and caught Lilah off guard," Everleigh tried to explain the reason behind Lilah's outburst of energy.

Todd poured a cup and joined them at the table. "He's always been a loose cannon, that one. I'll talk to him."

"How's mom and dad?" Lilah's voice was barely above a whisper. "Are they mad?"

"At you?" Todd's shock was evident. "No, they are not mad at you. They're fine. Uncle Brian, not so much."

Hearing her uncle's name, Lilah cocked her head to the side. It stirred something, but she couldn't quite recall what. Everything was returning to normal except her mind. She couldn't remember most of the day before, and she couldn't control her emotions as easily anymore.

"What is it?" Everleigh saw the turmoil on Lilah's face.

"Nothing. It's just that I can't remember, but it's like its right there."

"It's probably something to do with Brian then. Maybe you saw him do something." Todd took a drink. "If that's the case, it might be best if you don't remember."

Lilah put her face in her hands and groaned. She lowered her hands down, pulling at her skin until her face looked deformed like a horror movie monster. A sideways look at Everleigh and Todd showed they were amused by her gestures. She let her hands drop and gulped her refreshed coffee then slapped both hands on the table. "What's the plan for today?"

"What plan?" Todd asked.

"The wolves. That's why you're here isn't it?"

Todd glared at Everleigh who raised her hands in innocence. "Secrets aren't our way," she told him casually.

"It would've been learned anyway," he commented, looking troubled.

Lilah easily deduced that Everleigh had been told not to keep her up to speed on the new events, but it looked like it was more than that bothering her uncle. "What's wrong?"

"They...want a meeting," he looked her in the eye.

"Well, that's nothing. I mean, even I expected that." Lilah's brows wrinkled together expecting something big to fall from her uncle's mouth.

"Yes, well they want a few representatives from each Elemental group to meet."

"To speak for the group?" Everything was clicking for Lilah, and she really didn't understand her uncle's attitude toward it. Unless of course, her family wanted to stay out of mixing affairs with the others. *That was probably it,*' she confirmed to herself.

"Essentially, yes. It would be a chance to share what we know concerning the northern wolves movement, and to learn all the information they have."

Lilah put her hands together and clasped then unclasped her fingers repeatedly. "I don't understand how this is not a good thing," she finally stated.

"Each Elemental group is to choose two representatives to attend."

"Oh," Lilah had it now. "And there's only Luke since we don't know where Fire is hiding out."

"No, there is another vampire who can attend."

Lilah's eyes grew wide, and her entire posture straightened as though her eyelids were attached to a string that pulled everything up with them. "Another vampire?" she asked excitedly.

Todd waved his hand to dismiss the question. "That is not the concerning part of the meeting."

"But still. There's someone other than Luke? That is exciting news."

"Lilah," her uncle was growing frustrated with the conversation. "We have no way to determine how many vampires are remaining. They're in hiding and rightfully so. As we come together, more will come to light."

She thought it over and knew it was true. It had been mentioned in one of her family's meetings before she was sure of it. News of another vampire being located was still cause for excitement and almost celebration in her mind. It would do no good to gush about it with her uncle, but she would have time to talk it over with Everleigh later.

"Then what does concern you?"

"Apparently word of your abilities has already managed to spread." Todd took a drink of his coffee, and his face reflected the turmoil he felt. Theirs was not the kind to share so openly about themselves. It was understandable he didn't appreciate the gossip. "And they would like for you to be one of the representatives from Air."

"Me?" Lilah was in shock.

Todd looked at her apologetically. "I know a lot has been put on your shoulders since the move. Including the move for that matter. I hate to add more weight to the load."

"No, I can't do that. It should be you and one of the other Elders. Uncle Joseph maybe?"

Todd sucked his lower lip in and looked out the window. "Let me be perfectly plain. It's not exactly a request, Lilah. They're insisting on it."

"Why me? Get upset and throw one little storm, and people lose their minds."

Everleigh snickered which caught the looks of Todd and Lilah who didn't find anything funny about the conversation. "I'm sorry! Wrong time. I know. It's just that..." she didn't finish her thought.

"Just that what?" Lilah wanted to know.

"Oh, come on! Like I have to spell it out for you? It wasn't one little storm for one thing. Plus from what I've been told, your little storms are nothing the rest of your family could compete with on their own."

Lilah knew what she was saying was true as much as she would like to be able to deny it. She wished it wasn't that way, but there was nothing she could do to change it. "I don't want to do it."

Her uncle crossed his arms on the table. Lilah waited for him to speak, to object, but he didn't. Not saying anything bothered her more than if he argued with her over it. The silence became awkward, and Lilah was desperately trying to find something to talk about that wouldn't seem too obvious she was trying to change the subject.

"I know you don't want to, Lilah," her uncle finally said. "And I can't make you do it. All I ask is that you at least consider it carefully."

She agreed knowing her answer would still be no. "When is the meeting?"

"Late this afternoon. I will need an answer preferably by noon. The two chosen to attend will need to have time to prepare."

Time to hear the demands of the family is more like it. "By noon," she agreed.

"Well, now," he turned to Everleigh. "Where's that aunt of yours?"

"Haven't seen her. Probably still asleep."

"She won't be for long." He left and headed upstairs.

Everleigh waited until he was far from ear shot. "Why don't you want to attend? I would kill to go."

"It's not my thing. I don't like being the center of attention like that."

"Of course," Everleigh got up taking both of their mugs with her. "I bet none of you would be comfortable with that."

The words stung Lilah, but she didn't know why. It was the truth. "Why do you want to attend?"

"Mostly because I'm tired of being treated like a kid even though I'm grown. Know what I mean?" she asked, topping both mugs off with more coffee.

"Do I ever?"

Everleigh set the mugs on the table. "I'm going to make another pot. If Todd wakes my aunt, it'd be better to have it ready."

Lilah stared off down the front hall toward the door thinking about nothing until Jackson appeared. Her face lit up, "Good morning."

"Morning," he replied with a smile.

"I'm surprised you're up so early," Everleigh said from the counter.

He walked over and playfully nudged her side, tickling her. "But I love spending time with my Lee-Lee," he teased.

One look from Everleigh was enough for him to stop. He sat next to Lilah and leaned in to kiss her on the forehead.

Lilah saw Everleigh from the corner of her eye waving frantically at her. When she turned to look, Everleigh mouthed the words, "Tell him."

It caught Jackson's attention, and he turned. "What do you need, Lee-Lee?"

"You are one Lee-Lee away from being stabbed with a fork," she told him, pulling one from the drawer and holding it in front of her.

Jackson threw his hands up like he was being robbed. "Alright. Alright. Can't I be in a good mood?"

"Not before coffee," Lilah answered.

"It's illegal," Everleigh continued.

He hopped up and got a mug, waiting until just enough coffee had brewed to pour a cup then sat back down. "Something go down while I was asleep?"

Worry hit Lilah fast, but Everleigh motioned for her to breathe. "Why do you ask?"

"I woke to voices in the spare room that Meredith and Luke stayed in, but it didn't sound like Luke."

"Oh, that's my aunt's friend," Everleigh shrugged trying to make it out to be no big deal. "He came asking for her a little while ago."

"I'm surprised you haven't emptied the fridge looking for breakfast yet," Lilah wanted to change the topic.

"Too early. Not awake enough to eat yet," he said nonchalantly.

"You? Not wanting to eat? That's new," Lilah teased.

"Well, I'm going to hit the shower. I'll be back," Everleigh headed to the stairs giving Lilah a sly wink of encouragement.

Lilah tried to clear her mind and focus on what she would say to him...how she would say it. Once she had something that didn't sound too crazy, she had to try to see into the future. She needed privacy for that because if Jackson tried to get her attention while she was in her mind's eye, it could have an adverse effect.

She excused herself to use the bathroom where she sat on the edge of the tub. Her hands were shaking. She had never attempted to do this before by herself. There had always been someone around in case something went wrong, and it was usually her mom. Even then, she had only done it a handful of times.

Taking a deep breath, she closed her eyes and focused on what she needed to know. She saw herself leaving the room and pulling Jackson aside for a private chat. *'There's something I haven't told you,'* is how she began. Alternate outcomes were already popping up in her mind. Versions without this conversation, and versions with frenzied actions. It wouldn't be possible to follow them without going too far inside her mind. The focus could only be on telling Jackson the truth. This needed to be simple with as few parallel paths as possible for it to work without consequence.

The conversation seemed to be going well. Jackson wasn't at all frightened or panicked by the news. Lilah's eyes opened. She didn't risk going farther into the future and didn't feel like she needed to. If she had seen what was coming after their little talk, she might not have talked to him at all. She would have been too busy warning the others.

Lilah returned to the kitchen where Jackson was cooking several large pancakes on a long electric skillet. It seemed he was always munching. She had seen this timeline. *'Wait until he's eating,'* she reminded herself. You don't want the pancakes to burn or for him to be distracted by hunger.

"Want any?" he offered.

"No, thanks."

Jackson flipped the pancakes onto a plate and filled the pan with circles of batter for a second time.

She checked his cup, and it was empty. Taking the carafe from the coffee pot, she filled both cups then got the syrup out for him. This was so far one of the best scenarios she had seen. Honestly, it came down to whether he dropped the fork at this point. If he does, he will accidentally step on it before picking it up and slightly injure his foot. It distracts him throughout everything she says. If he doesn't, they're golden.

The pancakes finished cooking, and Jackson added them to his plate. He put the plate on the table and pulled out the drawer for a fork. With one hand he closed it, and with the other he gently tossed the fork up into the air. Lilah watched him and held her breath until he caught it easily and joined her at the table.

Anxiety was welling up inside her, but she needed to stay as calm as possible. A freak storm right now would easily be distracting enough to derail any chance of saying what she needed to say.

"Jackson," she wanted to get his attention before she started.

"Hmm?" he looked up with a mouth full of pancake.

"I need to talk to you about something."

Panic hit his eyes quick, and he swallowed. "About what?"

"There's something I haven't told you."

The panic increased momentarily then faded away just as quickly as it appeared. "You're a man?" he asked dryly.

"No," she said rolling her eyes.

"You're a witch!" his eyes twinkled at the joke.

"Close."

Jackson turned his head to the side intrigued. "How can you be close to being a witch?"

"It's a long story. I'm...different."

"You have a tail?"

As much as she was glad for his sense of humor at any other time, it was aggravating her this morning. Even knowing what was coming didn't help her appreciate the jokes.

Jackson put down his fork and gave her his full attention. "So if you're not a witch, what are you then? Vampire? Werewolf? Leprechaun?"

"I'm psychic."

He looked at her like she had told him it was Tuesday. It was noticeably not a big deal.

"I'm from a line of immortal psychics."

"Now we're talking," he rubbed his hands together. "How old are you?"

"Twenty-one."

"Not in appearance, but how long have you lived?" Jackson rephrased.

"Still twenty-one."

There was disappointment on his face. "I always wondered what it would be like to be with an older woman."

Lilah looked off annoyed while he laughed at his own joke. "You're taking this much better than I would have guessed." In fact, Jackson didn't seem to miss a beat over anything she was telling him.

Jackson shrugged. "My best friend is a witch. Now, my girlfriend is telling me she's a psychic who will live forever." He finished the pancakes with one large bite, and chewed it down. "Typical day as far as I'm concerned."

He carried his plate to the sink and rinsed it with hot water. There was a bowl of fruit on the counter, and he grabbed a banana before returning to Lilah.

"There's something else," she told him as soon as he sat back down.

"But wait!" He clapped his hands together loudly. "There's more!"

Lilah chewed the inside of her lip waiting for him to finish his infomercial imitation. This was harder for her to say than anything else because she felt like she was defining their relationship for the both of them without discussing it first.

"What?" he asked, but she was still contemplating her words. "I promise I'll be good," he added when she didn't answer him right away.

"My people have only one true match in their lifetime."

"Like a soul mate?"

"Exactly."

"And I'm yours? Is that what you're trying to say?"

She nodded because saying the word yes was suddenly very difficult for her. It was like owning some deep dark secret even though this should be considered amazing news.

Jackson's face lit up, and he took her hand. "I like that."

"Like what?"

"Knowing that we're soulmates. Not having to question if we're with the right person."

"Yeah, there is that."

"But it must suck for you."

"Why do you say that?"

Jackson went back to the counter with his cup for more coffee. "Finding me so young. If you're immortal, you will have the rest of time to live alone after me."

"After you die? Is that what you mean?"

He poured the last bit of coffee from the pot into the sink and rinsed it out before filling it to start a new pot. "Yeah, I have maybe fifty-sixty years if I'm lucky. Plus to other people, I will look like I'm your grandpa. They will think I'm rich, and you have a sugar daddy," he winked at her over his shoulder.

"Our matches are immortal too."

The water slowly poured into the pot. He grabbed the filter basket and started filling it with fresh grounds. It took an eternity for him to speak again, "How does that work?"

"I couldn't tell you how or why. It's the way of my line. We each have one true match, and when we find them, they is granted all of our abilities."

"So you're telling me I'm psychic."

"Baby steps," Lilah laughed easily at how well he was taking the news. "Let's start with simple things."

Jackson finished up and put the coffee away before joining her.

"I didn't expect this conversation to go this smoothly," she confessed to him.

"Why?"

"I don't know. I thought you'd think I was lying or something."

He reached over and lifted her hand to his lips kissing the back of it gently. "My oldest and dearest friend is a witch. She's told me that there is all manner of supernatural beings in this world who are nothing like the myths. Why wouldn't I believe you?"

Lilah hadn't thought of it like that. She leaned in hoping for a quick kiss while they had the room to themselves, but no such luck.

Todd came running down the stairs with the others in close pursuit. He ran into the kitchen, "We have to go! Now!"

They jumped from their seats with Jackson's chair crashing to the floor so hard Lilah was sure it busted. "What's happening?" she asked Todd who had already made his way toward the front door.

"I don't have all the details, but my hunch? Brian has been fed to the wolves."

Chapter Nineteen
Desperate Times

Leena sought refuge in the forests on the eastern edge of Bavaria nervously awaiting to hear word of Earth's fate. Fire had led his clan to safety days ago and had returned to help Earth free her coven. They should've returned by now, and with each passing hour, Leena worried she waited in vain.

There was no doubt Earth would come through it, but her coven was a different matter. The Elementals had taken so many hits in recent years. They feared losing any more of their numbers.

It had taken them several months to make it from their home in the western hemisphere across the Atlantic Ocean. That was after having to wait out the winter before it would be safe to venture this far. The last Return was the first Fire had attempted to make in many years. It was he who spoke of the fate befalling his people and Water. Earth had long been caught in the trenches of witch hunt after witch hunt, but most missed her and her coven completely as the ones murdered for being found guilty of witchcraft were almost never witches.

Upon arriving in Bavaria, they quickly learned that would not be the case here. Earth's family were being rounded up, home by home. The guards knew exactly what evidence to look for and where to find it. It was the same as what had happened to Fire's people. Leena watched in horror as Earth and her descendants were locked away awaiting sentencing that would be far from fair. They had to act fast if they hoped to save any of them.

Once they made it down from the cities above to the cover of the trees safely, Leena would help with the escape. Marcus had feared taking her with them and asked her to wait on lookout instead. This is where Leena stayed even now hoping for some sign of their arrival soon. She had no indication of what was happening. Marcus had blocked his mind from everyone because of the unknown threat trying to take the Elementals out.

Water's tribes were the only ones to escape unscathed. The wolves were being hunted by the towns that dotted the countryside, but their reluctance to stay in any one place for long had saved them this time. The tribes that had settled the area had already moved on before the persecution began.

She tried again with her mind to hear something. Any small sign that the rescue party would be making their way to the checkpoint safely. It was no use. She could sense nothing. There was one other option that she had been trying to convince herself to avoid. Three days had passed since Marcus and Fire left her behind to aid Earth. *'It was time,'* she decided.

Leena sat beneath several tall spruce trees and closed her eyes to concentrate. This had to be done delicately and was dangerous to do alone which made it even more necessary for her to practice extreme caution. Emptying her mind of everything, she tried to project herself into the future where they would join her in the forest. There was nothing on her first attempt. The only imagery she saw was her continued wait with very little variation between the pathways.

It frustrated her to see nothing new and only her continued wait in the future. It gave her no information to determine what was happening in the village on the ridge above her. The only thing she would be able to foresee was their return, and that would only be shown to her if it happened swiftly enough before the pathways pulled her down, drowning her in her mind and trapping her there. It had happened to one other before her. Their son Otto had met this fate many years ago.

The only way for her to see how the others were faring would be if she could scry a future where she went to their aide. It would be far riskier, but she felt there was no other choice. It was this or leave the shelter of the forest and actually seek them out. This would have to be brief, and she would have to plot it carefully. If only she could pick up on the other Elements or their people, it would be much easier.

Leena shook her head. If I could pick up on the other Elements, this wouldn't be necessary. She needed a plan since she didn't know where to look inside the village. The least risk would be if she first ventured in her mind to get the layout of the area. Then she could try again once she knew where to concentrate her efforts. She would stick to the shadows and survey the landscape, so she would know where to look for them next time she plotted hoping she may stumble on some clue that would lead her to them.

After trying to reach Marcus again without success, she closed her eyes and saw into a future where she went to find him. The ripples into the timelines were minimal as she saw herself begin to make her way to the village. There along the cobblestone streets the ripples became more frequent, but she had nothing yet. Not one indication of what was happening to her love and their companions. Leena continued to search the village hoping for something that would direct her on where to look for them.

A carriage came careening out from a side street onto the road near her. The horses were out of control, and the buggy tipped to the side. The occupants cried out, and the horse dragged the driver away through the street. His blood curdling screams stopped forever after hitting a statue as the horse made a sharp turn sending him flying to the side.

There had been a torch ablaze near where the carriage toppled, and it caught fire quickly. Soon chaos was everywhere as those inside scrambled to get free. Leena saw every version of these events including ones where the carriage managed to make the curve even with the runaway horses leading the way. The pathways spread around her like wildfire. It began as only a few then one fleeting moment created a number so vast and so quickly, she couldn't return to her body in time. In her mind, she saw herself standing on the edge of the cobblestone street where her form was deteriorating as it broke apart being wrenched down all the different timelines at once. It was growing more shadowy, and the rate would increase by the minute as new offshoots continued to branch along each one creating an endless array of possibilities.

In the woods, her body convulsed and thrashed along a spruce root that stuck up through the ground. It would be minutes before she lost consciousness and lay on the forest floor in a virtual sleep. By morning, they would learn if his undefined immortality extended to her as his match, or if there were in fact limits on her as there were on their children. That is of course unless Marcus found her first.

MARCUS TRIED TO REACH his wife to let her know they would soon be nearing the forest, but he couldn't make contact. He motioned for everyone to stop while he tried again. He was leading the way for Earth's coven with Fire bringing up the rear. Their efforts would be in vain if the woods were found to be compromised when they arrived. Taking a moment to make sure his mind was clear, he focused and tried again. Leena couldn't be located anywhere.

A tremble went through his lower lip, and he clamped his mouth tightly to suppress the scream building in his throat. As an Element, he could not be blocked by his family the same as they could each other. There were only three souls on this earth whose thoughts were safe from him, and two of them were behind him trying to reach the woods before they were all caught. If he couldn't find Leena in his mind's eye, there were only two explanations. Either she was unconscious, or she was dead.

He balled his fists and place one in his mouth biting his hand until he drew blood to avoid releasing the cries that would lead to their capture. An empty rage ignited within him, and he raced to the tree line to see what became of his beloved. Twenty yards from where the road curved along the edge of the forest, he went sprawling to the ground knocked down by an unknown force. It held him tight as he bucked and fought to break free.

"Be still," Fire bellowed in a hushed voice. "You are behaving like a madman."

1. http://www.clker.com/cliparts/7/6/9/b/13309573511112670181decorative-lines-2_large-md.png

"It's Leena," Marcus gasped.

Footfalls were just behind them when Earth breathlessly said, "Why didn't you say something, Marcus? We will help. What do you need us to do?"

Fire began to lift his weight, and Marcus sprung into motion headed to the trees again. There was no time to explain what was happening. He needed to act. He could hear Fire directly behind him, and he was sure Earth was following as fast as she could manage.

Inside the cover of trees, Marcus scanned the area looking for a sign of what befell his wife. There had to be a clue.

"Marcus-"

"Find her!" he interrupted Fire.

Fire's eyes filled with concern as Earth caught up to them. Marcus headed farther into the woods while Fire told Earth to help look for Leena.

It didn't take long to find her laying on the ground convulsing. Her condition could only be the result of one thing. Marcus let out a low whistle for his companions to trace to him, and he collapsed onto his knees. He had only seen this once before with Otto, and his fate had not been pleasant nor did it end well. They knew the risks of looking into the future which is why they only did it when absolutely necessary.

"What happened?" Earth asked.

"She's trapped in her mind's eye," replied Marcus as he rubbed his forehead trying to think of a plan.

"Mind's eye? Trapped?" Fire asked.

"It can happen if we're not careful when we try to see the future."

"What can happen?" Fire didn't know what Marcus meant.

Earth stepped forward and knelt by Leena lifting her head to her lap. "This," Earth told him.

Fire didn't have the gift of sight like Marcus and couldn't use any other powers of divination like Earth. He didn't understand that the future was never a solid line one must follow. It was a labyrinth of maze like paths ever bending and changing.

"We will save her," she told Marcus.

"I might be able to reach her if I..." his voice trailed off.

"If you what?" Fire was ever the pesky curious one.

Marcus shook his head. "I'm not sure it can be done."

"Go to her, Marcus," Earth guided. "You have to try."

Holding Leena's hands in his own, he leaned his head down to hers. Before their heads touched, he paused and looked at Earth. "If my light dims, pull me back."

Earth nodded.

"What light? Will someone explain this to me?" Fired demanded, but as he finished asking his questions, he saw it. A blue light began to shine from Marcus' forehead where he rested it against Leena's. Slowly it grew brighter until it was a ball of blue electric waves about the size of his head.

Fire dropped to the ground and raised a knee in front of him resting his arm on it. "Now I've seen everything," he said to no one at all.

"Not quite everything," Earth told him. "Come. Help me hold her legs, so she doesn't knock him off of her."

He did as Earth instructed kneeling by Leena's feet and holding both ankles steady, being careful not to apply too much pressure. "Do you know what is going on here?" he asked her.

"Yes."

A moment passed while he waited. "Would you be so kind as to fill me in?" he asked with growing impatience and crossness.

"What don't you understand?" she asked, genuinely unsure because matters like these were more commonplace in her experience.

"Oh, I don't know. Why does Leena act as though she is possessed by an evil spirit? And perhaps you could explain why our friend is glowing like the lights of the north? All of it, woman! I don't understand any of it."

Earth glared at him. "When Leena tried to see into the future, she went too far. There were too many alternate timelines. This is what happens to them."

"How does he get her back?"

"He doesn't," Earth said solemnly. "At least there is no known way to save her."

"Is he seeing into the future then?" Fire tried to understand.

"The future she saw...the place where she is trapped...it is now the past. There is no way to reach her except through her mind. It may work." Earth didn't sound hopeful.

"What will happen to her?"

Earth looked over the top of Marcus' head and even in the darkness, she was able to meet Fire's eyes. "If he can't bring her back, she will die."

"But she is immortal."

"Yes, but she is not an Element like you or I. There are ways in which she can perish."

"She can die like their children," Fire understood all too well that the Element's limitless immortality didn't carry over to their people.

"No one knows for sure if she can. No one wants to find out." Earth corrected him.

"Will this work?" he asked fascinated by the light surrounding Marcus and Leena.

"It has never been attempted."

Marcus' voice rang out. "I see her! She is stuck!"

"Where?" Fire asked.

"In the village near the fountain."

"Stay!" Earth ordered before Fire had a chance to react to the news.

"I can get there in no time," he insisted.

"Her body is here, you fool! What is trapped is her consciousness."

The light started to reduce in size. "I'm not sure I can get her to snap out of it," Marcus told them.

"His light," Fire looked at Earth worried.

"There's still a little time left."

"A little time for what?" Fire yelled.

"Time for him to try before I separate him from her."

"What would happen if you don't?"

Earth looked at Marcus. The light was now half the size it had been. "Marcus will become trapped in her mind alongside her."

"But Marcus cannot die. This we know," Fire declared, growing more agitated at his lack of understanding of the situation.

"True, but he will be trapped until she does."

Fire watched the ball of light reduce smaller and smaller. In slow motion, he saw Earth's hand begin to raise to push Marcus back from his wife. He took action.

In a blink, he hit Marcus off of Leena hard enough to send him sprawling into the trunk of a nearby tree knocking him out. He bit into his wrist and pulled Leena's head back dripping his blood into her mouth until he was sure it had flowed down her throat. Then he grabbed her head and twisted it hard breaking her neck. All of this he had accomplished before Earth could react to him jumping up from the ground.

"What have you done?" she screamed as she looked at Marcus and Leena both lying perfectly still on the ground.

"I found a different solution."

Earth put both hands over her mouth, and her breathing quickened to a near hyperventilation state. "Marcus will never forgive you."

"I beg to differ. I think he will be quite pleased with the end result."

Earth rose to her feet and squared off against Fire making him laugh that she actually thought he could be a threat to her. "He will never forgive you turning his wife into a vampire," she hissed.

"Marcus will never know unless you tell him."

The laughter that flowed from Earth's mouth was hysterical as one would sound who had gone insane. "I won't have to tell him! I'm pretty sure he will figure it out."

"Would you think it through? A broken neck can't kill Air. I saved her and got her out of wherever it was that had her trapped by doing it."

Earth's eyes lowered, and she circled around, trying to decide if it was possible. "Then why feed her first? Why give her your blood?"

"You said it would kill her if she stayed trapped. It happened before. To Otto, right?" he nodded. "I know about Otto although I never truly understood what happened. I gave her my blood in case whatever was happening was too far gone for her to come back from it."

"And if it was? What then? She is still a vampire," Earth spat as she paced around worried about her friends.

Fire shook his head. "Only if she were human. In our kind," he said, motioning to all of them, "The vampirism has to be triggered."

Earth stopped walking. It was true. Leena would have to feed again for it to trigger. Humans would wake from their death needing blood to survive the transformation. Elementals did not. She would survive the transformation if there was in fact one taking place without the need for blood. Fire wouldn't be triggered in her until she drank blood, and not just any blood. She would have to drink again from Fire himself to make the transformation complete.

He could see that Earth was realizing what he already knew. "You see? A different solution."

"But Marcus can read her mind."

"Leena has no memory of it. There is nothing for him to discover."

"And he can't read us because we're Elements," Earth began to understand.

"Exactly. Marcus will never know unless you tell him like I already said."

"Tell me what?" Marcus groaned from the ground nearby.

Fire's eyes pleaded with Earth not to say a word.

"This fool," Earth said as she bent to assist Marcus into a sitting position. "He panicked when you started to move away from Leena, and his sudden jerking sent you flying into the tree."

Marcus looked up at Fire, "You what?"

He played along. "When you moved, I thought you were starting to convulse. I tried to grab you back, but...I panicked and forgot my strength."

It looked like Marcus wasn't believing their ruse then Leena groaned. All else was forgotten. He went to her side and lifted her up until her head was to his chest. "Shh, my love. Be still. Don't move," he told her.

Leena's eyelids batted several times before opening for good. She looked around vaguely unsure of what had happened.

Earth and Fire stood over her with baited breath to see how it would play out.

"You're going to be fine, my love."

"What happened? I remember the village." She gasped and turned up to see her husband's face. Tears fell as she said, "I'm sorry."

"It's fine. I brought you back."

Leena clung to him staining his shirt with her tears. Her mouth was parched, and she licked her lips. She grimaced, "I taste blood."

Fire sucked in his breath waiting to be discovered so soon.

Marcus pulled his wife's chin down gently and looked into her mouth by the light of the moon. "You probably bit your tongue during your ordeal. No bother. If that is the worst you suffer, we are fortunate."

Earth shot Fire a glance and leaned in to whisper, "You lucky devil."

"What was that?" Marcus asked.

"I was saying we are lucky," Earth told him.

Fire smiled impishly, "How very true."

Leena said up, and rubbed the back of her neck moaning in pain. "I feel like my head has been cut off and reattached."

"You were thrashing about quite violently," Marcus offered as an explanation.

"I'm going to go check on my family," Earth made her exit.

Fire stood awkwardly feeling like Marcus could see into his soul. "I think I should go too in case there's trouble," he told him then followed Earth out of the woods.

Chapter Twenty
Meeting of the Elementals

Everyone was already out of sight before they got their coats and jumped into Jackson's truck. "I get to be a part of this now, right?" he asked, pulling out of the driveway.

Lilah looked at him confused.

"Or am I only dropping you off?"

She smiled at him. "You are a part of everything from here on out."

He shifted the truck into drive and sped off down the street. In the hurried frenzy over Uncle Todd's news and the rush to leave, neither of them noticed that Everleigh wasn't among the group who had left first.

The tension from the farmhouse could be felt a mile out. Lilah recognized it as soon as she sensed it.

Jackson groaned, "I think I'm going to be sick."

What a time for this to happen she thought hoping it was just nerves getting the best of him.

"Maybe the milk I used in the pancakes was bad."

It struck her then from out of nowhere. "You're not used to handling what you're capable of yet. It's the tension that's making your stomach flip."

"What tension?"

"From the farmhouse," she said as he turned onto the drive.

"I could feel it all the way back at the edge of town."

"I know. Things must be very bad up there." The beautiful house loomed in front of her, but it looked more like a frightening backdrop now.

They were the last to arrive, and the others had already gone inside. Lilah walked up to the house uncertain how she felt about returning after what happened. She was equally uncertain about how she felt about her Uncle

Brian and what would happen to him. As soon as the thought entered her mind, she dismissed it. This wasn't their way. In time, they would be cordial again, but she would never trust him.

The porch swing still hung haphazardly with one side touching the wood flooring beneath it. It's funny the things you take notice of in extreme situations. The swing should be the last thing to mind, but she still wondered why no one had gotten around to fixing it yet. There were close to twenty people in the house. Someone could do something for a change besides sit around the living room arguing all day.

"Are we going in?" Jackson snapped her out of her thoughts.

She took a deep breath and swung the door wide open, "Yeah, come on."

No one took notice as they stepped into the room. Everyone was talking at once. Voices were growing louder and louder until they were virtually yelling as they tried to be heard over the din. It was mass chaos.

A sharp whistle shattered the room, and everyone stopped in their tracks.

They all turned their eyes to Jackson including Lilah who was just as surprised by his intrusion.

"Hey," he waved and smiled at everyone.

The faces in the room were still focused on him, but no one returned his greeting.

"Now we can hear a little better. Don't you think?" Jackson shifted his weight nervously.

"What happened?" Lilah asked the crowd.

The murmur started at once with everyone trying to state their view on what had occurred. Jackson whistled again.

"One at a time," Lilah announced after he regained their attention.

Todd approached them. "Brian is missing. No one has seen him since shortly after I left last night."

"They just noticed him gone?" Jackson asked.

It wouldn't be difficult on a normal day since there are so many here Lilah thought, but he would have been the focal point of everyone's argument. "Why didn't they tell us sooner?"

"From what I gather, they thought he left voluntarily. He went outside for some fresh air and never came back." Todd explained.

"And he's not with the rest of the family at Aunt Sophia's?" Lilah knew that option had certainly been exhausted, but there was no harm in asking.

"He'd never step foot in the same house as Chloe. You know that," her dad looked defeated.

"But, yes, we did check," her mom added before Lilah could ask again.

"Why do you think he's in trouble and didn't just leave? For good. He could've left and blocked us all." Lilah felt like she had missed some important detail.

Her dad walked to her and took her hand. "He's been trying to communicate with Abby. The messages have been difficult for her to receive, so they must be hard for him to send. It would appear as though someone is blocking his telepathy externally, and he's in distress."

"What do you mean difficult to receive?" Lilah asked.

"They cause her migraines."

Lilah's mouth fell open. Her people didn't suffer migraines. Their minds, with all their psychic abilities, were always sharp and pain free.

There was a knock at the door which made Lilah jump. Worried looks flashed between the people in the room as they were not sure who it could be.

Jackson immediately opened the door without caution causing many people to jump to their feet.

Lilah wanted to move to stop him, but it was already too late. She held her breath until she heard him speak.

"Hello," Jackson greeted warmly, "Lee-Lee."

The entire room collectively exhaled when they realized the person on the porch was not an enemy.

Lilah approached her new friend and apologized for not realizing she wasn't already here. There was little time to fill Everleigh in on any of the new events before the arguing picked up again, and her attention was once more focused on the matter at hand.

Behind her, she could hear Jackson lay it all out for her in a nutshell that took about five seconds to convey.

"There's more," Abby said. "I think he's trying to reach me, but he's being blocked somehow. It's giving me massive migraines."

Lilah was confused. Their people never got migraines. It was too hard to think over the noise in the room.

The arguing was getting out of hand. It didn't take more than seconds for it to grow to a fever pitch. Air had never been singled out before for an attack by anyone. This was unchartered territory for them, and none among them seemed to be handling it well.

Lilah motioned to Jackson who let out another shrill whistle. The fighting stopped, and everyone looked to her expecting her to have something important to say on the subject. There was nothing new for her to contribute, and she stood there awkwardly feeling the stares from her family until Meredith stepped forward, offering a suggestion.

They listened as the idea was proposed for someone in Air to search the minds of the rest of the family to see if anyone knew anything about Uncle Brian's disappearance. Uncle Joseph was in firm and fast agreement, wanting to be the one to check considering he was the eldest of them present. There were nineteen of them present, so it wouldn't be an easy or quick task, but it would give them the answers they wanted. Most of the family were only pointing fingers at each other. They thought one of the others had to know more than they let on because that was the only way the wolves would be able to find them.

As she was trying to figure out why no one thought to accuse the southern tribes, she heard her name. Uncle Todd was suggesting she be the one to search the minds of her family, and he would in turn read hers when she was finished. *"Why me?"*

"I think you know the answer to that," her uncle answered while he defended his plan to his brother Joseph. *"Your powers are greater. They'd have a harder time hiding something from you."*

Meredith was standing back watching the decision being made, so she took advantage of the few seconds she had to approach her. "Meredith, if my family knows nothing-" she began.

"Already on it," Meredith told her, lifting a finger to quiet her. "I'm working on something to see just how far we can trust the newcomers who are supposed to be on our side."

Uncle Todd called for her, "Lilah!" He nodded when she looked his way signaling she was to begin.

Lilah went through her family one by one. It was the most difficult thing she'd ever had to do. The process was long. She had to first check to make sure they weren't keeping part of their mind closed off. They would be capable of blocking part of their memory from her, but allowing her to see the rest. They could even create a false memory for her to see. Once that was done, it didn't take long to learn that no one had anything to do with it. Most of them didn't even realize Uncle Brian was no longer on the property until that morning. They assumed he was hiding somewhere on the grounds.

That wasn't the hard part. Everyone had an opinion on what he had done, and it was next to impossible to not find out what their opinions were, given what she was doing.

"It was frightening to be around her."

"He did us a favor, really."

"If he had talked to us, he'd have found most were in agreement with him."

"The only reason anyone is mad is because he didn't have prior consent. The out lash against him was ridiculous."

There were so many more thoughts even worse than those. Most of her family felt the only wrong he was guilty of was not getting the family approval first. It was clear they would have given him that approval too. Aside from her parents and her Uncle Todd, the only ones against it completely were Sara and Gene. If it had gone to a vote, her family would have helped him subdue her through medication.

By the time she was through, an uneasiness had taken hold in her gut and was making her feel physically ill. She was still calm. There was no threat of her losing control. At least not for the time being. But she wanted to be as far away from these people as she could which meant going back to Jackson's. As hurt as she was, she wouldn't run away when her family's very survival was at stake.

At the end, it was Uncle Todd's turn. Lilah sat on the recliner to relax while he went through to make sure she hadn't covered for anyone. It might be petty, but she screamed the hurtful thoughts of others at him making sure he heard them as she did. When he was done, he let the others know that it was true. No one here had helped the wolves capture Brian.

"How did they know where to find him, then," Joseph asked still skeptical.

"That's easy," Matt stepped up.

The family recoiled collectively to the sight of a wolf addressing them. Some prejudices never die.

"You've said the wolf movement from the north has stopped. Correct?"

"Yes," Todd answered. "They stopped a few hours northwest of here yesterday."

"They aren't aware you have figured out a way to track them. They believe they're undetected."

"We were hoping for that advantage," Todd was the only one engaging him.

"We may learn more when we've had a chance to talk to the tribes from the south, but I believe it's a temporary base. This is the location they've chosen to plan their next move," Matt explained.

"That was our thinking too," Todd looked at his family nodding.

"They would send out scouts to not only find you and the witches, but to gather as much information as they can about your numbers and preparations."

"How would they find us?" Abby asked.

"I'm not sure," Matt was honest.

"There could be a mole," Uncle Joseph snipped.

"It's possible," Todd told him. "And it could be one of us."

"Hardly! Not with the brain scans the two of you forced on the lot of us," Joseph wagged his fingers at Todd and Lilah.

"I believe you were in favor of the idea, Joe," Todd said, knowing his brother hated the shortening of his name. "Besides, we only read through last night. The information could've been leaked at any time even before we arrived."

There was a low buzz like an electric current that went through them. It was as if they at once couldn't believe the hint of an accusation was there, but also the understanding that the traitor could be in the room with them.

"It could've been Brian," Myles contributed.

Todd pointed at him excitedly. "Yes, it could have been him. The image Abby picked up on could be a red herring."

"What do you think?" Abby asked Matt.

"I wouldn't rule it out necessarily. I was going to say it was more pure dumb luck than anything. Brian went outside alone while the scouts were near, and they took advantage of the situation."

"You think it was happenstance," Myles was thinking it over.

"I did, but what you've suggested makes sense too. He could have left voluntarily to join them, and they're sending signals to throw you off," Matt furrowed his brow and looked away.

"But you don't think he did?" Myles saw the look on Matt's face.

Matt took a moment before answering. "I think everyone is already upset concerning the events that involve Brian. It would be easy to place another strike against him. I don't want anyone to make rash assumptions which could affect him horribly only to find out their wrong later."

"Spoken like a wise man," Todd looked approvingly at Matt. "Let's put our heads together and see what we can find out," he said to his family.

After the discussion started, Lilah told her parents she would be heading back to Jackson's house if they needed her. It was obvious they didn't want her to go, but they weren't going to try to stop her.

Todd reminded Lilah they would be meeting soon. He wanted time to talk to her alone beforehand.

"Do we know who is representing the witches?" Lilah asked.

"I believe it will be Eloise and Rita, but I could be wrong."

Lilah was stunned. "I thought for sure Meredith would be one of the two."

"She will be representing the vampires," Todd informed her.

"But she's not a heriditary."

"There are too few left to be found." Todd's gaze fell from the weight of his words.

LILAH NERVOUSLY FOLLOWED her Uncle Todd into the apartment building where the meeting would be held. Luke, Matt and Rita were with them. Matt was chosen since he had already established some form of trust with some of the Elementals in the area. Meredith was bringing Eloise, and they might already be here. She wasn't sure. The only person she didn't already know was Irving who was the leader of the southern tribe.

Todd knocked on the door which was swiftly opened by a much older man. He appeared to be in his late fifties at least. The five of them filed inside. No one else had arrived yet. The wolf leader motioned for them to have a seat at the large table in the corner of the apartment. It only seated six, but two off chairs had been pulled up to accommodate everyone. Luke sat in one of the smaller chairs ensuring Meredith a good seat, and Lilah took the other. It wouldn't be wise to make Eloise feel out of place from the stories she had heard.

Moments later, Meredith and Eloise joined them. Once everyone was present, the old man began by introducing himself. "My name is Irving, and I represent Water. I have been the leader of the tribes in the southern region since my father's death almost ten years ago. Each of the tribes has a pack leader who reports to me. They have entrusted me to speak for them at this meeting."

They went to his right which meant Lilah would speak last. It was a blessing and a curse. It gave her a little time to listen to the others to figure out exactly what she would say, but she would rather get it over with first.

---

1. http://www.clker.com/cliparts/7/6/9/b/13309573511112670181decorative-lines-2_large-md.png

"My name is Luke, and I represent Fire. There are very few of my kind left whose whereabouts are known and hard to find representatives."

"I am Eloise, the leader of my coven. I represent Earth."

It was Todd's turn next followed by Matt. The nerves were mounting inside Lilah as she regretted not asking her uncle what she should say.

"I am Meredith. I was born an Earth Elemental, but I am here today to represent Fire. I was turned over three centuries ago. As Luke stated, their numbers are low. I am here to be their second representative since there are no others stepping forward."

Lilah barely breathed while Rita spoke. She was next and had nothing to say except her name and Elemental faction. The others all had a little something extra to bring to the table. They were a leader, or among the last of their kind. What was she supposed to say? *'Hi, I'm Lilah, and I've had my powers less than a week.'*

All eyes were on her. "I'm Lilah," she began.

"Lilah," Irving drew it out like he was savoring the taste of her name on his tongue. "We've heard all about you Lilah."

The tone of his voice made her feel very uncomfortable.

"I'm glad you could make it."

"I was under the impression my presence was a requirement." Lilah heard a couple gasps, but couldn't be sure who they were from as her eyes were staring directly into Irving's. One thing was certain about her powers. They definitely increased her confidence.

A slow smile formed on Irving's lips. "And this is why, Lilah. Not only does talk of what you are capable of precede you, but you are a force without your abilities."

Lilah took it as a compliment even though she would bet that some of the others didn't see it as such.

"Let's begin," Irving addressed the group. "Tell me what you already learned, so I know where to start."

The Elementals looked at each other unsure who should go first. Luke leaned forward. "The vampires have been killed at an alarming rate. Fire's blood has a mind control effect when consumed. We believe this blood is being used against our own kind, but..."

Irving waited before encouraging him to finish. "Take your time."

"I've never heard of our blood being used against us before, and it would mean..." Once again, Luke stopped mid-sentence putting his face in his hands.

"Go on," Irving told him.

Luke sat up and looked down at his hands. "Fire is involved."

Irving smiled creepily at Luke. "That's right."

"They have Fire, then?" Luke asked.

"The wolves don't have him. At least they didn't the last time I was updated on anything, but they do have access to his blood."

"What? How is that possible if they don't have him?" Luke's voice was growing loud to match his anger.

"In time, son," the creepy wolf leader told him.

It was Todd who spoke next mainly to give Luke a chance to control his emotions. "The wolves from the north have set up a base camp about three hours northwest of here."

"A base camp?" Irving questioned.

"For lack of a better term," Todd continued. "We know their plan is to come after the witches next then it will be our turn."

"Good." Irving told the group. "You are mostly caught up to speed. We need to work together if we are to defeat them. Their numbers are vast."

"How did their tribes get so large?" Eloise asked, but Lilah caught a fleeting look in her eyes that made her believe she already knew the answer.

"They've been turning a lot of people the last few years," Irving answered her with a smile.

"That is what I struggle with understanding," Matt contributed. "It's hard to create wolves."

"Explain." Meredith was demanding an answer more than asking a question.

"Water has to be in wolf form to create new wolves. Attacks almost always result in death. For every new wolf, there would need to be a hundred dead. Those numbers would be noticed."

"Very true," Irving nodded. "They have devised a way to amplify their success. That's not important now. What is important is how we are to defeat them."

"Do you have any ideas?" Todd asked.

"There are many ways to defeat the wolves. Their advantage is purely numbers. Taking out Fire was a strategic move that is going to play into their favor immensely."

Luke tensed up at the words. "Why would they want to attack us? Any of us," he added looking at the other Elementals in the room.

Irving stroked his beard while considering his reply. "It isn't Water who wants to destroy the rest of you."

"Then who?" Rita's voice hinted at irritation.

"That I don't know. I'm not entirely certain how the wolves were convinced to take part in these attacks, but I do know they are working for somebody."

"That makes absolutely no sense. Who could possibly have the power and influence to stage something of this size?" Todd was not buying the theory.

Lilah and her uncle had agreed to leave their minds open to each other before they went to the meeting to be able to communicate at all times. His opinion was loud and clear. It was a smoke screen. This old man wanted to throw everyone off the trail, so Todd believed he was feeding them false information. Todd wasn't one hundred percent sure the two regions of wolves were working together, but this man definitely was trying to protect the wolves reputation.

"How?" Lilah's voice came out low and weak. She cleared her throat and tried again. "Who would know about us?"

"What kind of absurd question is that?" Luke snipped.

Lilah shifted in her seat nervously.

"The entire world knows about us!" he continued.

This is why she had been against attending the meeting. The fear of not being able to contribute, or not being taken seriously if she did. The door wasn't far away from her, and she couldn't take her eyes off of it.

"Let her speak!" Eloise scolded Luke. "Go on, child. What are you trying to say?"

"The whole world doesn't know about us. They know the myths and fairy tales they've been fed. Luke is a vampire, but the sun doesn't faze him."

"I am not a vampire," he spat the word as if merely saying it was disgusting. "I am a Fire descendant."

"A Fire descendant who can use his echo command to control the minds of others. You're a damn vampire. Now shut it!" Meredith ordered him.

Luke leaned in his chair hooking his thumbs around the frame of the back, looking up at the ceiling, but he kept quiet after that.

"Who would know about our existence and want to eliminate us?" Lilah asked then continued. "With enough pull to sway an entire Elemental group?"

"Not an entire group," the leader of the southern tribe quipped.

"Well, mostly then. It would have to be one of us."

"How's that?" Eloise asked.

"It would have to be someone with extensive knowledge of who we are and how to harm us. Someone who would know how to turn Water against the rest of us."

"There's always been an underlying quarrel with the wolves," Matt reminded her.

"There are those who have issue with the wolves, Matt. I won't act like that's not true. But wouldn't it be us attacking them?" Lilah pointed out.

"She has a point. Just because some factions hold them responsible to this day isn't a reason for what they are planning," Rita told her fiancé.

Eloise leaned in and clasped her hands in front of her mouth. "Lilah, I agree. If Water is taking their orders from outside their Elemental, it would have to be one of ours controlling the situation." It looked like there was more Eloise wanted to say, but she held back.

"It's not mine," Luke snapped, leaning back into the conversation. "I can count on one hand the number of Fire I know are remaining, and it wasn't any of us."

"That you know are remaining," Matt emphasized.

"It would seem unlikely," Eloise agreed.

"That leaves Air and Earth," Irving stated.

"Or Water," Lilah added.

"I thought it was clear they were working for someone else," Luke told her patronizingly.

"It could still be someone in their Elemental calling the shots."

Irving leaned in on his elbow and was obviously preparing to give Lilah a piece of his mind when Eloise stepped in.

"We do need to figure out this mastermind. It will give us a leg up. We also need a game plan. How can we defeat them?"

"With the witches of course," Irving answered while glaring at Lilah. "Earth is the only one with the numbers now. The rest of your people need to join us."

Eloise looked forlorn. "I can't force anyone to fight."

"You need to try a rally cry," Todd encouraged.

"I've been in contact with many covens. Some are in hiding already. They're scared."

"We're all scared," Irving turned to her his voice softer. "But if we don't try, we're defeated already."

Eloise nodded. "I will do my best. How much time do you think we have? It would be best to meet with them in person. There are a lot of areas to cover."

Irving raised his hands and shook his head. "It's hard to say at this point. If I hear anything, I will let you know. They will soon realize our involvement here and cut off communications with us."

"I suppose I will just have to visit as many as I can until I'm needed back here."

Meredith turned her entire body to face Eloise. "I know you and I have had our differences," she started to say.

"I will appreciate all the help I can get. Perhaps, you and Everleigh can visit some covens together." Eloise smiled.

Lilah's mouth dropped in shock. This was not the Eloise she had heard about where Meredith was concerned. It was further evidence of the dire straits they were all in for her to be willing for them to work together.

"Alright, then," Irving clapped his hands. "Let's talk plans."

They strategized for almost two hours. Most of the time was spent arguing over mindless details. The biggest key was gathering as many Earth Elementals as possible. The mixed blood in the southern tribes and covens meant there were a large number of witches who could use their magic on Water.

The benefits to that were endless. Divination spells to learn their next move. Tracking spells to find them. Blocking spells. Revealing spells. If there was something anyone could find helpful, those Earth covens would be able to find a way. The rest of the witches could assist making the spells more powerful.

There were rumors sweeping through the south that Wolves were using the blood of Fire to make new vampires and control them. This was the most frightening piece of information they heard. Water was smart going after the vampires first. In physical combat, they were the closest match to Water. It would be harder, but not impossible for them to defeat Water without the assistance of Fire. But to go against them both? It felt like a suicide mission.

Irving wanted to gather enough Intel to plan a surprise attack. That would be their most likely chance at victory. They would need to be in control of where and when they strike and would have to take out or overpower as many as they could at the start. Once Water was able to regroup and rally against them, there would be no turning back. Their plan had to be solid.

For now, everything hinged on gathering as many of Earth as possible. Eloise and Meredith planned to leave shortly after the meeting to convince them to fight with Everleigh in tow. They would target the most influential covens first. The ones who could potentially sway others to join the cause as well. It was the best way to recruit the most numbers, but if they didn't succeed, the backlash would be ruinous. Newer covens would never come if the others bowed out.

Luke was not without his own mission. He had to find any surviving members of his clan that he could. It would be difficult. Meredith had already used locator spells trying to hunt down remaining vampires with mixed results. This time even Eloise offered her assistance in getting Luke on the right track.

The meeting adjourned with Irving requesting the eight of them send regular updates of the progress they were making to each other. Lilah wondered if he had real military experience, but never asked. Everyone had the mindset of going to war with Water, but Irving took it to another level. It frightened her at times, and maybe that was all the reason for his approach. Maybe he just needed to drive the gravity of the situation home for everyone.

Chapter Twenty-One
Finding Fire

The seven Elementals who left the apartment did so in silence. Without discussing it beforehand, they all met up at Eloise's house. There would be much to get done before anyone could begin their quest to expand their numbers. Lilah thought it strange her uncle would go there knowing they couldn't assist with the spells, but she supposed there were other tasks they could do to help out.

She was the last one in the house, and it was already filled with voices overlapping each other. There were several young witches filled with excitement over finding out they would be doing real spell work tonight instead of merely learning about it. Eloise and Meredith were doling out orders to everyone to collect ingredients and prepare a space.

Voices like that act like a muse for Air. It's like a crowded restaurant at peak dinner time when the patrons are all talking at their tables. The noise level rises creating a swirl of conversation all around. You may hear bits and pieces of it from time to time, but not so much that anything would make sense necessarily. That type of volume clutter acts as white noise which is a medium through which psychic energy can flow.

Many psychics and mediums can use this energy to aide them during their preferred means of divination. For Air, it acts like a conduit through which many means of psychic abilities can heighten. Being a novice and not yet trained to handle her powers, she had no indication how much of an influence the white noise could have on her and what precautions she should take to ignore it.

There was no intent to the wandering of Lilah's thoughts. She had drifted into a full trance without even acknowledging how the level of commotion could work to her favor like this. There was so much activity and hurried movement all around that no one paid any attention to the lone Air in the hallway who hadn't even yet removed her coat. If anyone had taken notice of her, they would probably have just assumed she had spaced out for a moment. Their attempts to get her to snap back would have failed. A trance like this was unshakable until the person's vision ended.

Lilah was pulled from the home through the far wall of the living room and across the town. Not physically, but through her mind's eye. It was slow at first like a tug on an invisible rope, but it increased with speed as she went. She would not remember the way to the building where it stopped, but there were enough clues to figure it out. It stopped in the middle of a large bright room, and it was freezing cold. The movement ended so abruptly she felt like she would topple over, but back at Eloise's house, she stood straight without a tremor.

The room looked like something in the back of a butcher shop or a meat locker. There were large metal hooks on chains that hung from the ceiling. Some had slabs of meat dangling from them. It confused her. She didn't know why she was there or how she arrived. A noise from the other side of the room caught her attention. She became aware there was something she was supposed to find, something of extreme importance, but she didn't know what.

Moving the slabs of meat to the side, she walked through the room toward the sound she had heard. The noise came again. It was the sound of a single drop of water dripping into a sink, but the echo was loud and twisted distorting the noise grotesquely.

At last, she moved a side of beef and a man came into view. It scared her, and she stepped back instinctively even though she knew she couldn't be seen. Peeking out again, she could see the man's back was to her, and he was sitting in a chair. Lilah walked up behind him, and as she neared, the full scene became clear. She cried out, and her voice garbled bizarrely. The echo came back to her ears like the sound a maniacal horror character would make before an attack.

It wasn't anyone she had seen before, but she recognized who he was eventually all the same. The man was strapped to the chair. His arms were gashed, and below him were two large metal containers collecting the blood that dripped down. The blood flow had all but stopped. All color was gone from his face. Lilah had never seen someone who looked that pale. There were clumps of dark brown hair clinging to the side of his face, hardened from the amount of sweat that had poured down for a very long time before being exposed to the cold in the room.

The wounds on his arms had almost healed completely she noticed as she circled around him. This was the Fire Element. It had to be she thought as she saw the amount of blood collected. There was no reading off him which meant he was an Elemental at any rate. Besides, no human could live through this.

His eyes fluttered, and his head rolled side to side. *'Could he sense me?'* she wondered. It would be impossible for him to actually see her as her body was still at Eloise's house. Only her spirit had traveled on the astral plane. Still his eyes focused on her after several attempts of keeping them open. A low guttural grunt came from his throat. Lilah leaned in closer. There was something about him. Something familiar. She knew she had never seen this man before, but she somehow recognized his eyes.

Voices in the hall caught her attention. The instinct to hide runs deep even in this state, and Lilah went back to the shadows and protection of the slabs of beef without thinking about her visibility. It was better this way she thought when she was out of sight. If he could sense me, whoever is in the hall might be able to as well.

The sound of two people talking grew closer until they stopped outside the door. Lilah could hear the echoing of metal on metal as locks were being opened. There were at least four locks. "Now, step back," she heard a woman say.

A chant began in the hallway, but she couldn't recognize the language. It was a short verse, and she knew what it meant. The door was spelled. There was a witch involved in this man's capture.

Lilah peeked out as the door opened and saw two women wearing long leather aprons enter the room. One of them examined the man in the chair who began to violently try to bust loose.

"Don't waste what little energy you have," she told him, shining a light into his eyes. "You know you're not going anywhere."

The other woman began laying out tools and supplies on the metal table that sat between the man and the windowless door. Together they moved the metal containers of blood to the table and tested it under a microscope. "It's still working," the second woman said.

"You still doubt her?"

"It's not that I doubt her-"

"It is," the first woman cackled.

"Think what you want. Let's hurry. I hate this room."

"Agreed."

The containers had a drainage spout on the bottom of each one. They took the blood and filled several plastic bags with it. It looked a little like the blood bags hospitals use, but much larger. IV bags perhaps. Lilah couldn't tell. They packed them up in a rolling cooler. The second woman began cleaning up the table while the first returned to the man carrying a large syringe.

He began to thrash about in the chair again trying his best to free himself.

"Stop," she told him. "You'll hurt yourself."

The needle entered his arm where a PICC line was in place, and she injected a clear liquid into his vein. "And that's my job," the woman added.

He continued to fight and thrash but it steadily slowed. Within a minute or two, he was out.

"I think you enjoy this too much," the second woman told her.

"It's not possible to enjoy it too much." She walked back to the table and helped finish putting everything away.

"No cutting today?"

The first woman shook her head. "He's drained. We need to let him recover a little to get anymore out of him."

The second woman looked over at the man and said in a low voice, "You know how risky that is."

"We'll do it tonight when his body has replenished some of his blood."

"We?" she asked. "I'm not sure I want to be in here when he's not weakened."

"I gave him a double dose just for that purpose. It'll be fine."

The second woman continued to stare at him. Even at this distance, Lilah could see the terror in her eyes.

"We need to remember to bring more anticoagulant," the first woman noted out loud dismissing her partner's concerns.

They took the cooler and headed out the door. Lilah could hear the locks clicking, and a chant being spoken again. She listened as closely as she could, hoping to be able to remember some of the words to ask the witches about it.

Once their voices and footsteps retreated down the hall. Lilah inspected the man in the chair again. His head hung to his chest. No movement. She would fear he might be dead except the only way to kill a Fire Elemental is with Fire.

She wondered what could possibly have been in that syringe. The cabinet doors were closed, and she couldn't open them physically in this state. With her eyes closed, she concentrated heavily on what was behind each one. There were countless bags for the blood. Bandages. That was strange they would have bandages because it doesn't appear like they get used. Finally, she saw multiple bottles of the liquid the first woman had injected. The image in her mind was distorted like looking through the peephole of a motel room. It had to be due to her metaphysical state. The front of the bottle was turned, and she couldn't read it all just the letters 'Pent.'

Lilah turned back to the man who sat unconscious and bound behind her. There was something distinctly familiar about him that she couldn't quite understand. She leaned in, examining him closely. The wounds on his arms had completely healed, but he was still extraordinarily pale and would be considerably weak if he were awake. Something about his jawline resonated with her, and she tried to remember why she felt like she knew him.

It hit her hard when she finally understood, and she reeled backward with a very loud gasp. It resonated off the cold concrete walls until it sounded more like the echo of shrill laughter returning to her ears. The last thing she saw before being violently pulled back to her body was the man's eyes shoot open as though the sound of her voice was powerful enough to wake him, even with whatever it was the woman had pumped into his veins moments ago.

Then she was gone. An invisible rope yanked her back to her body so forcefully the wind was knocked out of her. In mere seconds, she had returned to her body, fighting for her breath on the floor. "They have Fire!" were the only words she could manage to cry out.

Chapter Twenty-Two
Who's Who?

Lilah sat with Jackson and Everleigh sipping more juice and trying to recover a little bit of strength. Jackson had come quickly after Everleigh called him and filled him in on what happened. Normally she would feel slighted for being assigned babysitters thinking it showed the childlike way people treated her. Not this time. She was thankful to not be left alone.

Most of the others had left with a plan to rescue Fire. The details of the plan were not shared with her, and she didn't mind that either. There were only two thoughts on her mind. One was the chilling way he looked directly at her as if he could see her through the plane she was in at the time. Maybe he could. He was an Element who was born and lived for most of eternity on the other side of the veil. Perhaps the barrier didn't exist for him as it did for the rest. The other was the frightening knowledge that she could travel outside her body without intent. It had terrified her so, and it was something she didn't want to experience again.

The four newly called witches were still here too. They were packing and gathering essential magical items for Eloise and Meredith, so they could depart soon after Fire was safe. Everleigh would be joining them, but she was doing her own packing while stopping every few minutes to check on her once more.

Jackson looked miserable, and she felt responsible. This poor soul had been going about his day to day grounded in the normal human aspects of life occasionally testing the waters of the paranormal. His best friend was a witch stemming from a long line of Earth descendants. He knew supernatural creatures were real, but he didn't entertain them in the everyday world. At least he didn't until she came along and dragged him into this life. At least that is what she assumed was the cause for his quiet distress.

They'd known each other less than a week. They'd spent very little time hanging out doing things other couples might do. Normalcy was something Air always attempted. Blend in and fit in. It was what kept them safe for a millennium. Instead, Jackson had learned of her background and what it meant for him to be her match. She had been drugged and a less risky rescue than the one unfolding tonight was carried out to save her. Now there was this. She was shaken up over what she had experienced tonight. If she were him, she would be wondering why she had been the one chosen to be caught up in this mess. She wouldn't blame him for having these thoughts himself.

"Whenever you're ready," he told her, looking down at the floor.

"Take your time," Everleigh reminded her gently. "Your Uncle Todd doesn't want you to overdo it."

Lilah smiled at her. Again, it was something that would usually agitate her, but not now.

Everleigh looked like there was something on her mind, but she wasn't talking whatever it was.

"You can say it," Lilah told her.

"Say what?"

"Whatever it is you're thinking about."

"It's nothing," Everleigh gave a weak smile.

"It's not nothing because I see it in your face that something is bothering you."

"It's just... Are you sure it was Fire you saw?"

Jackson's head lifted and looked at her like he was wondering the same thing.

Lilah had wondered that herself many times since it happened. There was no way for her to be certain when she didn't even know what Fire looked like. "No. Uncle Todd was pretty convinced by the description I gave though."

Everleigh nodded like she had thought that too.

"I do know the man was a Fire Elemental regardless."

"How can you be so sure?" Jackson inquired.

"He had to be a vampire. His healing was fast and without scarring, and the women wanted his blood."

Jackson looked back down at the floor then said, "That would make him a member of the Fire faction."

It was more a statement than a question, but Lilah answered him anyway. "Three Elements have a high healing rate. If he were Water, they'd be after his saliva not his blood. I know he wasn't an Air. That only leaves vampires."

He nodded and took a deep breath like he understood.

"All right, lady. We should probably be heading to the farmhouse soon. I'm not sure how long it will take the others to join us, but I don't want them worried if they arrive and we're not there," Everleigh coaxed.

Lilah agreed and headed to the bathroom before leaving. Her reflection worried her. She looked like she had seen a ghost which is a silly phrase considering she sees them all the time. This must be what people are describing when they say it. She looked as pale as the man in the meat locker did. She splashed some cool water on her face and rubbed the back of her neck trying to encourage some circulation. When she joined the others, Everleigh was giving instructions to her cousins, and Jackson was waiting by the door with her coat. He was still visibly shaken. It added to the guilt Lilah already felt. It was terrible what she was dragging him through.

"If you'd rather go home," she began to say.

Jackson interrupted her. "Not a chance. I'm coming with you."

They piled into the cab of Jackson's pickup and headed out of town to the farmhouse. It was dark outside which surprised Lilah as she hadn't realized how much time had lapsed since the meeting that afternoon. There was an urgency building, telling her to get to the farmhouse as fast as they could. She didn't have to say a word to Jackson about it. The truck was already being pushed to its limits careening down the road.

As they headed up the drive, Lilah could see her parents on the porch. They had obviously been filled in on what happened and looked exhausted. There were no cars belonging to Uncle Todd or Meredith which meant they had arrived before the others did. Lilah had thought it would make her feel better, but the relief was fleeting. Now, she would wait and worry with the rest of her family hoping they returned successful and unharmed.

"Is this you?" Everleigh opened the truck door, and a blast of icy wind hit her.

"No, I'm fine," Lilah was too drained still to even think about becoming upset.

"There's a nasty winter storm headed our way," Jackson explained.

"Let's get inside quick before I freeze," Everleigh bounded up the steps.

Lilah smiled and walked up slowly behind her. Her parents rushed to her and hugged her tightly. They didn't use their voices to speak to her.

"I'm so glad you're alright!" her mom practically yelled at her.

Her dad wasn't as loud. *"We were worried to death even though Gene told us you were okay and would be here soon."* He gave her a quick hug then moved away letting her mom continue to mug her.

"Gene?" It was no surprise as word always traveled fast in her family.

"Yes, after Sara got the call from Todd," her mom stepped back, giving her more room to breathe.

Everleigh had stopped halfway to the door and was doing a slow circle looking around bewildered. She saw Lilah and paused. "What is this?"

"What?" Lilah pretended to not know what she meant.

"Why is the porch so warm?"

Lilah stood beside her friend and looked out over the lawn. Trees were bending from the force of the wind and snowflakes were swirling in the air, dancing their way to the ground. On the open porch, it was toasty and too warm for the heavy coat Lilah was wearing.

"Mom?" Lilah didn't take her eyes off the snowfall.

"Yes." She was still standing nearby and was quick to Lilah's side thinking she may need help.

Lilah turned to her with a twinkle in her eye, "Can you show Everleigh why the porch is so warm?"

Abby smiled at her. Normally her mom would scold her over such a request. Their powers aren't meant for parlor tricks. It could be because Everleigh was an Elemental herself which is why her mom didn't get upset. Maybe it was because of all Lilah had been through in the last few days, and her mom didn't want to add to the frustration.

"Come," Abby motioned to Everleigh.

Lilah smiled at her when she looked to her for reassurance before following Abby down the steps. Abby led Everleigh several feet from the porch where the air was still icy and sharp then spun around where the others could see. Everleigh followed her lead and faced the porch too.

Everleigh had just crossed her arms over her chest to combat the cold when her face widened in surprise. The puff of air that could be seen exiting her mouth disappeared before she was through exhaling. She waved her hands through the air like you might do in the water off the side of a boat. "How?" she managed to ask, full of wonder at the nature defying manifestation taking place around her.

"We can control the temperature of the air around us," Abby explained, slowly dropping the temperature until Everleigh got a chill then warmed it again.

Everleigh spun around laughing. "This is amazing!" Her eyes were still wide in awe. She looked more like a little kid who had finally been allowed to play in the snow after pestering her parents for hours than a young woman standing in the beginnings of a late autumn winter storm.

Abby laughed with her seeing it through her eyes. It wasn't often that any of them received a reminder of how truly magical their gifts could be.

"You would never have to pay a utility bill," Jackson commented from the porch.

"Not having to and actually not doing are different," Lilah told him. They have to live as normal a life as possible to fit in. Normal people run their AC in the summer months which means they do as well.

"I would be taking advantage of this," he continued, marveling at what Everleigh was experiencing.

Abby and Everleigh came back to the porch. Both of them still giggling from the fun they had playing in the storm. The porch was still warmed by Myles and no one needed any outer gear for the weather.

"What else can you do?" Everleigh asked Lilah excitedly. "Do you have any more literal tricks up your sleeve?" she added with a chuckle.

Before Lilah could answer, she heard it. They all did. Well, her family did at any rate. Her Uncle Todd was relaying a message. They were on their way, but they would require urgent medical assistance.

"Did I hear him right?" Lilah asked her mom.

"Hear who?" Jackson looked around to see if he missed something, but Everleigh looked just as confused.

"Yeah," her mom said weakly, walking toward the door. "We need to prepare for surgery."

Lilah didn't have time to explain, so she gave them a glance that unmistakably displayed the exigency and nodded toward the door. Given what their friends had set out to do, it wasn't hard to get a good indication of what had happened.

The house was already abuzz when they stepped inside. People were scrambling to get supplies and prepare an area. The kitchen was being turned into a makeshift operating room with what they could find to gather.

Lilah knew it had to be Rita, but wasn't about to say anything. The rest of the Elementals had some quality that would speed their healing. Even the wolves although theirs wasn't quite as quick, but Matt would still fare a severe injury easily.

In minutes, the door burst open, and part of the group filtered inside. As expected, Matt was carrying Rita who lay slumped and lifeless in his arms.

"In here!" Abby called from the kitchen where she and Joseph were getting ready for whatever might be needed.

Matt didn't go in their direction. Instead he sat down on the sofa still cradling Rita in his arms. Tears streamed down his cheeks as he rocked her. "I'm sorry," he softly said over and over.

Everleigh cried out and knelt in front of them. Her shoulders were starting to shake from her sobs. The scene playing out around them was dismal. Seeing Rita's motionless body was more than any of them had been prepared to handle.

The room was too busy. Her family were trying to keep a respectful distance, but it was still too many bodies for the small downstairs. Voices began to hum from every direction, and Lilah felt the room sway around her. She had to remove herself from the epicenter of the attention before there was a repeat of what happened at Eloise's house earlier that night. Or worse she could manage to bring on another storm to wreak havoc on the town.

It was easy for her to slip outside mostly unnoticed. Everyone's attention was on Rita as it should be. Questions swirled through her mind about what had happened during the attempt to free Fire from where he was being held. Todd had sent the warning call to the family, so she could assume he escaped without serious injury. Luke and Meredith were in the house near where

Matt sat cradling Rita in his arms. That left Eloise and Fire. No one had said yet whether they had been successful in freeing him.

There was also her Uncle Brian to worry about. It was hard for her to find any sympathy for him at all after what he had done to her. It was still something that would need to be addressed. They couldn't leave him to the wolves, literally. Lilah knew she would have to help her family find a way to save him as well.

Leaning against the post at the top of the stair rail, she closed her eyes and tried to think of anything that could keep her mind off of what was happening. She desperately needed to find something to take her mind off of it all, but it seemed the harder she tried the less she was able to distract herself. When she opened them, the first thing she saw was the snow being blown by the wind. It's crazy how in just a week the weather had gone from chilly to snow, then below zero temps to barely needing a jacket, and now back to freezing cold with some snowfall. *'No thank you,'* she thought. *'I will stick to my beautiful all year round southern climates.'*

Her eyes didn't leave the blowing snow once she discovered it emptied her mind. There was a beauty in it she had never noticed before because her family didn't usually live in the colder climates. Now she couldn't stop focusing on the thin trail of white dust that would blow around with the wind changing its final destination. It was nature's artwork to view and also something that could be so very dangerous in the right conditions.

The door opened behind her, but she wasn't ready for anything more than the sight of the wind out in the yard. Even so, she turned to see who had finally come to join her on the porch. Jackson stepped out from the house with her mom close behind, but she couldn't meet their eyes.

"Rita-" he started to say.

Lilah shook her head and turned away and saw what she hoped was her uncle's car approaching down the highway. It was too much for her to hear. She concentrated only on the car and didn't notice when Sara came out on the porch to join them. Nothing broke her train of concentration this time until Jackson placed his arm around her shoulder and spoke softly next to her.

"Your uncle should be here soon. He left soon after Matt got Rita in the car," Jackson filled her in part way.

'*Good*,' she thought. '*Maybe Uncle Todd can help me remain calm when I learn the full story of what happened.*'

'*That's exactly what I was thinking.*'

Lilah's eyes grew large, and she whipped her head around to face him. The smile on his face told her he didn't realize he could hear her until now either.

Headlights of the car from the road turned onto the gravel drive to the house. There were only a few moments left before everyone would be called to action again, and she would have to face the reality of what transpired that night whether she wanted to or not. She placed her hands on Jackson's chest and leaned in to kiss him not caring who was around, but a sharp pain ripping through her abdomen reeled her back.

She bent over suddenly grabbing her stomach. She felt dizzy, and she felt like she would be sick. Something had happened, was happening. It was too hard to understand right away. Her mind filled again with overlapping voices. It was like trying to hear a friend yelling to you from across the sports stadium. Her mom and Sara were at her side in a heartbeat, holding her steady. It was lost on her that Jackson was no longer next to her. Lilah's eyes rolled back into her head, and she almost passed out.

As the deafening roar in her head began to quiet down, she could hear the car come to a hurried stop near the porch sending gravel flying everywhere. It felt like her mind was about to split in two as she tried to concentrate on what was happening around her to stay in control. Doors started to open and slam shut as people exited the vehicle, but she couldn't count how many there were as the porch began to spin around her faster, making her fear she would soon lose consciousness.

Then it stopped. The footsteps and voices coming up the steps were frantic, but barely over a whisper in Lilah's ears as one thought alone pushed everything else aside. One voice made its way through the hum and took over, forcing every other thought from her mind. "Leena," Lilah finally managed to gasp.

Lilah's eyes shot open and she looked to her mom, but her mom was staring in fright at something on the other side of the porch. Lilah managed to straighten up enough to see what her mom was looking at. In the corner on the other side of the still broken swing was the white squirrel. It was convulsing and growing larger in size. It started slowly taking a few seconds to reach the size of a dog then in an instant, it changed as Marcus materialized.

"They have Leena!" He cried out to the small crowd now gathered on the porch.

A low guttural growl from behind Lilah sent a chill down her spine, and her eyes widened in fright. The terror grew inside her as she slowly turned to see what had made the dreadful sound. It was unlike anything she had heard before be it man or animal. Nothing could have prepared her what she was about to see.

Not more than two feet from her stood a man like beast on two legs. The arms were unusually elongated and covered in longer hair than found on a man. The face was disgustingly deformed and extended out with a full muzzle. Other changes were easily noticeable including the thickened layer of hair covering every visible part of the body. And the teeth. The teeth that bared from its mouth could easily tear a person apart without much effort.

The white sweatshirt and blue sweatpants were torn beneath the broadened frame of the body, but even without the clothing, Lilah would still recognize the man beneath the beast. The eyes were all she needed to identify her love. The ripple she had seen come across his face that night on the couch. This was it. It was the wolf inside of him starting to appear. That was what she had seen that occupied her mind for so long after wondering what it meant.

Slowly and without realizing she was doing it, she lifted her hand to the side of his face. Just before she made contact, a voice screamed from behind her with an urgency that suggested it wasn't the first attempt to catch her attention.

"Lilah!" her Uncle Todd yelled.

It snapped her to her senses, and she dropped her hand as she turned to see the people gathered on the top of the stairs. Her uncle and Eloise were well known to her, but the man standing between them she had only seen one other time when she left her body and visited him while he was being held against his will.

The last thing she saw before she passed out was the gaze of Fire staring deep into her eyes. He was filled with concern and something else she couldn't quite make out at first. *'Gratitude,'* she thought as darkness took hold and she collapsed.

Earth
The Elementals: Book Two
Available May 2020

"Did you hear me, Everleigh?" Judd asked.

She opened her eyes, and tried to say, "No." It came out as a hoarse whisper.

"I said it's time. I'm going to lift you to the wheelchair. The nurse insisted I not carry you all the way out."

"Okay. Go ahead."

Judd leaned over and carefully lifted and carried her to the wheel chair that was waiting by the door. He did it so effortlessly one might think he was a health nut and a regular at the gym if they didn't know better. He removed the brakes from the wheels and started pushing her down the hall. "You really did give me a scare," he whispered to her as they headed toward the exit.

That couldn't be right she thought. She was the one who had feared for her life. If she was alive, it didn't bode well for what might have happened to Jackson. In the state he was in, there would be very few options to tame him. The most logical was also the most permanent.

The automatic doors opened, and Judd stopped, putting the brakes back on the wheelchair before coming around to lift her again. Everleigh laid draped over his arms while he walked her through the parking lot as easily as a person might carry a folded umbrella.

"Where's Jackson?" she mumbled, but there was no answer.

Judd walked to the side of Jackson's pickup truck and still holding Everleigh easily with one arm, he opened the passenger door with his other hand then glided her onto the seat. Making sure she was completely inside before he closed the door, he told her to sit tight, and she'd feel better in a minute.

He opened the driver's door and climbed up in the cab. "Ready?" he asked her.

Everleigh thought he meant was she ready to leave, so she nodded then fastened her seatbelt. When she looked up, Judd was extending his right arm exposing a freshly bit wrist dripping in blood in front of her face. She clamped her mouth shut and squirmed against the back of her seat trying hard to get away from it, but he only inched closer. Tears fell down her cheeks. This was the last thing she wanted.

"Look," he told her sternly. "The only reason we came here instead of doing this from the start is because the neighbors heard you scream and called the police. I had barely hid Jackson's body before they showed up. There you still were on the floor of the garage unconscious. Hell! They gave me an escort to the hospital!"

He had dropped his arm away from her, and she could see the wound was almost healed. "I don't want to, but thank you for offering," she told him politely.

"For offering?" he cried out. Putting both hands on the steering wheel, he took several deep breaths. "I know, Everleigh. I know why you don't want to drink." He sighed and looked at her. "But I am not sending you home in your condition. I am not facing the wrath of your grandmother."

He bit into his wrist again, and held it out to her. "Please."

Still she hesitated.

"Please don't make me do this the hard way," he told her sternly.

Everleigh nervously leaned her head forward to his wrist.

"That's it. You only need a few drops. It doesn't have to be much."

She parted her lips, and he brought his wrist to her mouth. The bitter taste of iron covered her tongue immediately, and she started to gag.

Judd pulled his arm away. "That's enough. You'll be healed before we get home."

The last thought she had before the hallucinations set in was she might be physically healed that quickly, but the effect of the blood in her system would take most of the night to fade.

About the Author

Jennifer Lush is a mother of three from central Illinois where she has lived her entire life. Aside from spending time with her children and grandchild, writing and traveling are her two main consuming passions. Luckily, they are mutually beneficial.

Writing has always been in her blood even if it took her longer than planned to do it. One of her earliest memories of longing to be an author happened in kindergarten when she told her parents what she wanted to be when she grew up. It took close to four decades, but she has finally made that childhood dream come true.

Jennifer is an entertainer at heart who is always making those around her laugh. She can turn any mundane event into a story worth repeating with flair. Inspiration for her fictional worlds comes from everywhere. There are more ideas floating through her mind than she has time to write, but she is determined to finish as many as possible.

Twitter: AuthorJLush
IG: AuthorJenniferLush
Tik Tok: AuthorJenniferLush

Don't miss out!

Visit the website below and you can sign up to receive emails whenever Jennifer Lush publishes a new book. There's no charge and no obligation.

https://books2read.com/r/B-A-GSKK-YDATB

BOOKS 2 READ

Connecting independent readers to independent writers.

Also by Jennifer Lush

The Elementals
Air: The Elementals Book One
Earth: The Elementals Book Two